THE SPERLING CHRONICLES 2:
SPLIT IMAGES

by

Dilsa Saunders Bailey

Good Show Publications, LLC

The Sperling Chronicles 2: Split Images

All Rights Reserved.

Copyright © 2011 Dilsa Saunders Bailey

Cover Design by Derek Omo

SAN: 920-0533

ISBN Print: 978-0-9839061-1-7

ISBN ePub: 978-0-9839061-3-1

ISBN Mobi: 978-0-9839061-5-5

Library of Congress Control Number: 2018903153

Good Show Publications, LLC

www.goodshowpublications.com

Praise for "The Sperling Chronicles 2: Split Images"

The Sperlings are back and up to their usual scandals. "Split Images" opens up grabbing the reader's attention and throwing you right back on the roller coaster that you were on with "Dreams Thrown Away."

Now it seems as though Kalli has her Happy Ever After. That is until a stranger is introduced and turns everything all around. Ashton has changed and isn't the family man Kalli has grown to love and the stranger has a special bond that no one can really explain. Something just isn't right but in typical Sperling fashion, the truth is uncovered.

I give "Split Images" a 5. The roller coaster ride this book takes you on will have you begging for more and I can't wait to see what happens next!
OOSA (Goodreads)

An easy read book number two of The Sperling Chronicles. It contains the same high-level dose of deceit, sex, murder, love and mayhem. A twist with the identity of the twins Ashton and Asa. The appearance of the mysterious Lazarus who intrigues everyone. This book leaves you ready to read book number three. Good story by DSB. Good read!
Olivia R. (Goodreads)

Dedication

This book is dedicated to my biggest and most loving supporters, my aunts and uncle, Charles Saunders, Olivia Saunders, Johnnie Foster, and Florence Lucas. You keep me motivated to make you proud. And, to my mom, Gladys Saunders who still brightens my world with her smile.

PART ONE

~ Southwest Colorado 1997 ~

PROLOGUE

"BOBBY, ARE YOU listening to me?" Ray was strapping on his gun. It wasn't easy being the guardian of an 11-year-old boy. It was just the two of them now. Bobby's mother had taken the wrong path early, and left the screaming baby behind with a note attached. After ten years of raising the boy alone, he was still trying to cope with his daughter's actions. He would never have guessed she would have turned out like that. It was the drugs, he told himself. But, he knew it was more than that. It was being without a mother herself all those years, too.

"Bobby!" Ray pinned his gold star on his uniform and slid into his heavy jacket. Winter had come early fall this year. It was freezing outside in the Mesa.

"I *heard* you, Grandfather," Bobby whined as he made his way in front of the television set to watch Saturday morning cartoons.

"Do NOT leave the house. Do NOT let anyone into the house while I'm gone," Ray said, hoping the words would sink into his grandson's brain. Bobby had inherited his mother's stubborn gene. Ray knew the minute his back was turned Bobby would push the envelope, but, this morning, he didn't have a choice. Of all days, the state troopers had chosen a Saturday to pick up his latest prisoner, a bad biker who had been wreaking havoc robbing liquor stores and shooting their clerks all over the state. His buddies had gotten away, and Ray wanted to get him out of their little town as swiftly and as quietly as possible.

"Why can't I go outside?" Bobby protested. He had been protesting since he woke up and found out his grandfather was leaving him behind. Bobby wanted to go into town to find more stuff to put around his volcano, as he was determined to win that $25 gift certificate at the science fair. He had had so much fun with his grandfather the night before putting it together. Now, all he needed was a few more rocks and a few objects to get knocked over in the lava pool.

"We will go looking for rocks when I get back and I will get back as soon as I can." Ray put his hand on the doorknob and looked back at his sulking grandson. *He even looks like her when he sulks*, he thought.

"Do NOT leave this house, Bobby," Ray said one last time as he walked out the door.

Bobby got up and turned the television up as he heard his grandfather's truck pull out of the driveway. He sat there eating dry cereal from a box through three cartoons. Bored, Bobby walked into the kitchen and stared out at the barren pasture. There were rocks all over, any one of them he could pick up and paint black to make it look like lava rocks. He only needed a few.

Bobby went back to his homemade volcano and marveled at the progress he and his grandfather had made the night before. Pulling out the baking soda, he thought about testing the ingredients for the eruption one more time, but decided against it, and put the baking soda back in the cabinet and stared out the window again.

This was his project, and he wanted to be the one to pick out the right rocks. He wanted them to have little holes in them like the ones in the pictures, but Bobby knew if his grandfather was with him, he would have to settle for the ones his grandfather thought would be just right. Bobby thought about it long and hard and, then, ran into his bedroom and got dressed.

He had heard his grandfather talking to the state troopers and they weren't going to be there until around noon and it was only about ten o'clock, so Bobby had plenty of time. He thought he could run out, find the right rocks, and hide them. Later, when his grandfather helped him pick out rocks, he could sneak in his replacements while they were painting them black. Yeah, he thought, that will work.

Bobby dressed warm in layers, not wanting to give himself away by catching a cold. He pulled on a wool hat and found something to prop the back door open so he would be sure not to lock himself out. He ventured around in the fenced-in pasture. It was all dirt with a few patches of weeds here and there, with little grass to offer any livestock. They lived above the tree line; vegetation didn't get much air or water up here, just a lot of rocks, a few sturdy trees, bushes, and mountain ranges. Bobby kicked around the dusty grounds and found nothing to his liking. He started thinking about the other side of the road. He knew his grandfather would have a fit if he crossed that road, but Bobby suspected there were great rocks on the other side.

Venturing over the fence that separated Ray's property from the two-lane highway, Bobby stared across the road where there was nothing but cliffs and deep ravines. He realized he couldn't cross from the angle where he was standing, as there was a deep, blind curve. A car or a truck would overtake him and he wouldn't have a chance.

Bobby walked down the long line of poles and barbed-wire fence until he came to an area of the road that was straight. If he crossed, he could see cars coming from either side. He stood there and stared. Just across that road was a wide enough patch to be called a shoulder on the road with part of a dead-looking tree sticking out of the side of the cliff. Beyond that was a long way down. Bobby knew that he would have to be extremely careful, but he also knew there would be some prime rocks over there.

The boy climbed through the fence, stood against one of the poles, and looked both ways several times. He saw nothing, heard nothing. Then, he took a deep breath and ran across the road, skidding as he lost his balance on the loose rocks that covered the shoulder. The dead tree stopped his descent.

"Whoa," he screamed, his heart throbbing from the excitement of coming so close to the edge. "Whoa," he said again, congratulating himself now for surviving his adventure.

He looked with disappointment at the rocks beneath his feet. They looked like the same rocks in his backyard across the road. He kicked at them absent-mindedly and began to think about getting back across the road. He put his arm on the tree, glanced over the edge to see where he would have fallen, just so he could tell his friends about his adventure Monday morning in school. And then, he saw him.

In the only large limb left on the tree that had died several years back, a man hung vicariously and bloodied. Bobby closed his eyes twice. Then, he looked down again. The man was still there.

Bobby began to run toward town. He was afraid to go back across the road, but more afraid to go back home with a dead man hanging in the tree across the road from his house.

Bobby had run about a mile when a tow truck passed him and then pulled over to the side. Manny, who was just returning from transporting the biker's motorcycle for the sheriff, jumped out of the truck and ran back to Bobby.

"Boy, what are you doing out here on the road? I know the sheriff don't know you are out here. Get in that truck and let me take you home before you get us both killed," Manny yelled.

"There's a dead man back there," Bobby yelled back.

"Stop lying, boy," Manny said. He had known Bobby since he was a baby and knew the boy was inclined to stretch the truth.

"I'm not lying, Manny. Go see for yourself."

"What are you doing out here anyway?"

"There's a dead man, Manny. I saw him. He's hanging from the tree."

CHAPTER ONE

MANNY PULLED THE tow truck up to the back door to an outpatient surgical clinic run by a man who probably shouldn't have been practicing medicine, but it was the closest thing they had to a hospital for at least 30 miles. The sheriff and Bobby got out of the cab.

"What we got here?" A tall, disheveled doctor met them at the door.

"My grandson went on an adventure this morning. He found a dead man across the road from my property. Manny and I just spent an hour getting him out of the tree, you know, that dead thing that's just before the turn-off."

"Yeah, I know it," the doctor said, because he had always marveled how sturdy it continued to look after all those years of producing nothing. He walked over to the body that had been tied down on the back of the tow truck and removed the scratchy, old woolen blanket they had wrapped the body in for transport into town. Dr. Blum leaned down and looked closely at the battered face. Placing his hand to the man's throat, he looked at Ray with a peculiar look on his face. He pulled the stethoscope out of his pocket and pushed the blanket back revealing a huge bloody mass. He stuck the stethoscope into the bloody goo and began to yell for the nurse.

"You idiots," he looked at Ray and Manny. "This thing's still alive."

CHAPTER TWO

EVERY DAY, BOBBY sat by the bed of the strange man and read to him. He read his homework, the newspaper, or a magazine. He just wanted the man to wake up. He wanted to tell the man that he had saved his life. Instead, the man just lay there week after week.

"Doc, when are you going to transfer him up to Durango?" Nurse Misty was making a note in the chart. "He hasn't changed, and all you are doing is operating, operating on a man who may never wake up."

"At least, he will wake up in one piece," Dr. Blum said. Until this monstrosity had presented itself, he had spent most of his days at the bottom of a bottle of scotch. He had been kicked off a hospital staff down in Texas for his impairment issues. But, his skills had been so renown that, even now, he found himself sought out by those who needed his skills and relied on them as either the last or the ultimate resort. So, he obliged them their cosmetic whims, their desires to secretly lose weight overnight, or whatever reason they wanted to go under the knife. At least, these patients, kept his liquor cabinet filled. Now, this man had presented him with a smorgasbord of surgical needs, adding some excitement to his lackadaisical life. Whoever had tried to kill this man had really wanted him dead. Never before had he seen so many injuries on one body.

"But, will he recognize himself when he looks in the mirror?" the nurse joked.

"He may not know himself at all," the doctor said. "Don't know how severely damaged his brain actually is. But, according to the MRI, there is some damage to the medial temporal lobe bilaterally. Could result in some form of retrograde amnesia or not. All I can say is, it's more than a bruise."

"I would be devastated if I woke up one day and didn't know who I was." The nurse flipped the pages to the chart and, then, she smiled. "Since when did John Doe become Lazarus Smith?"

"Since I got tired of referring to him as "It," and I hate the name John. It's so last year's fashion," he teased. "Besides, I have decided I am going to raise this man from the dead. Just watch me."

"Well, it's not like I have a lot more to do." The nurse put the chart down just as Bobby bounded into the room with Ray close behind.

"Can I finish reading now?" Bobby held up a Star Trek novel. "I think he likes Star Trek."

"How would you know?" the doctor asked.

"Because he looks like he is going to smile sometimes when I read *Star Trek*."

"Interesting, Bobby. Have you noticed anything else?"

"Sometimes he looks sad when he is in the room alone," Bobby said. He had been watching the man's face closely, even though one side was mostly bandaged and hidden.

"Don't listen to him," Ray shook his head. "He looks the way Bobby feels he should look."

"No, Sheriff, I think it is highly possible our patient is beginning to come out of his coma. He's beginning to feel things, possibly dream. It's possible he is listening to us right now. Read something, Bobby."

Bobby opened the novel and began to read a dialogue between Mr. Spock and Captain Kirk. The doctor pulled Ray out of the room. Nurse Misty followed.

"How long can Bobby stay today?"

"All day, if he is not in the way. I have work to do in the office. And, since it is Saturday, you know I don't want that boy at home alone."

"Let him stay. I have noticed a marked improvement in Lazarus Smith when Bobby is around. I think he thrives when he is present."

"Doc, Doc," Bobby began to yell as Ray was about to leave.

The three turned to see Bobby leaning over Lazarus. "It's okay, Mister. You are safe now. I saved your life," Bobby exclaimed. "Didn't I, Grandfather?"

The man with the worn, hazel eyes looked from the young boy to the Sheriff. Tears began to flood from those eyes. He tried to lift up and couldn't. A look of panic swept across his face. He tried to speak and nothing escaped his lips.

"Calm down," the doctor said as he touched the man's arm as softly as he could so as to not frighten him further. "The boy is right. You are safe. Here, let me remove the restraints. We were afraid you would awaken alone and get up too soon. Hurt yourself. You have had a lot of surgery. You have a lot of healing ahead."

"I'm Bobby. I have been reading to you, too. Did you hear me?"

"Bobby, give the man some space. Come on out," Ray reached for his grandson.

The man shook his head keeping his eyes fixed on Bobby.

"Let him stay, Sheriff. Bobby, why don't you sit outside for a moment, though, while Nurse Misty and I examine the patient? You can come right back," the doctor looked down at the man. "Is that what you would like?"

The man nodded.

"You have been through quite a bit, even more, I believe, before Bobby found you," Dr. Blum tried to move as slowly and deliberately as possible. The man was exuding fear and rightfully so, he thought. He couldn't imagine enduring what this man had endured and survived it.

"The reason you are unable to speak is because someone slit your throat. I have repaired as much of the damage as I could for now. In time, you will be able to talk. You may not recognize the sound of your voice, though. I expect it to be lower and sound a bit hoarse. It will have to do for right now, but maybe later on you can consider additional surgery."

Nurse Misty removed the restraints and brought a tray of instruments to the table. The patient recoiled at the sound of clamoring instruments.

"Not to worry. Nothing invasive, she just wants to change a few bandages. Is that okay?"

The man nodded and then looked around the room that had been painted pale green, probably decades ago. The place was clean but old; its thick windows blotted the sunlight. There was another bed in the room, but it was empty.

"You are in a small surgical center. Your condition was so severe I didn't want to chance transporting you further. Lucky for you, I am a board-certified surgeon."

"A half-way decent one, I might add." Nurse Misty laid a handful of gauze on the man's chest. "I have never seen him so excited to see injuries. I guess we are boring around here. He worked day and night patching you up. You were bleeding from every imaginable part of your body. But, look at this," she talked fast as she removed one bandage after another. "You are making a quick recovery. Your body must have been in great shape before all of this happened."

"I'd say," the doctor smiled. "Now, while she's working on you, let's talk about you. Who are you? What happened to you? I have never seen injuries to this extent before."

"Can he write?" Ray asked as he returned to the room with a small, spiral notebook and pen.

"Can you move your hand? Try to lift your arm," the doctor instructed.

The patient lifted his right hand and reached for the notebook. Ray opened the book and clicked the pen. He placed the pen in the man's hand and held the notebook firmly in front of him.

"Where am I?" the man wrote.

"You are in a little blip of a town in Southwest Colorado," Ray answered. "We call it Los Huesos Secos. Dry Bones."

"How did I get here?" he wrote again.

"We were planning to ask you that question. My grandson found you hanging on the side of a cliff. No car, no identification. Who are you? What is your name?"

The man's hand dropped and the tears poured out again. He began to make a wailing sound before he dropped the pen. Bobby ran into the room and picked it up. Squeezing between Ray and the doctor, he grabbed the man's hand.

"I know who you are," Bobby grinned. "Your name is on the chart."

Bobby looked back at his grandfather and winked at him, "Your name is Lazarus, Lazarus Smith. Ain't it, Dr. Blum?"

Everyone in the room looked at each other, and then looked at the anguished man.

"Yes," Dr. Blum agreed. "Your name is Lazarus."

CHAPTER THREE

"GOOD MORNING, LAZARUS," the sheriff dropped a blue duffle bag on the foot of the bed. "Sure, you are ready to break out of here?"

"I'm sure," Lazarus answered. The doctor had been right. He could speak, but barely above a hoarse whisper.

"Well, here is some break-out clothing. Can't have you wandering around town in my hand-me-down pajamas, now can we?"

"No, the sheriff might pick me up for indecent exposure," the two men laughed.

"Where's Bobby?" Lazarus picked up the bag and began to pull out some real clothes. He smiled, he couldn't remember the last time he had worn real clothes, not that he remembered much at all. Doc had kept him in the hospital for eight whole weeks.

"Bobby is at home cleaning out his mother's room and fixing it up for you."

"Wow, I still can't believe how kind everybody has been to me. I promise I am going to make it up to everybody one day," Lazarus said as he stood up with ease. Only five weeks ago, he would have needed assistance to just sit up. Now he could walk to the bathroom to dress himself.

"Oh, you are going to work it off. Trust me. By the time you finish working at the store, all those women out there who were giving you their blood will be lined up to collect. You know, you are probably the newest eligible bachelor to hit this town in decades," Ray teased.

While Lazarus dressed, Ray sat down in the only chair in the room. "I have exhausted every possible angle, Lazarus. I'm still looking. We will find out what happened to you. Your case has been turned over to the state troopers. Are you sure you are okay with sticking around in this area? The perpetrator could be somewhere close keeping tabs on you."

"Are you sure you trust me?" Lazarus asked, as he came back into the room fully dressed. "After all, you don't know what type of man I was to get myself butchered and tossed for dead."

"Trust. I don't know if that's what I'd call it. Call it instinct. I'm following my instinct," Ray shook his head. He couldn't really answer that question. Honestly, Bobby had driven the decision to take the man in. The two of them had no other family. Sure, his daughter was out there somewhere, still. But, he had been unable to determine her whereabouts. Maybe helping Lazarus find his home would somehow help his daughter find her way back. Like Karma or something. But, that wasn't it. Perhaps, having Lazarus close might help to produce some leads. Maybe, eventually, he would remember something that would help him crack the case.

No, for sure, Ray didn't know why he was taking Lazarus into his home, only that there was something about the man had a calming, positive effect on Bobby. He could see it when he watched Lazarus and Bobby interact, whether it was playing a game of checkers, watching sports on television, or just sitting together quietly talking about anything. Bobby looked up to him, and Bobby needed someone besides his grandfather to count on. Ray was going to give Lazarus a trial run. But, at the first sign of danger or anything abnormal, it would be hasta la vista in a hurry.

Ray had been right about the women in town. As Lazarus took over the duties of running Ray's little grocery store, there was always a woman with a question about an order in front of him. In the beginning, Lazarus enjoyed the attention. But, after a few weeks of stocking shelves, and placating the female customers, Lazarus was getting bored and the desire to find out who he really was, was taking hold. In the beginning he was afraid. He was afraid to go looking for himself because somebody had wanted him dead in the worst way.

Dr. Blum had described his injuries to him in detail. One, he had suffered a brain injury from blunt force trauma. Then, both jaws had been broken and his nose. When Lazarus looked in the mirror, he would not, nor could not, see a reflection of his old self no matter who that was. The doctor didn't have a picture to even try to attempt to make him look close to that person. His other injuries included being slashed and pierced at least 500 times on his upper torso, leaving thousands of small, keloid scars resembling raindrops. The assailant didn't stop there as he or they had gutted Lazarus, leaving him with a short length of intestines and a stomach smaller than the size of a tennis ball for the doctor to repair. As an afterthought, the assailant had burned away his fingerprints, leaving Ray with no means to match him in the law enforcement database. Since his teeth and his jaws had been shattered, no dental record would match him either.

Every day, Lazarus looked into the mirror at his distorted, uneven face with a huge scar drifting down the left side from his temple to his chin. He had been fortunate that the facial slash hadn't taken his eye. Lazarus slid slowly into his shirt, watching his pencil thin arms and big bones take cover, his long body barely holding on to his clothes. He likened himself to a stick man in a child's picture, but the people in Dry Bones didn't seem to care, and neither did the Sheriff nor Bobby.

Lazarus had grown to love them. He didn't know why they had so readily adopted him into their family, but he was grateful. He was especially grateful to Bobby. There was something about that lazy smile of his that made Lazarus feel at home. But, Lazarus knew it was coming time for him to venture out. Plus, there were the dreams. He hadn't told Ray about the dreams.

For the last two weeks, he began dreaming of a baby lying on his chest screaming. Every time he reached for the baby, he would wake up from the dream.

CHAPTER FOUR

I T HAD BEEN six months since he had made Dry Bones his home. He was still living with Ray and Bobby, but he was growing increasingly restless. Not that he wasn't busy or could find fault with his new life, he just needed to know, really know who he was. Ray had just bought the grocery store a few months before he had arrived, and Lazarus had agreed to run it while they tried to find out his identity. The transition had been like a fish taking to water. He turned that store into one of the most popular in the county. Instead of the local residents trekking far away to buy groceries and dry goods, people were flocking in from everywhere to shop at Ray's store. The money was flowing in and Ray was very generous in sharing it.

One day, after receiving another generous paycheck, Lazarus strode out of the store with a mission on his mind. He had seen a vintage Mustang with a sale sign on it at the repair shop in the middle of town. Lazarus walked into the greasy mechanic's office and leaned against the counter waiting for someone to notice a customer was inside.

"Well, hello there, Stretch," Lazarus turned to see a beautiful, young woman with long, dark red curls framing her face speaking to him. "You are the walking dead?" she asked, her pink laden lips smiling and her dark eyes teasing.

Lazarus now leaned in the direction of the young woman. "That would be me," he said as he looked at her breasts that were all but exposed. He admired the nice smooth cleavage of her huge mounds shoved into the tiny red shirt.

"What can I do for you?" She leaned in his direction, giving him a better view. Instinctively, he licked his bottom lip. She smiled.

"I was hoping for a test drive," he openly gazed at her breasts as he spoke.

Letting her fingers glide across the counter and gently brush his hand, she answered, "That might cost you."

"Be careful what you wish for; it might cost *you*," he said in his whispery voice.

"Oooh, why would it cost me, Papi?" The young woman flipped her hair behind her shoulder and stood her five-foot frame as tall as she could.

"Because, it's been a long time and I am in the mood to make a woman beg for more," Lazarus grinned realizing he had left the innuendos behind.

"Oooh, it's like that, huh?" She didn't back down nor was she offended. She looked intrigued.

"Go put some clothes on!" Both Lazarus and the woman turned to see a short, grease-laden mechanic walk through the door. Like the woman, he was short and young, and he had a dark ponytail hanging down his back. His denim shirt was sleeveless, and each arm was covered with tattoos. One arm was covered with the naked back of a woman, surrounded by colorful flowers; the other was covered with a woman in the midst of flames and chaos.

"I got on clothes," the woman yelled back, but left quickly as if this wasn't the man to stick around and have an argument with.

"What do you want? Besides her, that is?" the man asked.

"I wanted to take that '65 Mustang out for a test drive."

"Cash only," the man said sternly.

"Well, that's a good thing, because I only deal in cash."

The man threw him the set of keys and started to walk back into the garage area.

"You are just going to trust me with that car?" Lazarus was astounded.

The man kept walking, "I know who you are, and where you live."

Lazarus wondered if the man really knew who he was, and then dismissed it. There were probably around 200 people living in this area. This place had no secrets. Everybody knew everybody, and that was beginning to smother him. He drove the Mustang back toward Ray's and then about 15 miles further. That's when he started feeling sick to his stomach. This had been the road his murderers had hauled him down to what was supposed to be his death. He made a quick turn-around and headed back to the mechanic's to negotiate the price of the car.

Minutes later, he walked away with the keys and the title.

Every day after he closed the store, he took a ride. On his next day off, he took the ride as far out as he dared. He was driving the two-lane highways north into nowhere when he saw an abandoned Quonset hut just outside of Durango. He skidded into the dusty, rocky yard and got out of his car. He didn't know why he was curious, or why he was taking a chance like that since he was all alone. He didn't know if he had always been so cautious, but he was now, given his recent history.

Lazarus stood there briefly, overcoming his fear, and opened the door. The floor was dirt. He kicked it around a bit, and tried to adjust his eyes to the darkness. There were streams of light sneaking through the breaks in the wall, enough for him to see pretty clearly. He began to walk around the inside perimeter and found an area that once held a large rectangular item. The outline was still in the dirt with a deep crevice on one side, as if it were turned on its side before being lifted.

Lazarus knelt down and touched the dirt. He picked some up, smelled it, and quickly stumbled back. How do you recognize the smell of dirt? It all smelled the same, he told himself. As he was regaining his balance, he noticed a piece of torn clothing in the corner. He walked over to it and picked it up. It used to be a white cotton button-up. There was blood on the tattered cloth. Lazarus didn't remember the shirt, he didn't remember the place, but instinctively he knew it was where he had almost died. He stuck the shirt in his pocket and walked around the perimeter some more.

Then, he went back to where the large structure had been and found bits of dried blood and matter on the wall. He scraped a tiny chunk from the wall with his fingernail and stared at it. He knew now *where* it had happened, but he still needed to know why.

CHAPTER FIVE

RAY WALKED INTO the small office in the back of the store. Lazarus was sitting back in the chair with his feet propped up on the overhang, smoking a cigar, and looking very pleased as he blew perfect rings of smoke into the air.

"You're pretty good at that," Ray said as he entered the room and sat down in the chair across from the big metal desk.

"Yeah, I am, aren't I?" Lazarus put his feet down and turned toward Ray smiling.

"You read your fiscal report?" Lazarus let a slow grin creep across his face. Ray smiled back at him.

"You are a mad genius," Ray laughed. "Let me have one of those cigars. Smells too good to be something we sell."

"Yeah, I drove down to Santa Fe and picked these up," Lazarus said. As he pulled a box from his desk, the bell from the dock rang. "Delivery," Lazarus smiled and pushed the box toward Ray and jumped up.

Ray moved around to the other side of the desk to find a lighter. He opened the desk drawer and saw several loose packs of condoms. He smiled. Lazarus had asked him where the hookers were, and he had pointed him to Santa Fe. No wonder he was looking so pleased with himself these days. Ray found the lighter and then automatically stuck it in his pocket. His hand came out with an old receipt, which he threw toward the trashcan under the desk and missed. He bent down to pick it up, threw it towards the trashcan, and missed again. He pulled the trashcan toward him so he could retrieve the receipt and saw two freshly used condoms in the trash. His heart sank. The rumors were true. Lazarus was banging someone in town and, if the rumors were really true, he was banging a biker girl. Ray put the receipt in the trash and went back to his chair. He sat there trying to blow smoke rings as Lazarus returned, still smiling.

"So, Boss, how do you plan to spend your income?" Lazarus teased.

"By kicking you out of the house," Ray said staring Lazarus in the eyes, no longer smiling.

"Yeah, I guess it's time I found my own place. It's just not much to choose from around here."

"I'm serious, Lazarus. You know how I feel about bikers. I still think your situation can be rooted in something that happened with a biker."

"I thought you had dismissed the thought that I was a biker in my past life," Lazarus picked up his cigar again. "No tattoos, right?" He held up his arms.

"Just because you weren't one of them doesn't mean you didn't have dealings with them, with their women."

"What do you know, Sheriff? You telling me you found out something about what happened to me?"

"No, I am saying that I told you before you entered my house, no dealings with bikers or gang-bangers. Bobby lost his mother to that life, and to drugs. Don't want him exposed to it."

"What have I done to expose Bobby to that? To you, to that? I would never ever do anything to bring anything negative into your lives. I appreciate you two. I would do anything to protect you. I know this might sound kind of hokey, but I love you, Ray. I love Bobby. Why do you think I would jeopardize your lives?"

"You are banging a biker girl? Eventually, it's going to spill over into everybody's lives around here. They are very protective of their clan, especially their women."

Lazarus laughed. "You had me worried for a second, Boss. I thought you found out I was a killer or something. You can relax. I will get her to drop me today. No problem. Just needed some release."

"You laugh, but if you piss her off, her brother and his boys are going to come knocking. They are the kind that would destroy the store, kidnap Bobby. I'm serious. Not two months before you arrived, an old woman was run off the road by these guys. She had a little Chihuahua in her car. They took him out, slit his throat and sprayed his blood all over her and the car. You know what she did to deserve that treatment? She grazed one of their bikes with her car as she pulled out of a parking lot. Witnesses say it just bounced a little. Didn't fall over or anything. But, they took it that far. These guys don't play and I've told you that I don't play that way."

"I'm just a distraction for her. She is bored. She will become even more bored when I start to act like an old man. She will drop me. She won't even look back. Her boys will even laugh at her."

"What makes you so sure?"

"I don't know anything about my name, or my past life, but I know women. I know this one, and she will drop me like a hot potato. She won't complain to her boys because she will be too embarrassed. I will let her do the dropping, I promise. It won't come to that."

"No, it won't. Because you won't be here," Ray took a deep drag on his cigar.

"I'm really sorry, Ray. I will get my things tonight and be on my way."

"Yes, you will. You have a store to open down in Santa Fe," Ray choked as he began to laugh while still blowing out smoke. "I bought another store," Ray grinned. "You are going to run it. Heck, you won't be that far away from home. Bobby can go hang out with his Uncle Lazarus on the weekends, maybe give Grandpa Ray a break and I can find my own woman of the week."

CHAPTER SIX

LAZARUS MISSED RAY and Bobby, but he enjoyed living in Santa Fe. The store was large and busy. He had a knack for making things run smoothly. He often wondered if that is what he had done in his past life. He wondered if he had a large stash of money somewhere since he was so good at attracting it.

One day, as he was cutting open a box of magazines near the front counter, he saw a man he had seen at least twice before. He didn't know why he singled him out because it wasn't unusual to have regular customers. But, this man didn't fit. He was a tall, chocolate, bald-headed man. He looked to be in his late thirties, early forties. He always wore a suit and he always walked through the store slowly, occasionally picking up an item and reading the back of the product. *Twice*, Lazarus thought. And each time, he had bought a box of Macanudos, some mints, and a magazine.

Lazarus shoved the box of magazines under the nearest register. He took the stairs two at a time to get to the office overlooking the store. He plopped down in his chair and turned the security monitors toward him, watching as the man walked slowly around the store. Then, the man halted in front of the security camera, looked directly into the camera, and smiled. Lazarus was stunned, and a shiver raced down his back. The man picked up a bag of pork rinds and headed for the customer service checkout. Lazarus got up and ran down the steps. Before the man could get to the register, Lazarus relieved the cashier.

"Nice grocery store," the man said as he placed the pork rinds and mints on the counter.

Lazarus put a box of Macanudos on the counter before he was asked. The man grinned.

"Great customer service," he said, and then held up a finger. He stepped over to the next counter and brought back a magazine. It was a popular national magazine with a picture of the Liberty Bell on the cover.

"Have you ever been to Philadelphia?" the man asked as he tapped the picture of the Liberty Bell.

"Can't say that I have," Lazarus said as he began to ring up the items, remembering a night when he and Bobby rooted for the Philadelphia 76ers basketball team as they played against the Boston Celtics. They were playing at the Spectrum and, for some reason, it looked oddly familiar. It had been the first feeling of familiarity he had experienced about anything. But, he had dismissed it. It was a sports arena. What was unique about a sports arena?

"I grew up there. My father and my grandfather used to take my brothers and me out on cultural hikes they called them. I will never forget one time on one of our trips my older brother touched the Liberty Bell. Do you know that that is totally forbidden? Well, our chaperones were busy with our three other brothers and didn't notice. But, the park ranger was paying attention. He grabbed my brother — put the fear of death in both of us.

"We just knew we were about to get carted off to prison, and then my grandfather walked up. He was a tall, gentlemanly man. Never raised his voice to anyone, but when he spoke, people listened. It was the first time I saw a grown man shake in his boots. I have no idea what my grandfather said, he said it so quietly, and with a smile on his face. The man let us go, and we were so proud of our grandfather. I miss those days," the man said, still smiling as he pulled out a wad of bills. "You should visit Philadelphia one day. You look like the type of man that would like it."

Lazarus nodded and noticed that the man's nails were manicured, and his watch was an expensive brand. He listened to the man speak, and wondered why he seemed familiar.

"Can I ask?" the man pointed to his own face. Lazarus reached up and let his hand slide down the scar on the left side of his face.

"Car accident," Lazarus answered in his low, wispy voice.

"Your throat, too," the man touched his own throat.

"Yes," Lazarus slid the bagged goods toward the man.

"Philadelphia," the man said as he picked up the bag. "I think you need to give it a test drive."

For the rest of the day the man's voice haunted Lazarus. After closing the store, he remembered no one had restocked the magazines. The vendor would be picking up the unsold copies the next day. He pulled the box out and began sorting the new magazines for August. One of them was an *Ebony* magazine. On the cover was a picture of four men with one woman in the center of them, the cover title indicated inside you could read about Black America's power families, and this Sperling family was number one, owning a giant security firm called PDSI. Lazarus stared at the picture. The woman was beautiful with long, dark curls spread around her shoulders. He gasped when he noticed the man on her left side was the man who had just been in the store.

He held the magazine back and walked around to the counter to restock the rest of the magazines. In a minute, he was going to get a glance into what made that man look so familiar to him. He began to pull down the July magazines, all of which had an Independence Day theme. He flipped open the magazine with the Liberty Bell. It had several pictures of Philadelphia with various stories, but there was one picture that caught his breath. It was a picture of an old bench in a park; in the background was a large U-shaped apartment building, called the Banks Building. Suddenly, the magazine burned his hand as if he had stuck it into a fire. He dropped the magazine, his knees going weak. As he went down to the floor, a severe pain seared through his brain. He cried out, but no one heard. His world went black.

PART TWO

~ PHILADELPHIA ~

CHAPTER SEVEN

"OM, MOM," EIGHT-year-old Kacie tugged at her mother's coat sleeve. "Can we get an extra meal, some extra coffee?" They were standing in line at the McDonald's on Walnut Street.

"Are you that hungry, sweetheart?" Kali smiled down at her youngest daughter. There were days when she still couldn't believe she was the mother of four children. She and Ashton had finally gotten it right, at least for a while.

For 10 years, they had lived blissfully. Until now. Now, she didn't know whether she was coming or going. And, she definitely didn't know the man she was living with anymore. He had changed this past year obsessing over things that had once lacked importance to him, and spending less and less time with her and the children. It was almost as if he had turned on her and their family. Now, commonly, he spoke to them very harshly.

He routinely put them in situations that could have easily brought them harm, once by driving like someone deranged off the road while yelling at them. And, what Kali thought was even worse; he insisted that the children attend public schools, walking there and back without supervision. He knew they weren't safe. The man who had loved and cherished them, the man who had put them on pedestals, and cared for their every need, that man seemed bent on destroying them. And, she didn't know why, but she could almost pinpoint the day when he changed. It was just days after his father's funeral, the funeral she had forced him to attend. She had even planned the event and had regretted it every day since.

"Can we get two extra sausage biscuits, Mom?" Kacie was staring eagerly at the woman behind the counter.

"You heard her," Kali smiled at the woman and paid her for the order. Kali and Kacie strolled down the street. Kacie held the bag tightly with a smile on her face that melted Kali's heart.

"Can I hold the coffee?" Kacie asked as they approached the park area in front of their building.

"Be careful, Kacie. It's extremely hot. I can still carry it," Kali stood still as her daughter carefully removed the coffee from the carrier. "Kacie, I thought," Kali stopped short as Kacie strode over to the park bench where a disheveled man sat staring off into space. Kali gasped as Kacie climbed up on the bench beside the man, who turned to Kacie and smiled.

"Kacie," Kali yelled and stopped dead in her tracks when she noticed the scar down the side of his face. She was taken aback by her daughter's friendliness with this man who wore a dirty, army jacket. "Kacie, come here. Now," Kali said.

"It's okay, Mommy. This is Lazarus," Kacie said. "He's my friend. Lazarus, I brought you some breakfast," Kacie presented the coffee and the entire bag of sandwiches they had just bought. "Two of these are yours, plus hash browns, if you want," Kacie said.

"Thank you, Miss Kacie. I really appreciate it. But, why don't you remove them for me. I need to wash my hands," he said hoarsely.

Kali was stunned. She wasn't sure what to say, so she held her hand out to Kacie.

"Come. Here," she said again.

"But, Mom. I want to introduce you to my friend. My mom thinks you are a bum," Kacie giggled.

"Kacie," Kali was embarrassed and frightened by the man. His face reminded her of Frankenstein's monster, and she didn't like the way that he smiled. Nor did she like the way he licked his lips when Kacie handed him the sandwiches.

"I'm Lazarus Smith," the man offered his hand. Kali didn't return the offer.

"Mom, you are being rude. You told me never to be rude," Kacie protested.

"Kacie, I am going to say this once and then I am going to call your father. Go inside. Take the sandwiches with you," Kali put a hand on her hip and grimaced.

"Okay, but he's not a bum. He's been working all night. That's why he is dirty," Kacie turned to Lazarus and, then, kissed him on the cheek. "Right, Lazarus?"

"Right," Lazarus grinned up at Kali and shrugged his shoulders.

"Kacie."

"I'm going. But, don't you be mean to Lazarus, Mommy. He is my friend," Kacie took the bag and headed toward their building.

Kali stood there with her coffee and watched her daughter run toward the double glass doors leading into the Banks Building. "What are you doing with my daughter? How do you know her?" Kali pointed her finger in the man's face. "If you have touched her, I will make you pay."

"Calm down, lady. I'm not like that. But, from where I stand or sit, you are not that concerned."

"How dare you? What the hell do you know what I am concerned about? The only damn thing you need to know is to stay clear of my daughter."

"Lady, the only thing I have done is look out for your daughter, which is more than I can say for you." Kali's hand shook and a bit of coffee spilled on it, she dropped the cup.

"Lady, are you okay?" Lazarus stood up with the napkins Kacie had given him and tried to put them on Kali's hand. She jumped back.

"Look Lady. The only thing I did was keep your daughter from getting hit by a car. She was running from a group of kids who seemed to be running her into traffic on purpose."

"What?" Kali snatched the napkins and put them on her hand. "You are lying," she accused.

"A month ago, I was crossing that street," he pointed down toward the red light, "and she was running at breakneck speed. I grabbed her and then I chased the kids. Ever since then, I have been walking her to school every morning, and walking her home in the afternoon."

"You have been doing what?"

"Let me finish, please," Lazarus held his hand up. "I work down at the docks. I live in a boarding house on Carlisle Street. I am new to town. I work all night, come out here and wait until my roomies leave the house for the day. I go home, shower, sleep, and come back. Walk Kacie home and go to work. I don't have anything better to do. And, I enjoy her company, right here on this park bench in front of the world. I have never touched her in any manner that was not called for. She takes my hand, I let her take it. She sits on the bench. And today, today was the first day she ever kissed me. She is a very special young lady, and I would do anything to keep her safe. Even from your neglect," Lazarus voice was low, but harsh.

"You bastard." Kali didn't want to hear anymore. She had objected to moving back to the city. She had been even more opposed to the children attending public school and walking to those public schools. Everything had changed, because that is what Ashton wanted. And Ashton was making her too afraid to say no these days. Long ago were the days of *what Kali wants, Kali gets*' as he used to love telling his friends and family. Nowadays, it was what Ashton wanted and no one had better get in his way.

Kali stormed away from the man, then stopped and turned toward him. "Stay away from my daughter," she yelled, and then ran into her building.

Kali rushed over to the reception area and grabbed a phone. She called her brother-in-law, the only person in the world she could still trust. She paced the floor until she saw Micah get off the elevator, then ran to meet him. She tried to tell him the whole story all at once. Micah took her by the arm and ushered her out of the building. She tried to go straight toward the man still sitting on the bench, but Micah changed her direction. He guided her down the block and into the alley behind the building, next to the parking lot entrance to the building.

"What am I going to do with you?" Micah's bald head shone in the late morning sunlight. "You won't do anything I ask you to do, and now this."

"What the hell are you talking about, Micah? There is a man out there that has been befriending my eight-year-old daughter. This creep had the nerve to accuse me of neglect. And, I can't really argue with that," Kali started to cry.

Micah took her face in his hands, and smoothed away the tears.

"Kali, I got this." He swallowed and looked both ways to make sure no one else was around. "All I need you to do is seduce Ashton."

"Seduce him? Hell, we're still fucking every night. And, I mean fucking. He hasn't made love to me in so long," she sobbed. "He comes at me like a madman. It's like rape. It's like he is trying to hurt me."

"Turn the tables, Kali. Seduce him. You know how to seduce a man. That I know for a fact. Seduce him."

"You're crazy."

"When was the last time you really looked at Ashton? Really, really took a good look at him," Micah's breath moved the rogue curl from between her eyes.

"I see him every day, every night," Kali countered.

"Do you, Kali? Do you *really?*" Micah kissed the tears from her eyes. He kissed each one of her cheeks and then he kissed her full on the lips. At first, her hands went up to push him away, but then his tongue found its way inside of her mouth. She responded and tried to not think that she was kissing her brother-in-law, the husband of her only female friend. She didn't want to think about what Ruby would think. She shivered lightly as Micah's hand entered inside her coat, her body arched. Then he stepped back.

Micah knew how easy it would be to pick her up and take her on the spot. The first time they had made love, they had really needed each other's refuge. The confusion caused by their spouses had left them to commiserate, but not as expected. Micah had walked into the music room one evening in the penthouse to find Kali lying on the floor next to the piano. She was clutching the yellowed sheets of music her mother had written for her when she was a little girl. They had been ripped. One more act of torment delivered by her once loving and doting husband, his brother Ashton.

Micah had lifted her up and taken her to the bedroom suite next door. He had lain with her on the bed, holding her close to his chest, trying to calm her tears by kissing them away. Then one light kiss led to another and then to another. The last one captured her lips.

As for Kali, listening to Micah's every heartbeat was comforting. She had held on tightly to Micah as he coddled her in his arms. And then his face was next to hers and she thought his eyes were just as sad as she was feeling. She opened her mouth and let his succulent lips meet hers. Her fear began to melt as his warm body drew her closer to safety. It was as if the only life jacket she could find was finally in reach.

Micah tried not to think of any consequences as he lifted Kali to meet his loins. It had been weeks since his own wife had even looked him in the eyes. He didn't know who she was anymore.

"See, you still know what seduction is. Seduce him. Let the man on the bench be. I got this," Micah pulled out his handkerchief and began to clean up her face. "You think I would let your babies roam these mean streets alone?"

"He's a bodyguard?" Kali was beginning to feel relief.

"No, but a bodyguard was there. There were two sets of hands on Kacie that day, but when Lazarus presented himself, the bodyguard stepped back and watched. He still watches every day, all day. But, this man," Micah shook his head. "I promise you, he won't hurt Kacie. I have had him checked out. I am thinking about hiring him. So don't topple the cake, right now. Just do what I have asked you to do. That's all I want you to do.

"Please, do that, Kali. The sooner, the better, please."

CHAPTER EIGHT

LAZARUS HAD LET go of all things greasy from his diet. With only a short length of intestines, all he ingested these days were very small portions of something fresh, something lean, or a vitamin shake made with soy milk. He appreciated the child's gesture and then waited until both ladies were gone for awhile. But, as he picked up the sandwiches and home fries to put into the garbage, he was blocked by a tall, red-faced man with no coat on this blustery cold day. He had been out in the cold way too long and Lazarus had seen him before.

"Excuse me," Lazarus sidestepped him to get to the garbage can. The man turned watching him closely.

"Can I help you?" Lazarus dusted his hands. He had given all of his napkins to Kacie's mom when she had spilled the coffee on her hands.

"Someone would like to see you," the man answered. Lazarus smiled. Finally, someone was paying attention. Maybe, just maybe, he was getting ready to meet his would-be killer face-to-face. A fleeting picture of the woman with the curls ran across his mind. That was her, in the picture, Mrs. Sperling, the powerful woman from the Ebony magazine. Lazarus resisted slapping himself on the forehead.

He turned away from the man to pick up his morning paper, and a tall, dark-skinned man with the common sense to wear a heavy coat handed it to him. He had never seen this one before. He turned to see a car pulled over. The man without the coat opened the back door and a hand motioned to Lazarus to come. Lazarus took the bite. He slid into the back of the old Black Mercedes. The man with no coat got in and drove off leaving the man dressed for the weather out in the cold. Lazarus turned to his host and smiled. It was the baldheaded man from the store in Santa Fe and from the magazine cover. He was getting close, he thought.

Micah Sperling had no doubt that Lazarus would take the bait. He was a man looking for his identity, his home, and a man who was closer to the truth than he knew. At least, that was what Micah had hoped. Lazarus didn't know it, but Micah had as much riding on finding out his true identity as he did. But, how? That he hadn't figured out yet. Micah had been following his brother Ashton's trail since he had disappeared a few days after their father's funeral. He was trying to close the gap between Ashton's disappearance and the day his then seven-year-old daughter, Kacie, had found him shot in his bedroom weeks later. Poor little Kacie was still having nightmares about pools and lakes of blood, with her father trying to swim toward her.

Micah had found that, for some reason, Ashton had rented a small U-Haul truck the day after their father's funeral and returned it in the oddest place: Durango, Colorado. Why had he gone all the way to Durango? Driven even. His brother would never have driven that far, especially alone. He would have flown easily, got there, did what he had to do, and jumped on a flight back. There was nothing going on in the business that had been so clandestine that he would have had to travel by ground.

"You took my suggestion, I see," Micah smiled and extended his hand. "I'm Micah Sperling. I understand you have already met my sister-in-law and my niece, Kacie."

"Yes, yes I have," Lazarus took the hand and shook it.

"You really pissed her off, you know," Micah nodded knowingly.

"It was not my intention." Lazarus didn't know why but he didn't feel threatened at all. It was as if he had been picked up by an old friend.

"So, how do you like it?" Micah waved at the streets they were passing by. "The city?"

"It's a fine city," Lazarus chuckled.

"I want you to meet some other people. Are you up to that?"

"I need a shower. Don't know how they would like to meet a homeless-looking man like me," he joked, recalling Kali Sperling's reaction to him.

"I don't think they will mind," Micah patted him on the shoulder.

A few minutes later they pulled in front of a row house on a well-manicured street. The two men got out of the car and walked up to a large, gleaming black door. A black flower box filled with purple pansies hung beneath a large windowpane.

Without knocking, Micah let them in, Lazarus following close behind. Two men sat in overstuffed furniture that was too big for the room but set on an angle toward the antique fireplace and mantel.

Immediately, one of them got up and, then, stopped suddenly in his tracks. For a moment, Lazarus thought the man was going to cry. He was short, much shorter than the rest of them, Lazarus noticed, as the second man stood up. The shorter one had straight black hair and appeared to be Filipino or Spanish. He began to smile as he walked over and grabbed Lazarus' hands, both of them, and squeezed them.

The little man in a pair of green scrubs smiled up at him. "I'm Chico, I'm next to the youngest of the Sperling brothers, and the shortest and the funniest," he added. "Though, my big brother always thought his jokes were funnier, I am the funniest," he said as he nodded toward the other man standing there.

"This is my other brother, Ricky," Micah added. "Ricky's the youngest. Both of them are physicians. Chico is an OB/G and Rick is a plastic surgeon." Ricky, an impeccably dressed man with hazel eyes and tan skin approached Lazarus almost with a reverence that made Lazarus a bit uncomfortable.

Standing almost eye-to-eye, Ricky stared at him without speaking. Then, he reached up and took Lazarus' face tenderly in both hands. "Nasty scar," he whispered. "Both sides of the jaw have been broken. Both." He looked back at Micah, then ran his fingers through Lazarus' hair and began to run them lightly over the scars that the hair hid. "Surgical and other scarring on the head, too. Old and new," he stepped back. He never broke his gaze.

"Good diagnosis, doc," Lazarus said, looking back questioningly to Micah for an answer.

Ricky stepped back toward him and touched his throat. "Someone did this," he said, his voice broke. "Someone purposely did this."

Ricky began to take off Lazarus' jacket. Lazarus didn't know why, but he let him. Ricky threw the jacket to Chico who asked Lazarus if he could remove his things from the pocket. He said he was going to throw it in the washer. Lazarus nodded and watched as his few belongings, keys, a SEPTA transpass, and a couple of 20s were placed on the coffee table in full sight. He knew instinctively that these men weren't planning to rob him or hurt him. There was a surreal calmness in the room that he couldn't explain.

"Your torso. Your doctor said your torso had been brutalized."

"You talked to my doctor?" Lazarus stepped back, and removed Ricky's hands from his throat.

"We had to check you out," Micah walked up to Ricky and patted his shoulder hard. "Back off, will you?"

"Check me out for what?" Lazarus took a couple of more steps away from the two.

"Well, first, I had to make sure you weren't some child molester interested in my niece. And second, I decided to offer you a job."

"Before or after Santa Fe?" Lazarus looked toward the door and realized his jacket was now probably wet and full of suds. How dare he let his guard down like that, he thought. What was it that had taken him temporarily into la la land?

"Santa Fe was just coincidence. But, you did grab my attention on the park bench. Why that park bench? Were you looking for me?"

Lazarus shook his head. He had no idea where Micah Sperling lived. But, he did know where he worked. The first thing he had found out when he got to town was where his building was located, but he had done nothing with the information. It was still milling around in his head. But, the park bench, when he had seen it in the magazine picture, he knew it. He knew he had sat on that bench before. He recognized it. He recognized every carved initial, every worn-weathered board. That's why he had come to Philadelphia and that was why he was sitting on that park bench every day. He was waiting for it to tell him who he was.

"My brother is more than curious about your injuries. Like I said, he is a plastic surgeon. He wants to make your face beautiful for the ladies."

"For the ladies?" Lazarus was intrigued for a second.

"Yes, Mrs. Sperling, her daughters. And her sons and my son as well. I like the way you handled her this morning and the way you have been protecting Kacie. I want to make you their personal bodyguard. There are some things going on that they aren't aware of and I want to keep it that way. I need someone who can keep their trust and keep them alive," Micah put his hand on Lazarus' forearm and leaned closer to him. "I want to move you into the penthouse and have you protect them with your life."

CHAPTER NINE

RICKY POINTED TO the examining table, "You can just sit. I bet you are getting a little stir crazy."

"Thank you," Lazarus sat down on the table with ease. Micah had walked him through the office building to make sure he didn't run into anything. He had learned his way around the little row house pretty well. That first day, the Sperling brothers had just given him the key and left; there he had found everything he needed, even the refrigerator was filled with his favorite foods, fruits and vegetables. He wasn't much of a meat eater, maybe it was because his own flesh had been filleted and displayed. Maybe he had seen too many pictures of his own face split wide open, his gory chest and back cratered with deep slashes and punctures. Both Ray and Dr. Blum had let him take a look at the condition he was in when he was found. He had hoped to find the original man in that mess, but it hadn't helped. It had only made him sick to his stomach.

"Let's take these bandages off your face and see if we have a kinder, gentler looking Frankenstein underneath."

"Ha ha," Lazarus said, surprised at how much clearer his voice was beginning to sound. Ricky's friend had operated on his throat first, removing additional scar tissue that caused the low, hoarse sounds to emerge.

"Be still. I want to take in my work of art," Ricky looked back to see Chico Sperling walking into the office, holding up a large, black lace scarf. "And, what the hell is that thing?" Ricky chuckled.

"It's for his face, just in case you made him look worse," the four men laughed.

"See," Chico laughed. "I *am* the funniest."

Lazarus held onto the examining table nervously as Ricky removed the bandages. The room was quiet with anticipation. He watched their eyes as the last bandage was removed. They looked pleased. Ricky handed him the mirror.

"Wow, is that what I used to look like?" Lazarus smiled at himself.

"No," Ricky took the mirror from his hand. "We don't know how your jaws were before they were restructured, nor your chin. Your face could still look amazingly different from its original make up. But, you don't look so bad, now."

"No, I look kind of handsome, if I say so myself," Lazarus said, making the men laugh again. "Do you think Kacie will still recognize me?" he turned to Micah.

"You don't look that different," Micah responded.

CHAPTER TEN

T HE KIDS WERE sitting at the dining room table eating quietly. Kali tried to make conversation, but no one was having any of it. Ashton sat brooding on the other end, thumbing through the newspaper.

"May I be excused from the table?" Katie, the eldest girl and fraternal twin spoke up. She was always the first one to get the ball rolling.

"Have you finished eating?" Kali asked, noticing her daughter's plate was still full.

"I'm not really hungry," Katie glanced at her father whose eyes were still focused on the small black and white print of the *Philadelphia Inquirer*. "Daddy, you won't mind that I leave now?" she asked.

"No, go ahead," Ashton answered without looking up.

Katie sighed and shook her head. She stood up to clear her plate off the table just as Micah walked into the room.

"Hey, Everybody! Smells good in here. Aren't you going to invite your old uncle to eat?"

"I can make you a plate," Katie said, as she was happy to at least still have her uncle acknowledge her existence.

"Make two," Micah walked over to her and hugged her tightly. "Hey, son," he hit Ashton on his back. "I want you to meet someone." Ashton looked up at him impatiently. "Ashton, I want you to meet Lazarus. I just hired him to be the nanny." Micah looked back at Lazarus and winked.

"You, what?" Ashton looked up at the tall, lean man with the dark, dark eyes.

"You need Kali down at the office. Ruby is spending most of her time at her office, so I thought we needed someone to keep up with the kids and their schedules. I hope you don't mind. When I hired him for my Artie, well, I figured why not all the kids. That way, we won't have to worry about them when we are not with them, and the rest of the house staff can get their jobs done."

"A nanny?" Katie and her twin, AJ, protested.

"I'm 15, Uncle Micah," AJ announced as if that had been an

unknown factor.

"So am I," Katie agreed. "Neither AJ nor I need a nanny."

"And, we are perfectly capable of taking care of Kacie and Adam, and Artie, too," AJ offered.

Micah walked over to AJ and leaned his forehead against his. "You are growing up quite nicely, but would you prefer to babysit if, by chance one day, you have the opportunity to go out on a date?" Micah grinned.

"Too early," Kali gasped, "he is not ready for dating. And no one asked me about a nanny." Micah had been right. Lazarus didn't look that different to her without the scars and maybe a tweak to his chin, okay maybe something about the eyes, she thought. But, his presence made her very uncomfortable. She was about to say something when Micah stepped between them and smiled.

"Mrs. Sperling, I would like for you to meet Mr. Lazarus Smith. Mr. Smith, I want you to meet our children. This is Miss Kacie," Micah winked at Kacie who was grinning from ear to ear. "Miss Katie," Katie walked up to him and extended her hand. Kali sighed, recognizing Katie's immediate crush. She wondered how that was going to work out between Katie and Kacie. Before Ashton's change in behavior, there was already a competition between the girls for their father's attention. Now, he ignored both of them.

"This is my son, Artie, who didn't bother to call me to dinner." Micah squeezed Artie's shoulders as he still sat at the table. "And, this is Batman, oops I am sorry, this is Adam," Micah teased. "Adam is our 11-year-old hero; he rescues lizards and frogs from the banks of the Schuylkill."

"I'm Robin," Artie the 13-year-old grinned. "I may be older than Adam, but I am his sidekick, Robin. We are going to save the world one day, one lizard at a time."

"Yuck," Katie interjected. "I hate boys. And, Mom. They had that stupid lizard out of the cage again."

"And, my brother, Ashton Taylor Sperling." Ashton stood up and shook hands with Lazarus. He noticed that they stood eye to eye. They stared at each other.

"Well, if this is final, and, I have no say," Kali turned to see Kacie still smiling and on the edge of her seat, "when does he start?"

"I want him in the house tonight, especially since Ashton leaves on a business trip tomorrow. Is that alright, Ashton?" Micah deferred as he always did to Ashton's last say.

Ashton nodded and then stepped around Lazarus and looked back at him again giving him a complete once over. "Keep the kids quiet when I am in the study. I will be working and won't want to be disturbed."

"I am going to talk to Ashton for a few minutes. When I get back I will show you to your suite and through the rest of the place," Micah said to Lazarus as he nodded his head back toward the kids.

"And, then I am going to find out if everyone's room is nice and tidy," Lazarus said jokingly, but all the kids left the room quickly, except for Kacie. She waited until her father and Micah were out of earshot.

"What happened to your eyes?" she dropped her fork on the plate and began to climb over the chairs closer to him.

"Kacie, get down," Lazarus and Kali said simultaneously. She got down from the chairs and walked around the table.

"Well," she said, taking his hand.

"I hate wearing glasses," Lazarus kneeled down in front of her. "So I am wearing contact lenses."

"What was wrong with your hazel eyes?" she asked.

"I thought I would try black for awhile," he answered and turned to her mother. "Are you okay with this, Mrs. Sperling?"

"Her name is Kali," Kacie interjected.

"Yes, my name is Kali. It's okay for you to call me Kali," she said watching her daughter's face light up. Ashton used to make it light up like that.

"Okay, Kali. I didn't know that you weren't aware of the arrangements. So, if you have any objections, I won't take the job."

"It's okay, isn't it, Mommy? Mommy is okay with it. Please, Mommy. You are okay with it, right? I can be quiet, Mommy. I can be real quiet. I won't tell Daddy, if you don't want him to know I already know Lazarus," her precocious daughter was aware of the secrets being held in the penthouse. "I promise," Kacie crossed her little heart.

"That won't be necessary," Lazarus stood up and lifted Kacie into his arms. "We won't lie to your father," Lazarus said.

"It might be best, if we omit," Kali reached for Kacie and pulled her out of his arms.

Chapter Eleven

IMMEDIATELY, KALI NOTICED the difference in her children. They held their heads high again. Ashton was still doing everything he could to avoid them, but it no longer mattered. They were getting all the attention they needed. In the four weeks since Lazarus had moved in, she watched each child's light brighten a little more each day.

She walked out of her room and sat on the stairs near the picture of Ashton's grandfather, Jordan, the family patriarch that still overlooked the expansive living room below. She watched Lazarus walk through the hall into the living room with Adam glued to his side. Adam was talking and Lazarus was actively engaged. The same way Ashton used to be. Kali thought about how Ashton would set aside time to spend with each kid each day. And, even though some days he spent more time with one than the other, they didn't mind, they knew their father loved them.

They missed their dad, and so did she. She stood up and looked Jordan in the eye. She reached out and touched the painting of the man who began her life in this penthouse. She missed him, too. He would know what to do, how to get her out of this mess.

Jordan's eyes haunted her every time she passed that life-size painting. Some days she half expected him to reach out and grab her hand, ask her what was wrong. But, he didn't. So she stood there staring at him waiting, hearing his voice in her mind.

"Seduce him," Jordan's voice said clearly. "Listen to Micah, Kali. Seduce him. You have waited long enough."

Kali turned to look down the stairs as she heard footsteps coming toward her. Adam was a few steps ahead of Lazarus.

"Hey, Mom," Adam kissed her on the cheek and kept going up the stairs past her.

"Well, hey to you, too," she said to the blur as he sped by.

"Hey, Mom," Lazarus said as he met her on the stairs.

"Hey, Uncle Lazarus," she smiled genuinely at the tall, lanky stranger that had brought an element of safety and security into their home.

"I want to thank you," she said, not sure why she needed to say that right now. Maybe because she had just made a decision and she was scared.

"Are you alright, Mrs. Sperling? I mean, you did just say, thank you? Or, was I hearing things?" Lazarus stepped aside to let her pass, but she didn't move.

"You are such a tease," Kali slid down to sit on the stair, "but, yes. Thank you. My children are happy. You put order back into their lives. I have never seen a group of kids so excited to go to school each morning. What are you putting into those homemade lunches they are fighting over?"

"How about I make you one, one morning, and you can find out?" Lazarus licked his lips as he stared into her eyes.

"When are you going to take those things off your beautiful eyes?" she asked.

"I can't see without glasses or contact lenses," he grinned.

"You lie," she wrapped her arms around her knees, "but I am going to let you slide on that one."

"Honestly, is everything okay?" Lazarus leaned back against the banister.

"Yes. No. I was wondering, could you take the kids for an overnighter somewhere? I would like to spend some time with my husband. Alone." Kali looked away when she said "alone." That frightened her.

"If you are looking for privacy, I can just take the kids around the corner to my wing. This place is huge. I can keep them occupied. We can have music night since the music room is next to my suite, and do some history projects or something. When?"

"Tonight," she said, hoping she wouldn't lose her courage to seduce her own husband, the same man who had seduced her when she was 17 and then again when she thought she was legally married to another man. The same man who had made passionate love to her thousands of times was now the man who, literally, raped her every night. He had become brutal and mean, downright vicious behind those closed doors. She was afraid for her life. She was afraid for the children's lives as well.

"Okay, they will love the surprise. I'll take them around about

9:00. Will that work?" Lazarus asked.

She nodded and held onto the wall as she steadied herself up. She swayed a little. Lazarus placed his hand on her waist and she could feel the heat from his hand race through her body. He excited her. She gasped. It had been a long time since she had experienced that type of tension between her thighs.

"Mrs. Sperling," he said as he placed his other hand on the other side of her waist. He lifted her and placed her at the bottom of the stairs. He took her hand and led her to the sofa.

"Kali," she said, smoothing her skirt as she sat down. He sat down beside her.

"Mrs., sorry, Kali, I will take the children on an adventure right around the corner in my wing. They will be far enough away not to hear any noises of any kind, plus we will be making lots of noises of our own. Your children cannot sing," he grinned. "Beautiful faces, horrible voices."

Kali smiled. He was trying to make her feel better and he was. That was something else he had in common with her old Ashton, that and the need for adventure. She remembered the days when Ashton would take her on adventure after adventure long before the twins were born. Even though she had grown up in the south, she had never swum in a creek before. Ashton had taken her to Wissahickon Creek and pushed her in, then he jumped in and they swam most of the day in their underwear without getting caught and without getting sick from the Filthadelphia runoff.

Ashton had taught her how to climb the wall behind the Art Museum. He took her trout fishing on the Delaware River. They went scuba diving in the Bahamas. She started thinking of all the things they did back then, and even the safaris he used to take the kids on in their own backyard. She missed that yard in New Jersey. Had she only known how bad things were really going to get, she might have fought harder to stay in New Jersey.

"Kali, Micah hired me to protect you and the children," Lazarus touched her on the knee. "While the children are working on their projects this evening, I may on occasion walk the hallways to make sure everything and everyone is okay. Okay?"

"Okay," Kali answered. Lazarus stood up, and for a moment she thought he was going to kiss her on the head the way Ashton used to. Instead, he reached down and pushed her rogue curl from between her eyes and smiled. She watched him as he went up the stairs and began to think about seducing Ashton.

CHAPTER TWELVE

KALI LET THE hot shower give her the courage she needed to face the man she had once loved more than she loved herself. She was going to take Micah's advice and seduce him. She had to approach him just the right way, the way Ashton had taught her to seduce Jordan when she wanted to have her way. Jordan was loving, but strict and had rules that could list a mile long, but on more than one occasion she had gotten him to bend those rules. Ashton had taught her to pick her battles, so she did. She picked the rules that were important to her to break, then she would seduce him.

She had been thinking as much about Jordan as she did about her old Ashton these days. Maybe this was why, she thought as she prepared her body with her own homemade oils of strawberry and vanilla. She washed her hair and let her curls hang naturally around her shoulders as she slid into a black, silk gown with a slit up the side. She lit all the candles in the room and brought in some more. She took a few into the bathroom and lit those. She started a slow drip in the bathtub, so that the water would be just right when he walked in the door. She threw fresh rose petals in the bathtub and added a mildly scented bubble bath, and then turned the fresh linens back and waited.

The sudden knock on the door surprised her. Ashton wouldn't be knocking. Draping herself in a matching robe, she went to door, swung it open, and found her children standing before her with the biggest smiles she had seen in a long time. They had pillows bunched up in their arms and blankets draped around their shoulders.

Katie was holding onto Lazarus' left arm like she owned him, and Adam was leaning his head against his right arm. AJ and Artie flanked him from behind and Kacie stood in front of him.

"Mom," Kacie reached up and tugged at her robe, "we're going camping." All the children giggled.

"Camping? I don't believe I have given any of you permission to go camping and on a school night," Kali put her hands on her hips and tried to subdue a grin as she eyed the happy bunch.

"We will be just around the corner," Kacie announced. "Can we?

Lazarus said we had to ask first."

"Can we, Mom?" Katie looked as if she was going to pull off the poor man's arm.

"I know it's silly, Mom," AJ worked his way around the group and knelt beside Kacie. "We will be in Lazarus's suite and the music room. We are just sleeping around there. There's nothing wrong with that, is it?"

"Well, no. But, don't keep Lazarus up all night. He will need his sleep. You know old people?" Kali finally smiled back at the kids and they were immediately excited.

"Do you mind, Lazarus?" she asked for the benefit of the children.

"No, Mrs. Sperling. And I promise they will be at school on time tomorrow," he winked.

"Alright," Kali bent down and kissed Kacie, then got a good night kiss and hug from each of her children who took off running down the hallway.

Lazarus was still standing there.

"He must be due in soon," Lazarus' eyes scanned her body and rested on her breast area. She looked down as the oil had seeped through and the silk was clinging to her body. He absent-mindedly licked his bottom lip and it sent a shiver through to her core.

"You know where I am, if you need me," he backed away reluctantly.

Kali closed the door and went back to her bed. There was something about that man. Not only had the kids fallen for him, she was beginning to think she was, too. Ten minutes later, she rolled out of the bed to check on the bath water, and the door swung open. It was Ashton, a solemn look on his face. At first, she wanted to bolt for the door and run. Then, she remembered her mission.

"Hello," she said sauntering cautiously close to him as he began to peel off his suit jacket. "Let me help you," she said. She eased the jacket from his arm and then reached for his tie. He grabbed her hands almost squeezing them. She wanted to gasp, but didn't.

"I have run you a bath. I thought," she said as she gently tugged her hands free, "I thought, it's been a long time since I made love to my husband." She reached for the tie again.

"We screw every night," Ashton said.

"Yes," Kali began to loosen his tie. "We screw. You have had to deal with so much this past year. I want to help you, Ashton. I want you to know you are not going through this all alone. Let me," she stood on her tiptoes and kissed him under his chin. "Let me take care of you."

"What are you up to?" he stepped back and glared at her.

"My goal is to help ease my husband's pain. I see it in your eyes," she stepped closer to him and began to unbutton his shirt. "Let me make love to you the way I used to make love to you. Let me ease your pain," she kissed him lightly on his cheek and began to remove his shirt.

"Your pants," she tugged at his belt and he began to help her. He stepped out of his shoes and then his pants. "Come on," she grabbed his hand and led her naked husband into the bathroom. He leaned forward and tested the water and then got into the tub.

"Aren't you getting in?" he asked.

"No, I am going to bathe you from right here," she said as she lathered a sponge and began to soap his head and his neck. Dropping the sponge, she began to massage his head, letting her fingers massage every inch and then feel around the back of his head. There was a scar, but not the scar she had expected. Ashton had had two head injuries that she was aware of, one from the prison attack when he was serving time for killing her first husband. Thank God he had been released for that wrongful conviction. But, the second had occurred when both of them had been shot by an unknown assailant, about the same time his personality changed drastically. A chill went down Kali's spine as she remembered that day, but their lives had changed weeks before that.

Kali's hand massaged the back of Ashton's head at the base of his skull where his first scar should have been, a keloid scar the size of a plump earthworm. He had told the kids a snake resided in daddy's head. They would sneak up and touch it and run. He would chase them around making crazy noises while they squealed in delight. She found a scar, one that was splintered and about the size of a quarter. That scar shouldn't have been there. He shifted uncomfortably and she began to massage his neck and shoulders. She looked at the mirrored tile and thought about her own scar, the bullet wound to her chest that had just missed her heart by an inch.

Kali took a deep breath and got through the bath, a sensual smile on her face. She led him back to the bed. "Stay here," she said. "Let me get some towels and I will massage you on the bed."

She was surprised when he obeyed her. She layered the thick towels on her bed and made him lie down. She picked up the heated peppermint oil she had put in a baby bottle warmer and began to pour it down the middle of his back. He sighed.

Kali took her time the way she used to before with Jordan and Ashton. She rubbed slowly and massaged the muscles deeply and then she kissed them lightly. She could feel his body relax beneath her as she straddled him with her bare bottom. As he relaxed she knew this was exciting him. She slid down his oiled body and lingered over his buttocks, reaching between his thighs teasing him with the tingly oil. She patted down his thighs and wondered when they had lost their tautness. All of his muscles had once been tight, massive, and strong. That was one of the reasons she was determined to never let herself go, whether it was one kid or four kids. She saw women who had gained weight and never lost it, or those who just had stopped dressing in a manner not only to please their men, but themselves.

Kali worked her way to the back of his calves and almost gasped aloud. She hadn't noticed it in the midst of the sudsy bath, but another scar was missing. Shortly after they had moved to New Jersey, they had bought horses. It had been Ashton's dream to own a horse. He had a bought a stallion named Nightmare.

Nightmare was jet black and as mean as the devil. The only person that could ride him was Ashton. He was determined to let Nightmare know that he was his master, and Nightmare seemed determined to let Ashton know that he was sadly mistaken. Every chance Ashton had gotten he would get on Nightmare's back, and whenever Nightmare got tired of Ashton he would either dump him on a trail or lead him straight back to the stables.

One day, Nightmare dumped Ashton in a thick brush and Chico spent the better part of an hour stitching Ashton's leg back together. Ashton was so angry he got right back on Nightmare and took off, bloody bandages and all. No one really knew what happened after that, but Nightmare never threw Ashton again.

Now that six-inch keloid scar was gone. Kali could feel her heart race, as she was eager to get this so-called lovemaking session behind her. She coaxed him on his back and began at his feet. Then, it was all she could do to keep from getting the .38 she had hidden in one of her boots and shooting the impostor. The third, most endearing scar was missing, too. Kacie had dropped a glass tumbler on his barefoot when she was three. Ashton had asked Kali to hand him his glass from the kitchen table, and Kacie had beat her to it trying to please her Daddy. She tripped as she tried to hand it to him, and Ricky had had to stitch him up. She had kissed and sucked that toe many times, teasing him about his little love scar.

She kissed and massaged and nibbled her way back up to his penis and took it in her mouth. She knew that it wasn't Taylor, Ashton's nickname for his most outstanding limb. She wondered if it was Thomas, Taylor's freaky twin. But, he was dead; at least, he was supposed to be. Whoever, he was, she thought as she did her best to please him, he was dangerous, but not as dangerous as she was about to become, now that she knew the man that he wasn't. He wasn't Ashton. She wondered if Micah knew. And, for how long?

The next morning Kali awakened with the man standing over her watching her sleep. "Good morning, what time is it?" she stretched, trying not to appear startled or frightened. He sat down next to her and smoothed her hair away from her face. She was surprised how gentle his touch was and even more surprised by the look on his face. He looked almost happy.

"Good morning to you," he said as he kissed her on the forehead. "Thank you," he said, his hand lay lightly against her cheek. It was warm and soft, almost reminiscent of Ashton's.

"For what?" she stretched again, then kissed the palm of his hand. "Let me at the bathroom."

He moved to let her up. "For last night," he said as she climbed out past him.

"It was way overdue," she kissed his cheek then ran to the bathroom. She tried to hold back the feeling of nausea rising up in her throat. She didn't want him to hear her throwing up. After all, she had only made love to her loving husband.

"What are you doing today?" she yelled from the bathroom.

"A couple of meetings in the office later on. What are you doing?"

"End of the month. Gotta closeout," Kali walked out with her toothbrush.

"No one," he stopped and turned to leave the room.

"No one, what?" Kali followed him to the door.

"No one has ever loved me the way you do," the fake Ashton said, and Kali could tell in his eyes that he really meant it.

"Oh, silly. What did that bullet do to you? To us? We used to make love like that all the time. I have always loved you like this. I'm sorry if you have been feeling alone. I have always been here. Will always be here," she said, wishing she was saying those words to her real husband. Where was he?

The fake Ashton leaned forward and kissed her passionately. She pulled up all her acting skills reminiscent of when she first had to succumb to Jordan. If Ashton hadn't coached her, she would have ended up becoming one of Jordan's sex slaves stashed away in some apartment. Instead, she became Jordan's favorite concubine, the one that had survived and walked away with millions. No other woman in his stables could have dreamed of that reward. And, the thought had never crossed her mind. At that time, all she knew was that she had no choice but to play it Jordan's way; plus, she had no objections to the perks that came with the game. She liked living in luxury, and as long as Ashton was a part of the game, she had been willing.

She leaned sexily against the door as he left. He kissed her again on the cheek. She blew him a kiss, watched him walk down the hall, and then ran back to the bathroom. Kali let the nausea rise and she threw up every last vile taste of the intruder.

CHAPTER THIRTEEN

LAZARUS KNOCKED ON the door to Dr. Ruby Sperling's office. She was Micah's wife and, after becoming a psychologist, had gone to medical school and was now a full-fledged psychiatrist. Micah had joked that she was a woman who always wanted more and was busy trying to analyze herself to find out why. Both Kali and Micah had said he should talk to her, since she was the family shrink, to see if she could help him recover his memory. But, he didn't know if could trust her. He wasn't really sure that he should trust any of them, especially the two doctors.

Ricky and Chico both looked at him as if there was something important not being said. At first, he had thought, since they were gay, they were competing for his attention. Both or one of them would stop by, just to hang out while the kids were in school. They would always hug him and touch him, but neither made a real pass at him. When he asked Micah about their sexual orientation, he had said that Ricky was definitely gay, but Chico was more bi-sexual. So, whatever they were up to, Lazarus stopped believing it had to do with sex. But Micah always acted as if life was normal. He made him feel at ease, as if he were in the right place. He had no problem with the oldest one, Ashton, who didn't look at him strangely or make him feel uncomfortable, because he was too wrapped up in himself. Lazarus wouldn't have been surprised if Ashton even noticed he was present in the Sperling household.

Now, Kali, the beautiful one that haunted his mind and his body, was another story. He didn't think it was in his nature to pursue another man's wife, but he knew it wouldn't take much for him to pursue this one. Her eyes danced and her lips pranced, he thought, as he visualized her talking non-stop and how her eyes lit up when her children smiled. And how, he didn't know, could he love someone else's children as much as he loved the Sperling children? When he was hired, Micah had asked if he would die for them. He had said yes, because he knew he would be willing to protect any child. But, he knew now that he would not just die for them, he would be willing to kill for them, especially for Kacie.

"You are early," Ruby answered the door. Micah's wife was a tall, attractive dark-skinned woman with almond-shaped eyes and long, straight black hair. The cadence in her voice was slow and sensual. He imagined all of her patients falling madly in love with her.

"I'm on time a little early," Lazarus joked, but Ruby didn't smile. She was strictly professional and had been aloof since the first day he had met her.

"My husband has told me you were an intended murder victim with amnesia. Are you still experiencing amnesia, or have you begun to get any memories back?"

"Well, hello. How are you? Nice meeting you, I'm Lazarus."

"Look, you are a freebie. I know all about you through my husband and my son. It's not like I haven't seen you around. Let's cut the bullshit and cut to the chase. Micah thinks you might get your memory back through hypnosis. I advise against it. I think you should allow it to return gradually, if it returns. Ricky gave me your medical records and it showed severe medial temporal lobe damage bilaterally. What I am trying to say is from the looks of your MRI, I believe it is likely that you have *pure retrograde amnesia*. Meaning you will never recover your past memories. All I have to offer is someone to talk to." She sat down behind her big desk, her eyes focused only on the notepad before her.

"Okay, since you put it like that," Lazarus sat down in the chair across from her and stared. She looked uncomfortable, and he wondered why. Either the two younger brothers or Micah's wife knew who he was and the others didn't, or this motley crew was unable to wear poker faces and pretend as well as the others.

"I am having recurring dreams," he leaned forward to see Ruby's reaction.

"What kind of dreams?" she picked up the notepad.

"I dream of a baby crying. He's not just crying, he's screaming at the top of his lungs and he's lying on my chest. Whenever I try to reach for him, I wake up. I have this dream at least once a month. Lately, I have been having it about once a week."

"Is that it?"

"No, I just recently started having another one."

"What would that be?" Ruby was scribbling feverishly on the

pad. Lazarus was tempted to lean forward to see what she was writing. He was equally curious as to why she refused to look at him while he spoke, so he leaned over on her desk. She sat up and pushed her chair back with a frightened look on her face.

"What is your other dream, Mr. Smith?" she asked.

"It's a woman's hand. It is reaching for a glass ornament on a Christmas tree. The ornament is like one of those snow globes, except it has gold glitter instead of white snow. It has a saxophone in the middle with an inscription on the base. But, I can't read the inscription. The woman is holding the ornament real careful like and, then, her hand seems to weaken or something. The ornament falls right out of her hand and crashes loudly. Then, I wake up."

"Very interesting," Ruby said. "Anything else?"

"No, nothing else," Lazarus says still leaning on her desk watching her breathe. Her chest was not moving evenly, she was agitated, but why?

"Those are just dreams of anxiety since you can't remember. They don't mean anything," she said getting up from the chair and looking at her watch.

"I have a paying customer due any minute. Do you mind?" she walked him to the door.

"Not at all," he looked into her eyes and she looked away. He knew immediately that she was lying.

CHAPTER FOURTEEN

LAZARUS HAD NOTHING better to do than to wait. He went into Ashton's study and turned on the computer. While he waited for it to go through its paces, he picked up a Personal Defense Systems Incorporated (PDSI) contract and started to read, laughing aloud at the rudimentary language and the giant loopholes. Then, the door opened.

"What are you doing in my office?" Ashton asked as he stormed toward the desk.

"How does your business survive?" Lazarus asked as he leaned back in the chair.

"What?" Ashton stopped in his tracks.

"You are giving away money," Lazarus pointed to the contract.

"What do you know about my business and who gave you permission to critique my contracts?"

"I was bored. So bored I thought a contract would be recreational reading. And it is. I have never seen such a poorly written one. What legal department wrote this?" Lazarus thought Micah couldn't have possibly seen it.

"I wrote it," Ashton admitted. "Ever since, well," he stopped talking. Kali and Micah were holding his hands in the business. They were afraid of him messing up. At first, he didn't care if it messed up. In the beginning his only purpose was to liquidate it. Now, he was beginning to like the power and the family that came with it. For a second, he could still smell Kali.

"Well, it's your business." Lazarus stood up, surprised at how intrigued he had become reading a contract.

"Sit back down." Ashton approached the desk and sat in the chair across from him. "Can you do better?"

"First, I wouldn't write any contracts myself, I would be using the company form. Your company is old enough and your brother is damn smart enough; I am sure there is a fill in the blank for most types of services you perform. If not, I can help put that together. Next, you need to renegotiate these terms. Like I said, you are giving away money."

"Come work for me," Ashton said out of the blue.

"I already work for you," Lazarus grinned.

"As a babysitter. How would you like an executive job instead?"

"I like babysitting." Lazarus wasn't about to let go of the kids. He didn't know why, but he had to keep them close.

"Think about it," Ashton gathered the documents and walked out of the door.

"What an interesting piece to this puzzle," Lazarus said to himself. "How the hell did a man develop such a lucrative business writing child-like contracts? Kacie could have done a better job. What am I saying? How the hell did I know about contracts? God, is that what I did? I know about contracts, negotiating. What else do I know?" Lazarus did a little victory dance and then walked to the door and looked down the hallway where Ashton had gone. "Where do I know you from?" Lazarus whispered, thinking about Ashton's angry hazel eyes and how familiar they had looked.

CHAPTER FIFTEEN

KALI SPED INTO the office with two things on her mind: the fake Ashton and the watch. She wondered if he was still looking for that watch. When he had first gotten out of the hospital, he kept asking for the watch Jordan had given him, the one that Ashton's father, Billy, had tried to steal when Ashton was in prison, the one that both Micah and Ashton had made sure was kept under lock and key until he came home.

Then, when Ashton came home, he put the damn watch back on every day. He knew it was a faux Rolex, but he wore anyway. He said it was his trademark. She said it was his choice, but she hated the thing. She knew within her heart, if she could find the watch she could find Ashton, her Ashton. The watch was with him. Sadly, she thought, he could be lying dead somewhere with the watch on his left wrist, then she shook the thought from her head. Ashton was not dead, she couldn't think that way. But, where was he? He wouldn't just leave her and the kids. Or, would he? He was disappointed in her and angry the day of his father's funeral. He had every right to be. Here was his wife orchestrating a funeral for the man that had tried to kill him twice.

She stormed into Micah's office. He was on the phone and didn't look startled by her grand entrance. He held up a finger for her to be quiet. He was listening to someone speak. He pulled open his drawer, pulled out a key with a white tag, and handed it to her. He put his hand over the receiver and mouthed the words, "Meet me there. An hour."

Kali ran into Mr. Fake as she was leaving Micah's office. He grabbed her around the waist and kissed her. She wrapped her arms around him and smiled up at him.

"Are we feeling better today?" she asked as she gave him a big hug.

"Yes, much better," he grinned like a man in love. Kali looked back and saw the woman occupying Ms. Elliott's chair staring at them. She missed Elliott. Elliott had been Ashton's executive assistant since the day the business had opened. Now she was gone, nowhere to be found.

"You better get to work," she whispered. "I have a meeting in an hour. I'll be back though, okay?" She patted his chest and stepped away, walking toward her office. She turned back and saw him still standing there. "Go to work," she teased. He smiled happily as he disappeared behind the double doors.

Kali sat in her office tapping her fingers on her desk. She needed to talk to Micah now. She had to find out where Ashton was and who was this man impersonating him. She pulled out a notepad and began to jot down places the watch could be, places where Ashton had left it before, and places where neither the fake Ashton nor she had looked.

Ashton's arm
The jewelry dresser in Jersey
Nightmare's saddlebag
Safe room

"The safe room," Kali sighed, really disgusted now. When was the last time she had been in the safe room? Over a year! She and Ashton used to use the safe room as a rendezvous place, a place that was kid free, phone free and, let's face it, Micah free. They would move into the safe room for a day, make love, read books, watch movies, and sometimes just sit there in total peace and quiet.

She ripped up the note and decided to focus on the safe room. She looked at the key and grabbed her purse. She couldn't get into the safe room right now. She wasn't sure if the fake Ashton had a clue it was there, and she didn't want to tip him off. She would try to check things out this evening.

CHAPTER SIXTEEN

KALI RUSHED DOWN the street on foot. She didn't feel like sitting in Center City's gridlocked traffic. She could get to the address on the tag faster if she walked, and she needed to take the walk anyway. Plus, she needed to drop her bodyguard. The guy was good, really good. Half the time, she didn't know he was there. But, then she would spot him. All of their bodyguards had to lay back. At first, she didn't understand Micah's logic, not until Ashton started getting really weird. But, she didn't want one tailing her today. She doubled back through another building and went through their loading dock to get back on track. She glanced around and realized she had lost him.

The address was to a little head shop off Samson Street. She walked into the small, dark shop with its drug paraphernalia dustily displayed. She wondered if anyone ever shopped there. She walked around waiting for someone to appear, but the store was eerily quiet and empty. Kali stood in the middle of the floor for a few minutes looking upward and around, trying to figure out the reason she was given a key to a door that was already open. She noticed a doorway to what could be an office; she walked over to it and knocked on the slightly opened door not wanting to startle anyone. She stuck her head in and found only a small cluttered office with no one in it, but there was a door in the rear that must have been an exit. She opened it quickly, and saw that it led to another door across an alleyway.

Kali pulled the key out of her pocket and wasn't surprised when the key easily slid into the new door and turned. She stepped into an older building; it was clean but bare. The entire first floor was empty. She ran up the stairs to the second floor and in the first room found a huge metal desk and a desk chair on wheels. On top of the desk was a computer. She turned it on and it asked for a password.

"John1111," Micah said as he walked into the office. "The password is John1111."

"Micah, my God," Kali ran to her brother-in-law and wrapped her arms around him. "I did it, Micah. I seduced that thing, that man. He is not Ashton. How long have you known?"

"How long have you known?" Micah freed himself from her arms and spun her around.

"I didn't. I thought the second head injury had blown his mind. Didn't you? He lost part of his memory, right? At least, that's what we believed. I believed," her voice trailed off. Micah was right, she had struggled with believing that, but she had had no choice. She had thought it was something she had to live with; after all, she couldn't run with four kids in tow.

"Kali, you brought it to my attention, how many times? You said, the way he touched you reminded you of Asa."

"I thought the part of his brain that took over had taken on Asa's personality. That's what Ruby said. And I knew that Asa was dead. Or, at least that's what you told me. You said you saw Asa's dead body in the hospital. And, I believed you," Kali moved away from Micah. She was suddenly afraid of the only man she had been able to trust this past year.

"I saw the body. I saw the flat line. But, I must have been deceived because there is no one else in this world that looks and acts as much like Ashton as his identical twin."

"Then where's Ashton?" Kali choked. She had tried not to focus on that since last night. If she had, she would have given herself away to the fake Ashton. Now, the tears began to flow down her face, and her hands began to shake. Ashton would never have willingly left her behind and especially not the children.

Micah reached out for her and she turned away from him. She walked around to the other side of the desk and thought about the small firearm in her bag. Was she on her own?

"Ashton's alive and well," Micah said.

"How do you know?" Kali didn't believe him. If Ashton was alive and well, she would know it. He would be in touch with her. She would have known that the imposter in her bed was another man. Was Asa.

"I got this, Kali. I got this," Micah began to walk toward her.

"For over a year? You let me be abused by Asa, for over a year."

"You let you be abused by Asa for over a year. I told you to seduce him."

"And, what difference does that make?"

"Asa is easily manipulated. You turn the tables, and you find out for yourself who he really is, you gain control."

Kali swayed a bit. The room had suddenly become warm. The ground beneath her feet was rocking. Micah reached for her again. She let him pull her close to him. She laid her head against his chest and listened to his heartbeat to help steady her own.

"Why haven't you exposed him, Micah? Why is Ashton in hiding? Is that where he is? You have to explain it to me, because I don't trust you right now. I never thought I could ever doubt you, but I don't trust you right now. Nor your wife."

"Kali," Micah took her face in his hands. "I love you, almost as much as I love my brother. You are a part of this family. Jordan loved you. I would never ever willingly do anything to hurt you. I'm not telling you to trust me, but I am asking you to give me some time to work things through."

"Like what?"

"Like keeping you, the children, Ashton, and Ruby safe. You and I know Asa is a dufus. So whatever he is doing here, he is not doing it alone. But, he is not totally stupid, either. He's paying people to watch us, the same way I am paying people to watch him. Two things. One, he is looking for Ashton's stupid watch."

"The fake Rolex?"

"Yeah, there's a code on the watch that he and Daddy had been dying to get their hands on."

"They almost got it when Ashton was in prison. I surprised them and got it back," Kali remembered threatening them with a gun in front of her children. Her babies had been exposed to a lot, she thought. Unfortunately, she thought, they were Sperlings, and there was a lot she wouldn't be able to protect them from experiencing.

"And, Kali. This one is totally dependent on you. When he liquidates the accounts he has his hands into, he will try to collect on your insurance policies."

Kali's eyes widened with the new information.

"I need to find out where the only other person that used to lead him around with a ring in his nose is hiding out."

"Redd?"

"Yeah, Redd," Micah nodded.

"Are you going to tell me where Ashton is, Molasses?" she remembered how Ashton used to say Micah was as slow as molasses and as deliberate as a pit bull with the taste of blood on his tongue. It had been Micah that had tracked her down when she was running, not once or twice, but three times. On the third go around, he had put his deceptive skills in place by manipulating her young husband into bringing her back into the Sperling fold. Ashton hadn't lifted a finger. She had just walked right back into his bed, a willing victim or a willing lover. For the last year, she had tried to shake the feeling of being a victim. But, every time that man had walked into their bedroom, he had ravaged her aggressively. Whenever they were alone, he had put her on the defensive. Last night, she had finally listened to Micah and went on the offensive. She was angry, but mostly angry with herself. All this time, she should have been searching for Ashton.

"Why can't Ashton come home?" Kali knew Ashton would never stand by and lose his family, let alone his money.

"Murder charges. About three weeks after the ambush, when the two of you were shot. Ashton, not your Ashton, but our impersonator..."

"Asa," Kali interjected.

"Watch it, Kali. I don't want either one of us getting used to saying that. We can't afford any slip-ups. For now, Ashton."

"Ashton A.B.," Kali offered. "Ashton after the bullet. Or, Ashton all beautiful to his face, if I slip."

"Okay, AB was picked up on murder charges by Camden police. They knew they had him."

"Murder charges? Why would he get picked up?"

"That security guard. The one that set our Ashton up in prison. The one Daddy paid to orchestrate Ashton's death and failed."

"But, he almost succeeded," Kali knew where this was going. She had prayed Ashton had let it go, but she knew he hadn't. Every time he had one of those debilitating headaches, it had been when someone or something reminded him of that incident. He had had that same headache the day after his father's funeral. He had crumbled to his knees in their bedroom. She had sat on the floor massaging his head all night. They weren't frequent, but they were chronic. She walked over to the desk and took a deep breath.

"Well, someone strangled him to death. That someone left a fingerprint."

"Oh, God. Ashton?"

"Yes, Ashton's fingerprint."

"On something where it happened? I mean, where did it happen? Maybe it was something Ashton had touched a long time ago," Kali grasped for straws.

"No," Micah shook his head. "He left a thumbprint on the dead body."

"On the body," Kali was amazed, trying to imagine a fingerprint on the body.

"On his neck, Kali. Ashton strangled him to death. The man was wearing one of those plastic ID holders strung around his neck. Somehow, Ashton left a clear thumbprint on it."

Kali's hands covered her mouth; more tears flew from her eyes. She knew without a doubt Ashton had murdered the man. When Ashton was angry, he always went for the throat. Though it had been 15 years ago when she was the one who had made him that angry, she could still feel his hands around her throat.

"Anyway," Micah sat on the desk next to her, "AB's prints didn't match. He's never been imprisoned or picked up before that."

"No, he just got away with murder playing dead," Kali was stroking her throat. She hated thinking about that era in her life. "So, they let him go," Kali crashed into the chair. She couldn't stand any longer.

"They had no choice. They attributed the prints to a mix-up, but they had a witness who thought that a man resembling Ashton was outside of Scully's house one morning. The morning he was found dead. But, he wasn't sure enough to testify."

"Can we make him, AB, pay for the murder?"

"Then what do we do with Ashton when I bring him home?"

"Oh, so that's what this is about?"

"Yes," Micah walked out of the room and brought in another chair. He sat in it and leaned onto the desk looking at Kali.

"Kali. I can't tell you where Ashton is. I can only tell you that if he knew what was happening he would be here."

"What do you mean?"

"He just can't be here. And we, you and I, are going to have to handle this on our own."

"And Ruby?" Kali wanted to know why Ruby was avoiding her. "Does she know about AB?"

"I don't know what Ruby knows," Micah was being honest. About the same time Ashton had started acting weird, so had Ruby. Kali was being raped every night and he had been going without. Ruby would barely give him a kiss, let alone a kind word.

"You don't think," Kali gulped. She didn't want to think anymore. She wanted Ashton to come home and end this. She looked at Micah's face. She had never seen him worried before. For a moment, she was even more frightened because Micah was looking like a lost child.

CHAPTER SEVENTEEN

IT WAS AN early dismissal for AJ and Katie. Lazarus had driven to pick them up and three young ladies had followed Katie home. He was expecting them. Katie had begged her mother to allow her to have guests, and when Kali finally had given in, Katie began planning the afternoon as if it were a major social event. Lazarus helped her plan as he noticed AJ was just as eager as Katie.

"AJ," Lazarus called as he entered the rec room with a tray of goodies for the girls. He placed the tray on a corner table and tried to get out of the way as the girls converged. Lazarus motioned for AJ to follow him, and saw the look of disappointment on the young man's face. AJ was in love and from the looks of it so was the young lady who was the subject of his attention.

"AJ," Lazarus called again, as the lanky teenager slowly backed out of the room. Lazarus grabbed him by the shoulders and lifted him out of the door. As he was about to close it, Katie came running toward him. She stepped outside the door and closed it, grinning from ear to ear. She reached up and hugged Lazarus, then kissed him on the cheek.

"Thank you, Uncle Lazarus," she said. She then punched AJ and ran back into the room.

"Uncle Lazarus," Lazarus chuckled. "That's new." He continued to usher AJ down the hall.

"Yeah, well, that's what Kacie calls you," AJ laughed. "Is there any food left?"

"No, I cleaned out the kitchen and gave it all to the girls, you knucklehead. I saw you looking at Marissa," Lazarus teased.

"That's my girl," AJ said proudly.

"Your girl?" Lazarus shook his head. "You had better think about your homework and forget about your girl. You are too young for your girl."

"She's my age," AJ protested.

"Naw, naw. That's not what I am talking about. We have already had this conversation, AJ."

"I'm 15. In a few months, I will be 16. By the time my dad was my age, he was having sex every night. He had plenty of girls."

"I think your father was exaggerating," Lazarus shook his head,

"Probably not," AJ arched his eyebrows. "You don't know about the family history, do you?"

"No, not past history," Lazarus thought that he had landed in the midst of a very interesting family, to say the least.

"When Katie and I turned 12, my mom and dad started telling us things. It looks like I'm going to be the one to tell Adam since they don't talk to us like that anymore," AJ grabbed his stomach. "I gotta get something to eat, Uncle Lazarus."

Lazarus and AJ parted ways at the stairs. AJ ran toward the kitchen and Lazarus started up the stairs. He stopped in front of Jordan's picture, the original patriarch of the family. The picture never stopped amazing him. The man's face seemed to change at will. Some days he would glance in its direction, and think the picture was happy; on other days the eyes would just look sad. Today, he stopped and appreciated the delicate strokes that made the man seem real enough to step out of the life-sized painting. He half expected Jordan to extend his hand for a handshake, and he was half expecting to take it. He stood on the stair, eye to eye with Jordan. Today, his eyes and his lips were smiling.

"That's my great-grandfather," AJ was coming up the stairs, loaded with a sandwich and some fruit.

"AJ, you are still not allowed to take food up to your room."

"Ah, Uncle Lazarus. Just this once, please," AJ begged, coming to a stop on the stair just below him.

"If you tell, I will have both your ears for dinner," Lazarus looked down at the boy who obviously didn't believe him.

"I'll be careful. And, I won't tell," AJ adjusted his meal in his arms.

"Let me help," Lazarus took the fruit and then looked back at the picture.

"He was the man," AJ said with pride.

"The man, huh?" Lazarus had figured as much. Why else would a life-sized painting reign over the entire penthouse?

"He was the reason my father had so much sex," AJ looked up at Lazarus for his reaction.

"Your father doesn't appear to be that big of a ladies' man," Lazarus shook his head and started up the stairs.

"Seriously. My grandfather was a pimp. That's where our money came from," AJ volunteered.

Lazarus stopped in the hallway and leaned against the wall.

"AJ, you shouldn't talk ill of the dead."

"I told you, my mom and my dad told us our history. Or at least, were telling us our history. They said we needed to know so that could arm ourselves. They said there were people out there who didn't like us for various reasons."

"Like what," Lazarus was now curious.

"For instance, people don't like you because they just don't like you. Personally, that is."

"Yeah," Lazarus said.

"Then there are people who don't like you because you are not in the same group, or race, or religion. Right?"

"Right," Lazarus couldn't disagree with any of that.

"Then, there are people who don't like you because you want to succeed or you do succeed. And, then there are people who don't like you because of something someone in your family did. Like hurt people, or take from people. Or succeed by making someone else lose," AJ was eating his sandwich.

"You're dropping crumbs, AJ. Take it to your room," Lazarus didn't know where the kid was going with the story, but he didn't want to be responsible for the crumbs in the hallway.

"The music room," AJ said excitedly. "Let me show you the pictures in the music room."

Lazarus followed AJ down the hall to the music room. He was surprised at AJ's height once again. He thought the boy had grown an inch in the few months he had been taking care of him. They went into the music room and, for the first time, Lazarus noticed the walls were covered with the shelves and filled with gold-imprinted, leather bound books.

"My mom put these together. She went through all the pictures and sorted them by people, events, and years. She says these pictures hold our entire history. Mom talks to us about the past, but mostly in metaphors about what and what not to do, and how to treat people. But, my dad. He used to tell us like it is. He used to tell me more because I was a boy. But, he told Katie things, too. And my mom would get so mad sometimes. She would fuss and tell him he was exposing us to too much too soon. He said we needed body armor and mind armor."

"Used to?" Lazarus asked.

"Yeah, a lot happened in the last year or so. First, my grandfather died, or was murdered or something. There was a lot of talk and stuff about that. It was all over the news. My grandfather was a big-time lawyer. He hated my father."

AJ pulled down one of the leather bound books.

"This is the Sperling men. My great-grandfather, Jordan Banks. He was an award-winning sax player and a high-end pimp. He made millions. He bought this building, which was unheard of for a black man back in his day; he had nightclubs, good ones and illegal ones. My dad said no man, no man crossed Jordan Banks. And definitely no woman. Not until my mom came along.

"My dad said the reason there were only men in the household was because Jordan wouldn't let my granddad keep any girl babies. My mom said Jordan wasn't a fan of women. Otherwise, he wouldn't have built his livelihood on their backs. Get it, on their backs," AJ chuckled as Lazarus began to flip through the book.

Lazarus was flipping through the bound leather book that had been embossed 'The Sperling Men.' He looked at the variety of shades first. The younger ones didn't even look like they belonged to the same race. Jordan was black, real black and wore a black suit with a stark white shirt and red tie in most of the pictures. It was as if he was ready to blend into the night, but said wait, I had better give someone a little warning and threw in the white shirt. Billy was the exact opposite; his mother's genes had to have been strong to produce such an extremely pale child with grey eyes and straight hair.

And then there were the boys: the tan twins — Ashton and Asa — with their hazel eyes and long, curly locks; the chocolate brown Micah; the short Filipino-looking Chico; and the tall Puerto Rican-looking Ricky. Lazarus had met everyone except Asa and Billy who were both dead. As he flipped through the pictures, he began to notice a theme. Ashton and Jordan were always together, and they were always happy. Jordan would have Ashton pulled close in a big hug; Ashton would have his head against Jordan's shoulder. They looked like a team headed in the same direction.

Then there was Billy and Asa, both brooding, both looking left out or angry standing next to each other. Sometimes Billy would have his arm around Asa's shoulder, but it looked forced, as if someone had directed him to do so for the picture. On some of the more casual pictures when the family wasn't really posing, or Billy or Asa would just happen to be in the background, you could really see the anger seething beneath the façade of those two. One or the other would be looking shadily toward Jordan or Ashton, or they would just be looking annoyed. Lazarus wondered why.

He closed the book and was about to reach for another when he noticed the time. "Ride with me to get the others, will you?" Lazarus wanted to get AJ out of the penthouse. He knew if he didn't, AJ would make a beeline straight to the girls as soon as he left.

"Can't I stay and do homework?" AJ begged.

"No," Lazarus pointed toward the door. He stopped and looked quickly at the names on the bound photo albums. He pulled one down that said 'The Sperling Babies' and another that read 'In the Beginning.' He tucked them under his arm and dropped them off in his suite as they headed for the stairs.

CHAPTER EIGHTEEN

LAZARUS HAD HAD to drive each one of the girls home with Katie and AJ in tow. Then he returned home to help Kacie and Adam with homework. On top of that, Kali was in some sort of mood that made her snap at everything he said during dinner. He was tired, and was ready to retreat from the Sperling clan as early as possible. He walked through the halls to make sure everyone was secure in their rooms; he stuck his head outside to see if the guard outside the door needed anything, and then he checked on Kali.

"Mrs. Sperling," he knocked gently on her bedroom door. He knew Mr. Sperling was in New York for the evening.

"What?" she snatched the door open, standing with her robe hanging open revealing a two-piece cotton ensemble that wasn't meant to look sexy, but it did on her.

"I was just saying good night," Lazarus bowed before her.

"Good night," she said as she slammed the door, leaving him standing there stunned. She had always been a little flippant, but never this outright rude. He started to knock on the door again, but decided against it. It was none of his business if she was mad about something. He knew he had done nothing to warrant her anger, not knowingly anyway and he was tired.

Lazarus went to his room, showered and shaved. He plopped down on the bed and picked up the remote. Suddenly, he changed his mind about the television and threw the remote over on the sofa. He decided to take a look into the Sperling psyche. He picked up the photo albums.

The first one made him smile so hard his face began to hurt. It was 'The Sperling Babies.' They were absolutely beautiful. He especially admired the family pictures of the growing crew, but fell in love with the one with just Ashton, Kali, and Kacie. All three of them were nude. Ashton's arm was draped tastefully around Kali's lower waist and the baby, a brand new Kacie, tastefully hid her mother's bare breasts. Lazarus let his finger caress Kali's face, then Kacie's.

They were the most beautiful females in the world, he thought. He closed that album and picked up the other. The first picture was a happy, much younger Ashton and Kali standing beneath a huge Christmas tree. Ashton wore a tux and Kali a white sleeveless gown. AJ and Katie wore matching outfits. Kali was holding a bouquet of red roses. It was their wedding. The four of them looked happy enough to float away into the atmosphere.

The first few pages were different angles and different poses in front of the same tree, so he began to flip past them quickly until something strange caught his eyes. He paged back to see the glittery gold ornament that was on the tree right behind Kali's head. It glistened from the camera's flash. Lazarus looked at it closely, but couldn't tell immediately if it was the same ornament in his dream. So he kept looking for other pictures with it in them.

And, then there it was, as clear as day: a close-up picture of Ashton with his '80s mullet hanging around his shoulders, and Kali with her big hair straightened and covering her shoulders. It was a close-up of the newly married couple, but since she was several inches shorter, it looked as if the ornament sat on top of her head and next to Ashton's face. It was the same ornament — glass, with a saxophone sitting on a bar that was inscribed. He could see where the ornament had been shaken just enough to have glitter covering the lower half. Lazarus dropped the book as a sharp pain shot through his temples.

Dropping to his knees, he grabbed his head. He had had that same piercing pain in Santa Fe and that fact was not lost on him. He knew he was trying to remember. He tried to pull himself up by holding onto his dresser, his hands weakened and he crashed to the floor again. He lay on the floor writhing in pain.

"Lazarus, Lazarus," Kali called softly as she was knocking on the door and feeling guilty about the way she had treated him earlier. She had walked around to his suite to apologize and that's when she heard the commotion.

"Lazarus, are you alright?" she tried the doorknob and it opened easily.

"Oh, my God," Kali ran to him and tried to pry his hands away from his head. She climbed on top of him trying to still his body. She pulled his head up to her and began to massage it. She climbed over him again and helped position him so that his head fell into her lap.

"It's okay," she whispered. "It's okay. The pain will pass," she said, remembering having to do the same thing for Ashton on several occasions.

"The pain will pass," she whispered again. He tried to reach for his head again and she blocked his hands. Gently, she began to massage his temple with one hand and the top of his head with the other until his breathing began to calm. They didn't speak.

At first, Lazarus didn't know who was in the room with him or why they seemed to be wrestling with him. His entire focus was on the pain, and he couldn't even grasp another person's presence, let alone their identity. But, then he felt the warmth of her breasts against his face. He began to relax under the pressure of her fingers as they made firm circles lifting his face and drawing the skin back toward his neck. He knew his head was in her lap and he breathed her in as he fell asleep.

Kali had done this before. She had sat in the dark with Ashton holding him and trying to help ease the pain. Her fingers skimmed through his hair. She was amazed that his hair lay in a way that was so much like Ashton's, so was its texture and the large, loopy curls. Her fingers continued to glide through his hair and put pressure on his scalp until they reached the base of his skull. She gasped as her fingers began to outline a large keloid scar. It was the shape of an earthworm in the right place, the place where it was missing on the fake Ashton's head.

"Ashton," she cried. He had been there all along right under her nose. How could she not have known? She tried to wake him and then decided against it, thinking about her conversation with Micah.

"He knew," she whispered. Micah had to have known. She had thought it strange that he hired a man off the park bench and brought him into her home, but she reasoned that Micah had arranged that, too.

Lazarus lay across her lap with a white sleeveless shirt and a pair of black silk boxers. She smiled, Ashton loved his boxers. Kali could see the scars on his chest. She lifted the shirt slightly and was astounded by the extensive damage he had endured. She tried to maneuver him so she could see the back of his leg, but he was too heavy and she couldn't move. So she sat there, her back against the hard dresser where she had found support when she was getting him to calm down.

Her touch had worked almost like magic, a lot quicker than it had ever worked on Ashton. Ashton's headaches would not disappear with medication. Ruby had said it was part of his post-traumatic experience and there was nothing that could help him. It was all mental and all mentally-triggered, but no one could figure out what triggered it, at least not until the day of Billy's funeral had she even thought of it.

Kali saw an elaborate cane standing at the end of the dresser. She was surprised to see it there. It had belonged to Jordan. She stretched until she could reach it and then used it to turn off the light. She exhaled slowly as the tears streamed down her face. What had happened to him? She knew this man truly didn't know who he was, and Micah had been blocking his ability to find out. She should have known something was up when Ricky and Chico started coming over and spent most of their time with Lazarus. She had just thought they were attracted to him and were trying to see which one of them could win him for themselves. She choked back a laugh. The one thing she knew the minute she had laid eyes on him, he was anything but gay. On more than one occasion, she had walked away from him because he was making her hot and bothered. Now, she knew why.

Kali sat there stroking his head. She truly believed he had no idea who he was. There was nothing in his mind to remind him of dragging her and the kids to Veteran's Stadium to see the Eagles in the freezing cold or a skinny dip with her under the moon on their rooftop pool. She could tell in his eyes, where the memories should have been was blank. But, he knew, she thought, as a tear slid down her face, his feelings knew where he belonged. She thought about how protective he was of the kids, even of her, as this man Lazarus. That was her Ashton, his love for them was so strong, he didn't need memories. She kissed his forehead lightly.

Lazarus awakened to a slightly darkened room. It was morning. He was surprised when he realized his head was still in her lap. She had come to his rescue and eased his pain with her skillful fingers and her warm breasts. At first, he was afraid to move. No, that wasn't it; he didn't want to move. He loved being that close to her. He had wanted to touch her since the moment he had met her and they had barely brushed against each other in passing. But, his body had longed for her every time she entered a room. He remembered wanting to take her finger in his mouth the day she pointed it into his face.

"I know you are awake," she said. "Your breathing's changed."

He rolled away from her slowly.

"Sorry, I was just trying to get my bearings," he lay on his back looking up at her.

"No problem," she sighed, looking into his tired hazel eyes. She smiled. She wanted to crawl over him and give him a big kiss, but that would give him a clue that she knew who he was. First things first, she thought. Somehow the fake Ashton would have to get sent up to the big house for Scully's murder, not Lazarus.

"How are you feeling?" she asked.

"Drained. But, no headache," he rubbed his temples and sat up slowly.

"Good," she made an effort to move away from the dresser and realized her back was aching. He pulled her up.

"Thank you. I don't know what happened," he was feeling more than a bit awkward. He walked to his bed and sat down, leaning forward he put his head in his hands.

Kali flipped the light switch and noticed the photo album lying on the floor. She and Ashton were smiling up at her. She reached down and picked it up.

"This must have given you the headache," she closed the book and laid it on top of the other.

"I doubt that was the case. The pictures are beautiful. The two of you looked happy. Your whole family looked happy."

"What happened, right? I know that's what you really want to ask."

"I don't want to pry. But, the kids have told me some things. So has Micah."

"They told you about my husband's condition."

"They told me someone tried to murder you and him. I'm glad they didn't succeed."

"Didn't they?" she sat down on the bed next to him. She wanted him to move so she could see the back of his left leg. She looked down at the big toe with the scar and a tear ran down her cheek.

"Mrs. Sperling," he reached up and wiped away the lone tear. "I think I may have tired you out last night. You must be really tired and uncomfortable after sitting against that hard dresser all night."

"Nothing a hot shower won't cure," she took his hand and steadied herself. She wanted to kiss it. She looked at it and recognized it. She hadn't looked at it before. Why hadn't she, she thought. Why hadn't she confirmed that the abusive Ashton was not her husband? He had promised her he would die before he would ever hurt her again. He had even added that to their wedding vows. And she had believed him, and he had proved it over and over for ten straight years. Then one day, he had changed. Even weeks before they were shot, he had changed, just more drastically after they were shot.

"What are you doing here?" he asked. "I mean, why did you come to my room last night? I thought you were angry with me about something."

"I came to apologize. I wasn't angry with you, but I took it out on you. I have been taking a lot of things out on you. I'm sorry. I just get frustrated."

"Your husband?"

"Oh, yes. He is the source of my frustration, alright."

"No, I meant, did he come home last night? I don't want him to think," Lazarus looked down at his boxer shorts and jumped up from the bed. As he strode away from her to get his pants, she saw the scar on the back of his leg.

"He is not due in for another…" She looked around for a clock and jumped up herself.

"The kids," she exclaimed and they both ran for the door. Lazarus and Kali had found the kids busy in the kitchen. AJ and Katie had prepared their lunches. Adam had filled all the cereal bowls, placed the fruit next to them, then poured the orange juice. Kacie was taking her place at the table, late as usual. They looked proud when the adults walked into the room.

"Wow, I am so impressed," Lazarus walked around like a drill sergeant inspecting his troops. The children stood at attention.

"Good. Very good," he patted AJ on the shoulder and gave Katie a hug.

Kali slid down in the chair. She was a good actress, but was she that good? She could feel the love her children had for Lazarus. She had noticed it right away. She had expected AJ to be sullen with him and Katie to be withdrawn. She didn't know what to expect from Adam, who never failed to surprise her. She already knew Kacie was in love with him. She had thought Lazarus was Kacie's first crush after her dad. But, Kacie's connection with her dad had drawn her right into his heart.

"Hmmm," she said. "I think we had better stop admiring our wonderful work and get a move on."

Suddenly she heard spoons hitting bowls and smelled toast

popping up out of the toaster. She wondered how she was going to get through this day.

CHAPTER NINETEEN

Lazarus was bored. He took the books back to the music room and placed them on the shelves. As he turned to walk away, something shined or glimmered from behind a book that had fallen over. He went back to the shelf, removed the book, and there was a safe. He stood staring at it and, then, instinctively reached for the knob. He turned it without thinking until the cylinders dropped and the door popped open. It scared him a little. He stepped back and stared at the contents.

There were more photo albums. He looked around to make sure the house staff wasn't entering the room. He pulled out the black albums. These were neatly put together, but nothing like the bound leather ones that lined the shelves. Lazarus walked over to the stuffed chair near the piano with the stack of albums. He opened the first one and found the most sordid pornographic pictures he could remember seeing. He thought about the kids and wondered why anyone would hold onto this trash. He couldn't help but flip through the others and found what he had hoped he wouldn't find.

There were nude photos of Kali. Thank God, she wasn't performing any of the acts the other women were. They were just pictures. Lots of them. In almost all of them, her eyes looked far away or they were closed. It was his guess that she wasn't aware that she was being photographed. Lazarus slammed the safe shut. He rearranged the other albums on the shelf to keep the safe from being seen.

Lazarus sped his car out to the Plateau. He didn't even know how he had gotten there. Taking the horrible albums to an iron grill, he set them on fire and, then, sat on a park bench and watched them burn to ashes. He left the park and went straight to a men's store on South Street. He bought two suits, some shirts and ties. One suit he left to be tailored and the other he wore out of the store. He stopped at a shoe store and walked out wearing the new pair. Lazarus drove to PDSI and walked into the executive suite unannounced.

Micah was leaning over Ashton's desk trying to explain

something. He had a look of frustration on his face until he looked up and saw Lazarus. Ashton jumped up from his desk and greeted him. He grabbed his hand.

"Now, here's a man that knows contracts," Ashton said. "And, I have hired him. You are here to work, aren't you?"

"Yes, sir. I am," Lazarus was surprised to hear the words come out of his mouth. He didn't really know what he was doing. He was scared. He knew the combination to the safe and that was still racing through his mind. If someone had asked him at that moment what the combination was, he wouldn't have been able to tell them. All he could remember was that the safe was locked, and he unlocked it with ease. Who was he?

"Come with me," Micah walked past the two men shaking hands. Lazarus nodded toward Ashton and followed.

"Ms. Sims," Micah stopped at the administrative assistant's desk. She was still in shock that Lazarus had ignored her attempt to find out who he was before he entered the suite. She looked frightened that she was about to lose her job.

"We are going to move our marketing director out of her office today. I want you to set up everything right away to Mr. Smith's liking.

"Mr. Smith, this is Ms. Sims. She will be assisting you with anything you need."

"Pleased to meet you and I apologize for rushing past you earlier. It was important," Lazarus said in such a sultry voice, the woman's hard demeanor melted right away.

"Let's go claim your spot," Micah started toward the office.

"Let me," Lazarus patted Micah on the shoulder. "I can handle it." Micah turned away smiling. He had no doubt that Lazarus could.

Kali walked in just in time to see Lazarus walking toward the other side of the suite.

"Micah, we have to talk," she said, tugging at his jacket sleeve. "Why is Lazarus here?"

"Claiming his territory," Micah grinned. "Give me an hour. You do have an appointment in an hour, right?" he winked.

"Yes, I do," Kali thought about the safe room and the watch. She stuck her head into Ashton's office and saw AB reading a photography book. Figures, she thought. He may be pretending to be Ashton but he is still into photography. Asa had been a master photographer. His pictures had been published in all the major magazines like *Ebony*, *Time*, and the *Rolling Stone*, and every major newspaper when he sold some current event photo to the Associated Press. She could never understand why he wasn't happy. He was skilled and sought after. He could have made a decent living on his own had he not followed Billy and Redd around like a little puppy dog doing whatever they commanded.

CHAPTER TWENTY

KALI WAS PROUD of herself. She had lost the bodyguard again. She didn't know if that was a good thing or if she should be worried about the man who was responsible for her safety. But, she had done it by going through Wanamaker's, her favorite department store since Jordan had introduced her to it. She had left her car in a nearby garage. She would either send someone for it, or go get it herself later on. She walked into Micah's hideaway and was not surprised to see that he had added another desk and chair. Plus, there was box on the floor holding a new computer.

Kali began to search in Micah's old desk for something to help her open the box. She found a narrow-serrated letter opener. She turned to attack the box and was startled to find Lazarus leaning against the door jam.

"What are you doing here?" She was both surprised and pleased to see him, but she was afraid to show it. She took a deep breath, hoping she hadn't shown it. She held up the letter opener and pointed it in his direction.

"I said, what are you doing here?"

"I could ask you the same question," Lazarus entered the room ignoring her veiled threat with the letter opener. He walked over to the box and moved it over a bit.

"Nice," he said. "Are you setting up office outside of PDSI? Or, is this some sort of clandestine, covert assignment?"

"That's none of your business. Aren't you starting a new job today? And, you still haven't explained why you are here?"

"I was just curious why a woman who is supposed to have a bodyguard is always trying to duck her bodyguard."

"How would you know that?"

"Micah made me head of the family bodyguards. I got the call when you lost him again."

"So how did you find me?"

"I'm not telling," Lazarus walked over to her and pushed the curl from her forehead.

"I'm safe. You can leave," Kali said moving closer to him. She gave his chest a small shove, but he held his ground and didn't even sway from her force.

"I'm not that easy to get rid of," Lazarus touched her chin.

She grabbed his hand and held it. They stood frozen, watching each other, waiting though neither of them knew why they were waiting or for what.

"No, no. No," Micah said as he walked into the door straight for them. They had to quickly part to allow him to get through, but it didn't break the gaze into each other's eyes.

"Lazarus, you are supposed to be working on a contract before you have to leave to pick up the kids. I just kicked someone out of an office for you to occupy. Why are you here?"

"Just doing my job, son," Lazarus said, the word son rolled off his tongue with ease as his eyes stayed glued to hers. He saw them brighten for a second. For a moment, he thought she was going to jump across the room into his arms and he wanted her to, in the worst way, he wanted to end whatever charade was taking place and make it real. There was no doubt in his mind he wanted this woman, and there was no doubt in his mind that he already knew this woman.

Micah had to break the tension between the two. It was dangerous and would throw his game plan off completely. "Make yourself useful. Put the computer together and then get out. I got her," Micah walked over to the box and kicked it. The loud thud broke the link between Lazarus and Kali only momentarily. Both reached for the box at the same time. Their hands brushed.

"Kali, come here. Now," Micah grabbed her by the arm and escorted her to an empty room down the hallway. He pointed to a large windowsill. She leaned against it with her arms folded.

"That's Ashton," she whispered as Micah moved closer.

"You didn't tell him, did you? Please tell me you didn't."

"No, I thought about what you told me yesterday. I don't want him to remember and end up in prison."

"Kali, it will be okay for him to remember. But, we have to guide him so that he doesn't explode and end up on death row or something."

"I think he's beginning to remember. He had a headache last night, just like the ones he used to have. He has the scar," Kali's voice got higher as she became excited. Ashton was alive. She had been rejoicing all morning, now she could say it aloud.

"Micah, I love you, Micah," Kali then began to cry. She was tired of crying, but today her tears were happy tears. Only a week ago, she had realized the man in her bed at night wasn't Ashton. She thought she had lost her husband for good. This morning, she learned her husband had been watching over them for the past six months.

She hugged Micah who smoothed her wiry curls. "Who did that to him?"

"I'm guessing the same person or persons who killed Daddy, tried to murder you. I don't think they were really trying to kill Asa. I think that was just some elaborate plan to cover his lack of memory.

"So, how? How did Asa survive? The first time, I mean?"

"Are you saying Ashton isn't Ashton? Then who is he?" Lazarus asked as he walked into the room, surprising Micah and Kali into silence. The air became heavy and still as they looked to each other and then to the brooding Lazarus.

"What are you asking?" Micah stood up and let his arm drop from around Kali.

"I have been thinking about this all morning," said Lazarus. "Everything you have said, everything the kids have said. Your reactions, Rick, Chico, the kids. Even dufus, and the pictures. And I kept looking for the missing piece. Am I the missing piece? If he isn't Ashton, then I am Ashton. Right? He is my twin? You," Lazarus pointed to Micah. "You lured me here. You knew who I was in Santa Fe."

"I was merely suggesting that you come here," Micah took a couple of steps toward him and stood between him and Kali who was still sitting in the window. He turned and waved her away from the window.

"You think I'm going to hurt her?" Lazarus asked.

"No, you would die first," Micah said.

"Then why are you suddenly in defense mode?" Lazarus was watching Micah's every move as if he knew what each movement meant.

"Because a little information is dangerous in anybody's hands. You don't have all the information. You can't automatically assume you are Ashton."

"How do you know I don't remember everything?"

"Because, I know you. You have figured out who you think you are. But, you don't remember who you think you are."

"Silly me. Trying to figure out my name and my place in this world."

"Silly you," Kali stepped around Micah and ran into Lazarus' arms. "You are my husband."

Micah threw up his hands and walked out the room. Kali let go of Lazarus and ran behind him.

"Molasses," she begged. "Molasses don't be mad."

Lazarus was behind her.

"Molasses?" Lazarus stopped and leaned against the desk.

"Kali, Lazarus. Everything I have done, everything I do is to keep this family safe. To keep you safe. Until Lazarus remembers everything, we are all walking a tightrope. We can't trust anyone. I mean anyone. I told you yesterday," he looked at Kali, "that Asa is not as dumb as you want to believe. Maybe, he's not a good businessman, but he is very good at deceit and he is still very dangerous. The only reason you and the kids aren't dead yet is because all of your funds haven't evaporated. But, he is working on it. In the 14 months he's been working at PDSI, he has liquidated and spent over six million dollars. And he just locked into a private account Ashton had in New York. He's made two one million dollar withdrawals. There's only $800,000 left. I got a lead on what's happening to the withdrawals. If I can follow that lead, I can follow it to the mastermind and, most likely, his partner in crime.

"My guess is, when the cash is gone, he will start collecting insurance and estate monies," Micah looked from one to the other.

"We are running out of time," Micah went over to his computer and pushed the power button on. "Kali, I need to know more about his trips to New York. They are never on his schedule. He just goes. I need to know when he is even hinting of going."

"He never, has never told me about his trips. He just started talking to me," Kali responded.

"You have to keep him talking. In bed," Micah emphasized the word "bed."

He didn't have to remind her. The bed was the only thing keeping the fake Ashton in line, for now. He was even looking at her differently.

"What the hell am I supposed to be doing? Keep pretending I don't know who I am?" Lazarus asked.

"You don't know who you are," Micah snapped. "Go to work."

"This is my life," Lazarus retorted. "My wife," he reached for Kali.

"Cut that shit out," Micah hit the desk so hard, both Lazarus and Kali jumped. "Kali, you have got to get angry with this man and stay angry."

"What? Why?"

"To mask the attraction." Micah pointed his finger at Lazarus who stumbled back into the computer box. "It's hard enough with the kids, but at least the kids are just viewed as impressionable. And you are just viewed as the happy go-lucky, paid uncle. But, what I saw when I walked into this room was two people seconds away from ripping each other's clothes to shred. I can still smell the funk and feel the tension. That's not going to work, not even in the penthouse. People will be able to pick up on it, Ashton especially."

"You mean, Asa," Kali hated referring to that insidious pig as Ashton.

"No, Kali. I mean Ashton. No mistakes, baby. We have endured this shit far too long for any mistakes now. You mess up and call him Asa and you will be dead in seconds. I won't be able to do anything about it. Neither will Lazarus. And remember, Ashton was no angel before this crap went down, and he is no angel now," Micah stood face to face with Lazarus, and then leaned closer so that his lips were near Lazarus's ear.

"A man's actions have consequences, consequences that are life-changing. When Ashton dies, he will be dead. I hope whatever you have lurking around in that messed up head of yours, it's not a dream of ever picking up from where you left off. You gave up that right. Murderers don't have rights," Micah spoke low enough to keep Kali from hearing, but Lazarus understood every cold word. His worst fear had just been confirmed: he would be alone for the rest of his life.

"Good day, Mrs. Sperling," Lazarus said as he turned to leave the room. Kali tried to run for him, but Micah caught her by the arm.

"What did you say to him?" Kali said, twisting away from Micah like a little child.

"What he needed to hear," Micah went back to his desk. "You need to sit down over there and conjure up some reasons to give

Lazarus distance; think of stuff that he does that annoys you and put that on the front burner."

"But," Kali wanted to argue, but she couldn't. Her mind understood the logic, but her heart wanted to go shoot Asa between his lying hazel eyes.

CHAPTER TWENTY-ONE

A FEW DAYS passed. Kali and Lazarus spent most of their time trying to miss each other. Lazarus would walk pass her in the office without speaking. He used the work he brought home as an excuse to skip dinner with Kali and the kids. He made up for missing dinner by spending time with the children before they went to bed. Everybody was adapting, but Lazarus was beginning to feel sad and anxious. He had one memory, the ornament, and he wondered if he could conjure up anymore, especially the important one. Who tried to kill him and who was trying to help Asa kill him? Micah acted as if he had an idea, but there were still missing pieces.

And, Micah refused to share the missing pieces. This was annoying the hell out of Lazarus. He was not a man to sit around and wait, but he had become complacent. He attributed his complacency at first to fear, but had to admit it was because of the children in his life every time. He hadn't wanted to lose Bobby and then these children, his children he couldn't claim because he had committed murder, and had paid for at least four others according to his conversation with Micah. No wonder he couldn't remember anything. What man in his right mind would want to? He thought about Kali and how or why she and the kids could love him so deeply. Even Micah. Why was Micah so loyal?

Kali's impatience was growing. She did not want to spend another night with the bastard pretending to be her husband. She wanted a means to get rid of him, but it was all out of her hands. She thought about calling the police many times, even thought about talking to Troy who was showing up more and more frequently.

"Detective Troy," Kali teased as she opened her office door. "You have been stopping by a lot lately."

"Don't you like seeing me?" He was as smooth as Denzel Washington.

"No," she said honestly. "Only my husband still likes you." She walked out of her office which had been her intention when she opened the door. She hadn't expected to see Troy. This was his third visit this week.

"Isn't Ashton in his office?" she pulled the strap of her purse higher up on her shoulder.

"Yeah, but I am here to see you today." He fell into step with her as she approached the elevator.

"We have already had Ashton's birthday party, and our anniversary isn't until Christmas. Oh, you wouldn't know that. You didn't attend the wedding," Kali flipped her hair back over her shoulders hitting him in the face. She turned to see him grinning down on her.

"I want to talk to you about your hired help," Troy got on the elevator with her. Kali held the button to keep the doors open. Another man stepped in with them.

"Troy, you know my bodyguard, Curtis," Kali announced and the man nodded. "You know Detective Troy Lucas?" Kali asked and the man nodded. "If I told you he was bothering me, would you be obliged to kick his cute little ass?"

"Yes, ma'am," the guard replied.

"What do you want, Troy?" Kali was point-blank. Troy knew her feelings for him. They hadn't changed. She would never forgive him for sending Ashton to prison for a murder he didn't commit. If he only knew the impact his blind justice dogma had had on them. She hated Troy even more now.

"I'd like to talk in private," Troy insisted as he walked her to her car.

"Get in," Kali unlocked the door and got in. She could see her bodyguard getting into his car to follow her.

Troy hopped in and looked at her earnestly.

"Ashton asked me to look into this Lazarus character Micah hired to watch over you and the kids."

"Excuse me."

"He was concerned. Micah didn't take the regular channels to hire this man. So he asked me to find out some things about him."

"So what is it that I need to know?" Kali asked as a large knot began forming in her stomach. Asa was getting suspicious. Why else would he bring Ashton's so-called best friend into the picture? Either that or he was getting ready to set Lazarus up. She had to get to Micah and to Lazarus.

"Well, it's not what you need to know. It's what I need to ask."

"Shoot," Kali said with an uncomfortable giggle. "No, don't shoot."

"Ashton said you have been angry with this man for the last few days. Any particular reason why?"

"Oh, maybe because my children will listen to him before they will listen to me. I don't feel threatened by him, at least not physically. We have differences over what the kids should be allowed to do and what not."

"You sure?" Troy was searching her face.

"Oh, and he is a freaking know-it-all," Kali said testily. "A lot like you."

Troy laughed. "That's all?"

"Yeah, that's all. Now, are you going to tell me what this is really about? Should I have any concerns, Troy?" she reached out and touched his tie. She saw the sweat immediately pop up on his brow. She knew she had that effect on him, but she didn't know if he realized that she knew.

He cleared his throat as he always did when she touched him.

"No, looks like everything checks out. He really does have amnesia. He used to live with the Sheriff and his grandson out there in Colorado. He says he is relatively mild-mannered. We can't trace him though. Maybe he's a brother from another planet," Troy chuckled.

"Well, do you want to me let you know every time he pisses me off or what?" Kali held open her hands.

"Not necessary," Troy put his hand on the doorknob.

Kali started fumbling around in her purse. "Darn it, I forgot something. Are you going back upstairs?" she asked sweetly.

"No," Troy shook his head as if he were too good to run an errand for her.

"I can tell you exactly where it is. I'll give you the keys," she pulled the keys out of the ignition.

"Get your boy back there to do it," Troy was getting out of the car.

"Come on, Troy. He has to go where I go," Kali pouted. Troy shook his head and backed away.

Kali walked back to the guard's car and told him she was going to be another hour or two. She took the elevator back upstairs and went straight to Micah's office. She had missed him. He was already gone.

"Damn," she headed for Ashton's suite and heard him talking to somebody. It was late and his assistant had already left. She started to open the door, but was stopped by the tone of his voice.

"Bitch, you can't keep calling here. Look, why don't you take your drunken ass back to bed and wait until I call you? I have taken all the money I can take openly. I don't understand. You can't be going through it all. Not this fucking fast," he sighed angrily. "Wait until you hear from me. I swear if I hear from you again this will be the last drop you get." He slammed the phone down.

Kali ran back to her office. She turned on the computer and turned the monitor away from the door. She picked up a folder and spread all of the papers from it across her desk. She picked up a pen and held it over the papers while peering back to the monitor hoping the desktop would hurry up and appear.

"Kali, I thought you had left," Ashton stopped mid-stepped when he realized he wasn't alone in the suite.

"Short appointment. Just picked up a check." She held up an old check, but he couldn't tell the difference. And then, she said, "I was walked to my car by Troy. What's up with that?"

"Nothing really. It's just that I wanted to learn more about Lazarus. It's almost as if he has run a big company before. Just wanted to make sure he wasn't a shark trying to steal the company from under me."

"Now, you would never allow anyone to do that," Kali got up and sauntered to the door trying to keep him from entering her office. She wrapped her arms around him and laid her head on his chest. He stroked her head gently.

"Are you on your way home?" she asked. "I can leave now, too."

"No, no hurry. I am going to New York on business for the next couple of days."

"Tonight?" Kali tried to sound disappointed.

"After this trip, it will be awhile before I take another. I promise," he lifted her chin and they kissed passionately. He backed out of the door and winked at her. She went back to her desk and played on the computer for about ten minutes waiting to see if he would double back. She got up from her desk to go to his office and heard the suite door open. She ran back behind her desk.

She heard Ashton's door open. She sat back in her chair with a plop. All she wanted to do was to go into the safe room unnoticed while she could.

"I give," she said to herself and put all the paperwork back into the folder.

She put her purse on her shoulder and closed her door. She needed to get to Micah anyway. She smelled smoke, cigar smoke.

She walked to the door and pushed it open further. Sitting behind the desk looking pleased was Lazarus. He had removed his shoes; his feet covered in black socks were propped up on the return of the desk. He was leaning back in the tall leather desk chair smoking a cigar, blowing perfect smoke rings. She smiled a wide, welcoming smile. His hair hung in loose fluffy curls around his shoulders. It was the same hair, with a few additional gray streaks that framed his now hawk-like face.

He licked his bottom lip when he saw her; she tried not to hold her breath as she breathed in the sweet smell of his cigar. It was one of his expensive ones she had grown to appreciate. A rhythm rocked within her soul as each step brought her closer to that desk. She knew she was walking to that rhythm and he was breathing to that rhythm as he blew out those sensual circles, throwing out all the warnings, all cautions, all reasons to steer clear of the man who had won her heart when she was only 17. He was her first and would probably be her last she thought as she stepped into the guest chair and catapulted herself onto the desk, crawling across. He put out the cigar and blew the smoke in her direction; she puckered her lips. He pulled her into the chair onto his lap and they kissed long and deep. She sat in his lap with one knee on each side of his legs. He began to remove her suit jacket. She began to untie his tie. They stopped, and then kissed again.

Lazarus lifted her with the ease of a man lifting a baby out of a crib, and sat her on the desk. He finished undressing her waist up as his hands continued to explore her, his tongue kept trying to find its way deep into the recesses of her throat. He came up for air and she sighed. He pulled her off the desk and was easing her skirt down her bare legs with her underwear in tow. He picked her up again and gently laid her on her back. He kissed her again holding her hands above her head, her back arched longingly, anxiously as he began to enjoy the taste of her flesh starting with her neck, between her breasts, her breasts, her stomach, and then she screamed.

There was no doubt in her mind whose tongue had just sent her to the heights above Mount Everest. She grabbed a handful of hair and tugged. He came up for air and entered her in one continuous fluid motion not unlike being caught in a current taking you out to sea. There was no turning back. She was out there. He was out there. There were no lifeboats. They held onto each other, taking each other under the water, and then giving each other their life-saving breath.

In one agile move, Lazarus picked her up, slammed the door to the suite. She leaned over him and locked it. He walked her with her legs wrapped around his waist trying to slide down to find Taylor who was teasing Niecy with its fierce hardness. He carried her into the private bath, opened the linen closet, and pushed hard on the third shelf. The shelves swung open into the small bedroom. He dropped her on the bed and dust particles flew wildly about like snowflakes. It didn't stop them. They were lost in each other as toes curled, bodies sighed, and the heavens gazed upon their lovemaking like it was the first time a man and woman discovered they could become one.

The intensity gained and gained as the two struggled violently to become one, to occupy the same space in the same place, with the same crescendo. The force of their passion catapulted them from the depths of an ocean to an eruption more powerful than any volcano on planet Earth. Their last climax sent them flying off the bed and into hysterical laughter while holding onto each for dear life. Both were too afraid to let go, and too exhausted to move. They lay there on the floor wrapped in its each other's limbs like a twist of pretzels.

"Let's get off this floor," Kali wasn't surprised by his strength as he again lifted her and moved her one fell swoop to the bed. Again, the dust flew.

"Eeew," she sneezed. "I guess it's been a long time since we cleaned in here."

"When was the last time you were in here?" He crawled over her and lay on his stomach. His arm fell over the bed, his hand hit the floor. He touched the carpet. It was stiff under his touch.

"Somebody didn't bother to clean up a spill, either," he complained as his hand kept feeling around.

Kali rose up on her elbows and turned on the lamp. "I never

realized this place could be so dark," she got up and closed the swinging closet doors and shut out the bathroom light.

"Oh, maybe I need to go back and get our clothes."

"You locked the door, right?" He had thought he had heard her turn the knob when they were making fast and furious love.

"Yeah, I think I did," she giggled. "I tried anyway."

She looked back to see Lazarus searching underneath the bed. This all seemed so familiar to him, the metal frame underneath the bed meeting the wooden headboard and a long screw. Something was hanging on the extended metal screw. He grabbed it and sat up quickly startled by a gold watch. Shifting himself, he leaned against the headboard, looked at the back of the watch and cried out.

CHAPTER TWENTY-TWO

LAZARUS CRAWLED OUT of the bed and stumbled into the kitchen. He looked at the rust-stained newspaper down on the floor. His knees weakened as he collapsed and fell to the floor.

Kali screamed as she ran to help ease him down. Lazarus laid his head on the newspaper and began to weep. Kali climbed over his body and tried to pull his head to her chest. He was resistant. He was remembering. He couldn't let her interrupt the memories. He lay there looking ahead, remembering the salty, thick taste of his own blood. Lazarus remembered watching a pair of women's boots pace around his face. He remembered feeling hate searing through the air as he heard the woman order Asa to do her dirty deed, and his brother shuffle his feet at her every command. Every last detail of that day flooded back. He knew who he was.

Kali lay on top of him trying to keep him from shivering, but there seemed to be no end, and then there was. Lazarus's breathing began to calm and the bones in his body ceased to rattle. They just lay there.

"Lazarus," she whispered.

"Get up, Kali," he whispered back.

She rolled off of him and leaned against the cold metal legs of the kitchen table. She watched how he agilely rose from floor, grabbing her hand and pulling her up with him.

"Are you alright?" she asked as she noticed her own hands were shaking.

"I'm fine. I remember," he said as he pulled her to him and held her tight.

"I'm sorry," he whispered in her ear.

"Sorry, for what?" she hated those tears welling back into her eyes.

"For leaving you angry," he reached up and wiped away his own tears. "The last time I saw you, I was mad at you. I don't ever want to walk away from you angry again. I swear, Kali. I swear."

"I won't let you," Kali held onto him tighter. She didn't want to let him go, afraid he would forget them again.

"I need you to go, Kali," he peeled her away from him.

"What?" Kali stood there helplessly, not sure if she should leave him.

"Go home."

"No, I am not leaving you."

"Kali," Lazarus shook his head. He needed to think and he needed to find out who all the players were, besides the two obvious ones.

"Kali," he said again as he picked up the newspaper. Those weren't rust stains; they were his bloodstains covering the article about Billy. "Refresh my memory. I am still a bit foggy. Who else knew about the safe room?"

"You, me. Ms. Elliott. Ruby and Micah."

"Micah! Oh, my God. Asa is on his way to New York," Kali put her hand over her mouth and looked around for the clock.

"Get dressed. Go," he took her back into his arms and kissed her deeply. "Go."

PART THREE

~ EIGHTEEN MONTHS AGO ~

CHAPTER TWENTY-THREE

THE DOORBELL RANG again, not urgently. But, whoever it was wasn't going away. Ashton stepped into his jeans and shimmied into them. He was going to have to answer the door. Kali and the kids had already headed to the stables. He glanced over at the little digital clock on the bed stand and sighed. They had let him sleep in; he knew he was at least two hours behind them. It had been way past midnight when he finally made it home from his business trip, so he had slept so soundly he hadn't heard the normally noisy crowd readying for a day outdoors. He hadn't planned to miss a minute of it.

He grabbed his boots and the rest of his clothes and headed toward the stairs. The doorbell rang once again as he hunched over to maneuver down the stairs of their old Victorian mansion. He shook his head as he looked back. Though there was plenty of space for living, most of the house was built around shorter people. He stared back at the stairs and made a mental note: he was going to remove the floor above the landing to give him and his brothers more headspace. Soon AJ and Adam would need that space, too.

Ashton swung the door open, just as a short, chocolate man was about to ring again. The man looked up at him with a wide, but kind smile.

"Mr. Sperling?" The man asked as he extended his hand. Ashton stared at him. He didn't have time for a door-to-door peddler. He wanted to spend his precious free time with his family and his horses.

"Yes," Ashton finally answered.

"I'm Reverend Mims. I'm your wife's and children's pastor," the man said with his hand still extended.

Ashton sighed. He didn't want to be rude, but he had not the time for religious debate. He hadn't stood in Kali's way when she had found the little church and began to take the kids to Sunday School. But, he had put his foot down when she had begun to talk about baptism. He didn't mind his children learning about religion, but he didn't want them addicted to the dogma he had come to hate during his 12 years in

Catholic schools. He could still remember how hateful those precious, Jesus-loving nuns could be. There was something wrong with a religion that hid hateful people behind restrictive and petty rules. And, then he thought there was something wrong with a man of God who murders his wife, her lover, and himself leaving a vulnerable young Kali behind to fend for herself. Kali could forgive her father all those years ago, but Ashton never could.

Here he was, holding a grudge against a man he had never met; trying to make up for all the hurt and injustice the man's daughter had had to endure. Not that he was an innocent; he had been the instrument to deliver her the most hurtful blows. Now all he wanted to do was to spend his life making her forget them by making her the happiest woman on the face of the earth. And, he knew he was close. Every morning when she opened her eyes they smiled and outshined the sun on its brightest day. He loved his wife. He loved his family with every molecule of his body and every whisper of his spirit.

"May I come in?" the little preacher was still smiling. "Mrs. Sperling asked me to come by this morning to speak with you and your brothers."

Ashton looked around a bit helpless, again he had no intention to be rude, but neither he nor his brothers were religious men.

"Let me see where she is," he stood back and let the man enter, regretting it the moment he let the man step across his threshold.

"Nice home," the preacher said. "I have passed this place almost my entire life, but this is the first time I have set foot in it."

"We like it," Ashton's long legs led the preacher to the rear of the home to the kitchen area where his family always congregated. The renovated kitchen was large with a long, sturdy wooden table in its center. It had to be long so that Ashton, Kali, and their four children could be joined by his brother Micah, his wife Ruby, and son, Artie, in addition to his two younger brothers, Chico and Ricky, who had moved back east. It was almost like old times in a way, with most of the entire Sperlings regularly assembling under one roof.

Only, instead of Jordan sitting at the head of the table lording over his son and five grandsons, it was Ashton enjoying the closeness and camaraderie of the Sperling crew, everyone except his father Billy and his long-dead twin brother Asa. His family had grown over the past ten years from the twins, AJ and Katie, and then Adam, to his precocious seven-year-old Kacie, who held onto his heart in a loving vice grip. She was his angel. She was the symbol that he and Kali had finally gotten it right.

Kacie had been the first of the four to be born in a hospital without Chico's assistance, and the first to be born without drama and without turmoil. She was truly his love child and she knew it. Everybody knew it, especially Kacie. She had him wrapped around her fingers and her toes. Whenever she called him Daddy, his world magnified his love way out into the universe. Whatever creatures were out there in the great beyond, they knew when Kacie took her Daddy's hand or whispered in his ear, she made him happy. He thought about it as he entered into the kitchen, he was happy, and he was not going to let anything change that this morning, not even a little religious banter.

"Have a seat," he waved toward the table, dropping his things on top. He stepped out of the patio doors and headed past the pool. He saw her running toward him in a pair of khaki shorts that were mid-thigh and in a white cotton-T. He barely felt the cool cement beneath his feet as he left the patio area to greet her. He grinned. Before she had become the traditional little mother, those shorts would have revealed the fleshy cheeks of her buns and that T-shirt would have revealed her curvy mounds. But now, even though her body was covered for its current role in their lives, he could still think of nothing else but the softness and the swell of her flesh beneath him.

"Slow down. I didn't chase him away," he opened his arms and Kali walked into them. She was sweaty and the sweet smell of her perspiration got him a little more than excited.

"Down boy," she whispered flashing her famous, hazel eyes up at him over a beguiling little smile.

"You are going to catch cold out here," he looked down at her. He rubbed her arms, but it was he who was cold. All he wore in the slight early autumn day was his jeans and he had just gotten out of the shower.

"You are the one," she scolded. "I've been out here moving all morning. And, I have already run five miles. Now there. Try to outdo that."

"Oh, just give me the chance," he followed her into the patio doors.

"Reverend," she greeted the man cheerfully. Ashton watched the man's eyes light up as Kali hugged him and kissed him on the cheek.

"Oh, my God, Ashton. Your boots," she grabbed his boots and clothes and shoved them toward him. Ashton slid into his shirt and then sat down in a chair to put his socks on.

"Ashton, show some decorum, son," she poked him with her elbow. He continued to get dressed at the table.

"I'm sorry. You have to forgive my husband. He used to be so formal. But, having four kids and living in the country like this seems to have changed that," she giggled. And, it had. Ashton used to be such a neat freak and a stickler for everything in its place, the same way Jordan had been in the penthouse, but four kids had changed that. Now, he would just shrug after tripping over another toy, or a misplaced sneaker and say that's why we hire people to clean.

"Can I get you something to drink? Lemonade or iced tea?" Kali sat down in the chair next to the preacher.

Ashton was buckling his belt as Micah sauntered into the kitchen, heading straight for the refrigerator. He opened the door and took out a jug of iced tea and began to swig it down heartily.

"Lemonade, perhaps," the preacher said as he arched his eyebrow.

"Lemonade, it is," Kali tried to hide her astonishment and went over to the refrigerator. She poked Micah in the waist with her sharp fingernail. He flinched.

"Excuse me," she said, working her way between Micah and the refrigerator.

"You are up?" Micah walked over to the table and sat the jug down shaking the tea.

"I was on my way out there. Why did you guys let me sleep so long?" Ashton looked back at the preacher thinking he would have gone away had no one been in the house to answer the door.

"Well, Nightmare and the kids can't wait for you to get down there," Micah protested.

"Oh, the kids," Ashton jumped up. "They shouldn't be down there alone with the horses. You know how Kacie spooks them."

"Calm down," Kali grabbed his shirtsleeve. "I brought the stable guys in to clean it out today. I figured we will have the horses out long enough. And, you know how Mr. Goodman is with the kids. They are fine."

"Oh," Ashton sat down with plain disappointment on his

face. "What's this all about?" Ashton asked. He was impatient now, and was not ready for any games. He was always working and didn't have a lot of free days to spend with his family. Plus, he had promised to take Adam up to the waterfall for a man-to-man talk. He was starting to talk about girls with a lot more fervor than he had only a few months ago.

"Well, Mrs. Sperling asked me to come speak to you. There are two more of you, correct?"

"Brothers?" Micah looked from Kali to Ashton. "Who's this?"

"Micah, I told you," Kali sighed with exasperation. "Reverend Mims, this is Micah Sperling. You have already met Ashton. Their younger brothers, Ricky and Chico, are both doctors. Chico had office hours this morning and Ricky had emergency surgery. These are the two decision makers for the family though. You can talk to them."

"Kali, you didn't tell me…." Micah gave up and took another long drink from the jug. Reverend Mims sipped his lemonade timidly. Kali wanted to tell him that no one had drunk out of the lemonade jug, but she decided not to say anything to embarrass him.

"Mrs. Sperling asked me to officiate at your father's funeral this weekend. And since I didn't know your father, I thought I could get a feel for him from his children. Is there anything special you think he should be remembered for?" the preacher toyed with his lemonade a little.

"Excuse me," both Sperling men said in unison looking directly at Kali.

"Troy called earlier," she turned to the reverend. "Troy is a family friend and a police detective in Philadelphia. He said the coroner had released Billy's body and that we had to make arrangements to move it. Well, since," Kali then looked at Micah, "since Ms. Elle is not capable…"

Kali knew Micah was touchy about his mother's condition. It had only been a few months ago when Billy had had to put her in a nursing facility for Alzheimer's patients. Elle had been acting strange for years, but it had recently worsened and then it had become obvious that Billy couldn't take care of her on his own. How so many things had changed over the last ten years, she thought.

"Released?" Reverend Mims asked.

"Yes, he was found dead in his home alone. The coroner had to perform an autopsy," Kali said, looking back over her shoulder at

Ashton who had withdrawn from the table. She could tell he was angry. She could only hope he didn't get one of those headaches he usually got when it came to dealing with this part of his life.

"So, let me get this straight," Ashton was now leaning against the railing that separated the kitchen from the keep room where the kids did their homework and watched television when allowed. "You want to have a funeral for the man who wanted me dead?" Ashton asked.

"Ashton, he is your father, your children's grandfather. And, all he has done these past few years is grovel at your feet for forgiveness. We have to put some closure to this. We need to bury him. You need to say a final goodbye," Kali wanted the kids to learn to put closure to things, and she wanted them to learn how to respect their family obligations.

"I said goodbye to the son of a bitch when he was living," Ashton walked over to the refrigerator and took out another jug of iced tea.

The preacher looked surprised.

"We have plenty of iced tea and lemonade," Kali offered, not trying to show how embarrassed she was by her husband's language.

"I don't know your history," Reverend Mims said, "but, I have to agree that you and your family will need some sort of closure. Mrs. Sperling had recommended a short graveside service. Could you live with that?"

"Micah?" Kali turned to see Micah staring at the jug of tea angrily.

"Why?" Micah shook his head.

"Well, what are you going to do with the body?" Kali thought of how she had had no part in her parents' funeral arrangements, nor was she allowed to put closure to Jordan when he died. She hadn't been allowed to even attend his funeral, nor even view his body. All she could remember of any of the people she had loved and lost was their violent ends. She didn't want that, not for her children. She rubbed her eyes. This wasn't going well, and all in the wrong order. Troy was supposed to come first, then Reverend Mims. Her preacher was a bit too eager. She was sure she had told him to come late in the afternoon. She looked at her watch and wondered when Troy was going to show up with the news.

"Burn it. Throw his ashes in the Deptford dump," Ashton said in a low growl that gave her a chill. Now he is really, really pissed, she thought. And he was rarely angry with her about anything.

"Miss Elliott already found the funeral home to pick him up. She even found a burial plot over here in Jersey. All I had to do was find someone to officiate. And since, since…" Kali didn't know what else to say.

"Gentleman, a small ceremony. A few words," the preacher held up his hands.

"Your mom," Kali reached over and touched Micah's hand. "Your mom will need to say goodbye."

"She won't fucking remember," Ashton shouted.

"Ashton," Kali shouted back and stood up and walked over to him. She wrapped her arms around him.

"Please, 15 minutes. Your father was a respected lawyer. How would it look to the city and to his peers to just throw him away? Think of it as a business decision, an image that Jordan would want to continue. That you need to continue," Kali whispered underneath his chin. His body remained tense, but she could tell by his breathing that she had hit the selling point.

"Ten," he said. "Ten minutes. And you can say he was a selfish, hateful human being that loved no one but himself." Ashton peeled her arms from around him and headed for the patio doors just as Troy was about to enter.

Micah killed off the jug of iced tea like an alcoholic killing off his last sip of scotch. He even made a face as if the tea had burned his throat.

"I'm sorry, Reverend. I'm sorry this is such a difficult time for us. Why don't I call you to arrange the time Saturday? I'm thinking early so we can get on with the rest of the day. But, not too early, in case some of his old colleagues from Philadelphia would like to come over the river to see him off."

"That will be fine," the preacher shook both her hands.

"I will see you out," Kali patted his shoulders.

"You know I couldn't help admiring the artwork on the walls," the preacher said looking back at the two sullen brothers in the kitchen joined now by Troy.

"Yes, this hallway is my children's special art gallery. Ashton is always teasing me for saving everything.

"You even framed them," the preacher smiled at some elaborate stick drawings of a happy family expensively framed.

CHAPTER TWENTY-FOUR

TROY HAD BEEN Ashton's best friend since college and hated stepping into his happy abode with more bad news. He looked at his old friend and wondered sometimes if being wealthy was more of a curse than a blessing. He didn't know anyone else who had more troubles than the Sperlings, but at least they had had a dry spell.

"Well, if it isn't Detective Troy Lucas," Micah chided. "Why didn't you call Ashton instead of Kali to break the news?"

"I did, but Kali answered the phone and began drilling me with a lot of questions," Troy shrugged his shoulders. He didn't like the way Ashton had just opened the door and walked away. "What's going on?" Troy could feel the tension in the room as he sat down at the kitchen table across from Micah. Ashton ran his hands through his hair before he plopped down in one of the chairs.

"Kali's holding a funeral for Billy," Micah replied as Ashton remained silent.

"Oh," Troy answered, not sure why that was an issue. He understood Ashton hated his father, and with good reason, but the man was dead after all.

"Did he die of natural causes?" Ashton asked looking Troy dead in the eye with an intensity that put his instincts on alert. Troy knew from his history with Ashton that he could pop like a solar flare.

"No, I'm afraid he didn't," Troy paused to let the words sink in. He had already told Kali, but it was obvious she hadn't shared the news. Maybe she hadn't had the chance to, but she had had the chance to arrange a funeral, Troy thought. He could feel her presence as she inched her way into the kitchen.

She walked quietly over to Ashton and placed her hands gently on his shoulders. She kissed the top of his head, and then laid her head on his. Troy noticed the tension releasing a bit from Ashton's shoulders. She was the lion-tamer alright, he thought. No wonder she had survived the Sperlings all these years. Few women had.

"So, how did he die?" Micah leaned forward onto the table.

"Old-fashioned arsenic poisoning. Looks like it was administered to the nth degree. It acted quick, created havoc on his body. But get this, whoever poisoned him, cleaned him up and positioned him so that it looked like he died eating a bowl of soup. Very creative," Troy shook his head.

"Very deliberate," Micah got up from the table holding onto the empty jug as if it were a security blanket.

"Any clues, leads? Who did it?" Ashton sighed as Kali was now stroking his neck and shoulders.

"We talked to the neighbors. They rarely saw Billy. But, a few days before Micah found him, they saw two tall people enter his house. The woman across the street said she had opened her door to pick up the newspaper when she saw Billy hugging them and letting them in the house. She said she couldn't tell by the way they were dressed whether they were male or female. But, she said Billy waved to her with a smile on his face."

"So he had visitors he knew," Micah sat the jug in the kitchen sink. "Why weren't they distinguishable?"

"She said they had on hats, and even heavy dark coats, and that they were both tall, but one of them was very, very tall."

"We have had a warm September, nobody is wearing a heavy coat yet," Micah stated as he began to swish water around in the jug rinsing it.

"Exactly," Troy nodded. "They wanted to hide underneath their clothes."

"Or, they came from somewhere where it was cold," Ashton reached up and grabbed Kali's hands and held them still.

CHAPTER TWENTY-FIVE

ASHTON WAS GIVING her the silent treatment. He had gone to the funeral, shook the extended hands, and stared off into space. It was so unlike him, it worried her. She had regretted the funeral the day the preacher had showed up too early, but she didn't think she could turn back. How she wished she had.

"Kali," Ashton said as he stormed into their bedroom the next morning. "You have to talk to Kacie. I have tried and tried to explain to her that I can't take her little surprises. I know she is playing, but…she just scared the shit out of me."

"Where was she hiding this time?" Kali watched Ashton pace the floor. Sure, he had talked to Kacie about her love for hide and seek and jumping out of nowhere, startling everybody in the house, Ashton especially. But, she had never seen him angered by it before. She wondered if he had yelled at Kacie. It would have been their first conflict.

"She was under the kitchen table," he marched over to the bed and sat down hard. He threw his head in his hands and began to rub his temples.

"Headache?" Kali went to him and tried to gently tug his hands from his head so that she could help.

"Get away," he shouted. Kali flinched and stepped backwards, almost tripping on her own feet.

"I'm sorry. I'm sorry, I'm sorry," he reached for her and steadied her. He pulled her into his arms and kissed her forehead.

"No, I'm sorry. I never should have had that stupid funeral. I'll talk to Kacie, I promise. We will get back on track. It's going to be okay," she was rambling because she was scared. She was afraid that the calm, peaceful, loving life they had been living for the last ten years was about to take an ugly turn.

"Kali, shush. It's okay. I shouldn't have yelled at you," he pushed her rogue curl from between her eyes. He loved that curl. "I'm sorry. We are okay. I promise you, we are fine."

Ashton let go of Kali and headed for the closet. He pulled out his black travel bag.

"Where are you going?" Kali was on her feet and in front of him, reaching for the bag. He held it up over his head and looked down at her. "You don't have any trips scheduled. Micah said that the two of you could relax the rest of the month."

"Not with Daddy's killer or killers lurking around."

"Troy's looking for the killers. So is the whole Philadelphia police department, aren't they?"

"But, do they know where to look?" Ashton stepped around Kali and threw the canvas bag on the bed.

"I will only be gone for a couple of days," he said throwing a few necessities on the bed near the bag.

"Is Micah going with you?" Kali didn't want Ashton to leave. That frightened her more than his mood.

"I'm a big boy, Kali. Micah is doing his research and I am doing mine," he picked her up and moved her out of his way. She was doing her best to block him again.

"Well, at least, don't leave mad," she walked up behind him and wrapped her arms around his waist. If she had had the strength, she would have subdued him and tied him up to keep him safe. That was it! For some reason, she didn't feel he was safe.

Ashton removed her hands again and headed back for the closet, but then his knees gave way and he crumpled to the floor, holding his head. Kali ran to him and pried his hands away. The headache was back. She climbed over him determined to help chase it away. There were no medications he could take for these headaches, no place for him to hide; the only cure was for him to think of other things according to Ruby. As a psychiatrist, she had plenty of test subjects living under the same roof with her. Jordan and Billy had messed the Sperling clan up big time, Kali included. She had diagnosed Ashton's headaches as part of his post-traumatic syndrome. Ashton was still affected by his six-month stay in prison for murders he didn't commit. Before the verdict was overturned, it had ended with a bold attempt on his life; a group of inmates had almost succeeded in beating him to death.

Occasionally, something would trigger the memory, creating a debilitating headache as its only outlet. There was no doubt that Billy's funeral had a lot to do with this one, so Kali felt responsible. She shifted his head into her lap and sat there holding him, rocking him for over an hour until he fell asleep.

He awakened with a start. He had been dreaming about the two tall people entering Billy's house in dark, heavy clothes. The tallest one was just about to turn around and look him in the face when he woke up. He looked up into Kali's worn, red eyes. She had been crying. He reached up and pinched her nose playfully.

"Ooooh, snot gut," he smiled up at her.

"You started it," she smiled back.

He rolled away from her and quickly was up on his feet. She was always amazed at how agile her long-limbed husband was and how beautiful. He was 13 years her senior, but kept himself in such great shape he looked younger than the men her age. He grabbed her hands and pulled her from the floor.

"How long have I been out?"

"Couple. Three hours," she corrected herself.

"And you just sat there," he took her face in his hands and leaned his forehead to hers.

"I wanted that headache to go away," she sobbed a little.

"I'm not mad at you, Kali," he said, but deep down he was still a little disappointed.

"Yes, you are," Kali countered, thinking she was mad at herself even if he wasn't.

"Okay, a little," he pulled her close to him.

"I've got to go, Kali. I have to find out if Daddy's murder had anything to do with us," he lifted her and sat her on the bed next to his things.

"I don't want you to go. I want you to let Troy do his job. And you stay here, and do your job," she purred into his ear.

"Very tempting. You keep that in mind for when I come home in a couple of days," he kissed her cheek and threw his things into the bag.

"Now, I know you are angry with me," Kali pouted. "You won't stay and make love to me."

Ashton laughed. She was partly right. All the two of them needed was a private space and a little quiet time, and they would be tearing each other's clothes off trying to occupy one body. But, the urgency he was feeling right now that had nothing to do with sex.

Kali followed him down the stairs like a child who had been

refused a special toy. Her hand slid down the banister as she took one heavy step at a time. She watched him take two or three at a time until he reached that short overhang from the second floor. She knew he hated bending over to clear the stairs at that point, but she was able to catch up with him then.

"Don't. Don't go. Please, Ashton," she pleaded one more time and he was out the door.

She walked onto the porch and watched him enter the large detached garage. All the doors were opened. She watched as he put his hand on the door of his Porsche and then seemed to change his mind. He walked past a couple of cars and got into Jordan's vintage black Mercedes. It was huge, just the kind of leg room he needed she guessed. She watched as he drove through their circular drive down to the gate. She waved, but he was too preoccupied to look back. She slid down the door jamb of the front door and cried as if she had just lost him forever.

CHAPTER TWENTY-SIX

ASHTON GRIPPED THE steering wheel. He refused to look back as he drove toward the gate. He knew there were tears in those eyes and he couldn't give in to them. If he looked back, he would have to stop the car and go home. He would have to pick her up in his arms and take her up that tight stairwell and into their bedroom suite. He would have to lay her on her back and lick her into a frenzy. He tried not to smile as he thought of it. That was what he would do, though, if he looked back. If he looked back, his anger would dissolve and he would lose his momentum for vengeance. He had to hold onto that anger now; he couldn't allow Kali to sap it out of him. He would make it up to her to the minute he got home. He would make it up to everybody.

Though Kali had moved them to South Jersey, all the way down near Atlantic City, it wasn't a bad commute to the city once he got off the back roads and hit the Black Horse Pike. They lived about an hour or so out of the city, down in the Pinelands. Although Kali never mentioned her upbringing in the south, he knew that this place reminded her of that. They were surrounded by greenery and peace.

He drove as fast as he could to get across the bridge into Center City, he wanted to hit I-95 and go straight to Aramingo where he had unfinished business. And it was time to bring it all to a closure.

Ashton parked his car right in front of the pawn shop that was located in one of the many strip malls along the bustling street. He flung the door open, a rolled newspaper under his arm, which he threw on the counter.

"Ashton," a thin man with long, neat dreadlocks appeared from the rear of the store.

"How's my cousin-in-law?" the two men shook hands.

"I'm fine. How are you and Ms. Alina doing?"

"We're doing good. She is still asking for Ms. Kalina," Jamal leaned over the counter and noticed the newspaper. "More work for me?"

Ashton shoved the newspaper toward him. Jamal picked it up and threw it in a chair behind him.

"Ashton, don't you think it's time to just let go?"

"One more time," Ashton said walking down the counter looking at the jewelry.

"That one," he pointed to an emerald ring.

"Kalina will love it, I'm sure." Jamal produced a set of keys and pulled the tray of rings out for inspection.

"No, this one is for Alina. Keep her motivated. Last time I talked to her she told me she had all A's."

"Just like Kalina," Jamal was proud of his cousin Kalina Denise Harris, who was now Kali Sperling.

"I hope not just like Kalina," Ashton shook his head. He had turned her into a spoiled monster. Whatever Kali wanted, Kali got. She would never take no for an answer. It was his fault, he knew it. He had wanted her to have everything he could provide. He still wanted that. He wanted his wife to be safe and happy and oblivious to the real world, their real world.

"Do you think she will ever come face to face with us again?" Jamal asked for the millionth time. Ashton had told him that Kali wouldn't even let him broach the subject about her other family nor South Carolina, the state where she was raised. That was the part of her life she could wipe out. He wished it could be that easy for him.

"Jamal, you know Kali's time in your mother's household was very traumatic. And she was so tied up in her own drama with Jordan that she missed all the hoopla about Mike's death. Jordan made sure she never heard about it," because, thought Ashton, he was busy seducing her. Kali was still in the dark about her little cousin's fate.

"What can I do for you, Ashton?"

"I need another delivery. You do know where he moved to this time?" Ashton had been tracking Scully, the prison guard, since he had awakened from his coma ten years ago. He had one mission in mind, other than making Kali and his family happy. He was going to make Scully pay.

CHAPTER TWENTY-SEVEN

AS SOON AS Ashton had walked into that prison for the murder of Kali's common-law husband and Troy's sister Rita, he knew there was a hit out on him. His cellmate, an old lifer, had confirmed it and schooled him on how to protect himself. Ashton took the old man's advice and took the bulls literally by the horns. He bribed them. He started a contraband business and kept everybody happy, at least as happy as you can keep a bunch of murderers and cutthroats. He started his own conglomerate, his own security setup with a mixture of inmates and guards, and walked through the prison like the king of the cellblock. But, he knew he could never let his guard down and he hadn't, not until that final week.

Micah and Kali had come as often as the prison rules allowed. Each time he saw Kali, it would chip away at his hope of ever getting out. He had had nothing to do with those deaths, but he had gotten pinned for them anyway. And, Kali's belly was getting bigger and bigger. Adam was going to come kicking his way out whether Ashton was there to catch him or not. But, then they stopped. It had been two weeks, almost three since a visit and the phones stayed ripped up to the point no calls were coming in and none were going out. He tried to pay for a contact, but that didn't work. It was working on him, he was feeling alone and desperate. He paid Scully to get information on Kali. He needed to know if the baby had come early, or if something had happened to his family. He was scared.

It was early one Wednesday morning when Scully signaled him to follow him. Ashton didn't wait for a bodyguard; he hurriedly followed Scully to the empty laundry room. They walked past the large washtubs and straight to the back door. Scully walked in first and then backed up. Ashton stepped in behind him and the first blow landed on the back of his head. His world had gone black as his head and his body were beaten and kicked on the floor of that back room.

When he awakened, Kali was holding a screaming, hungry Adam over his face. He was home in his own bed. He had been in a coma for seven weeks. And he had spent almost every waking moment over the last ten years thinking about how he would bring justice to Scully for almost taking him away from his family.

One by one, he had brought justice to the four others involved in the beating, one of whom was on his payroll. A man called "The Walker" because it was his style to walk over anyone who would let him. The Walker was the first one released from prison after Ashton. Two months later, The Walker was found in an alley with a needle in his arm. Nobody cared about a career criminal dying in an alley from a lethal overdose of heroin; they figured it was normal. The case was shut and closed without any fanfare. The other three never made it out of prison.

It didn't take all three for Scully to realize whose lives were in danger. It wasn't lost on him that he had led Ashton to the slaughter. But, he may have gotten his first hint when he received his first dead rat in the mail. It was a whole one.

Scully transferred to another prison in another city. It didn't help. Jamal found him, and had half a rat delivered to his home. That was two years ago. Ashton wanted him to get real comfortable and had waited patiently. Now, the headache was back and he couldn't bear it any longer than he had, too. Those damn headaches had come every time he thought about that beating, and each time he eliminated one of his attackers the headaches disappeared. Now, it was just Scully.

"The head," Ashton nodded at the newspaper. Jamal looked at it, knowing there was a lot of money lining those pages. He would never give Ashton a price; Ashton would just give him some outrageous sum.

"Put Alina's ring in a nice box, put a bow on it. Put a rat's head in another pretty box," Ashton smiled. "I think Scully will like that."

"Sure. To both," Jamal crossed his arms and leaned against a back counter.

"What are you getting ready to do, Ashton?"

"Just deliver it for me. Give me the address."

Jamal stood up straight. "You have never asked for the address before."

"Give me the address," Ashton's fingers tapped the glass.

CHAPTER TWENTY-EIGHT

ASHTON SAT IN the clunker that he had stolen off a side street in North Philadelphia. He had parked on a street that ended in a T section facing Scully's row house in a dilapidated Camden neighborhood. The streets were strewn with trash, the buildings blighted with graffiti. Scully had gone a long way out of character to hide from himself. He had been driven out of a neatly groomed yard and a nice little Cape Cod outside Harrisburg to this. Ashton thought it amusing that he was now hiding among the criminals he used to guard.

Jamal was a good enough investigator to work for him, but he didn't want to jeopardize the only family Alina had left. She certainly would never be able to rely on Kali. And, to think of the nerve Kali had yelling at him for ignoring his father. How hypocritical. But, at least he had reason. His own father had tried to murder him, not once, but twice.

Jamal had given Ashton a heads up regarding Scully's schedule. The man left his home exactly at 4:45 AM every morning. Ashton had pulled into a prime parking spot around two that morning. He sat there, staring at the house, playing out the deed over and over in his mind. He wondered if Scully would recognize him and then chuckled. Of course, he would. Who else was he running from?

Ashton walked up the concrete steps dressed completely in black. He had put on a pair of latex gloves under his sleek leather ones. He had opened and closed his hands many times in those gloves, grabbed things, shook them, and realized they didn't have that up close and personal feel. He put on the latex ones for two reasons: one to hide his fingerprints and, two, to get that up close and personal feeling when he was squeezing the life out of the bastard. He would remove the leathers just before he took the bastard's throat in his hands.

Ashton was standing in the doorway when Scully opened the door. He put up a good fight to close it, but Ashton had been pumping iron for over 20 years, even when he was in prison. He was strong and Scully looked like the only thing he had been lifting lately was a bottle, and he felt like it. Ashton slid into the door with ease, removed the glove from his left hand and lunged. Scully fought a good fight, but Ashton was on a mission, he wouldn't let go. Scully made one last effort to save himself. He grabbed a vase and tried to hit Ashton in the head with it. Ashton grabbed it and crushed it with one hand before the rest of it crashed to the ground. That's when the hope faded out of Scully's eyes. Ashton kept squeezing until the eyes went totally blank and the man's feet stopped scraping against the bare, splintered wooden floor. Ashton was still holding onto the man's throat, waiting to feel something.

Nothing, he felt nothing. He was surprised there was no excitement when the man stopped breathing. There was no relief; there were no bells and whistles, no adrenaline rush. There wasn't even a feeling of a spirit passing onto another world. There was an emptiness that hung in the room with him and the dead, pitiful looking body, the same emptiness that had lingered each time he had heard one of his assailants had bit the dust. And all this time, he thought it was because he had been so far removed from the act. Now, there he was, up close and personal, with nothing except silence and blank dead eyes.

Ashton eased out of the house. It was still dark. He saw someone delivering newspapers on the other end of the street. He walked away and turned the corner as soon as he hit it. He kept walking. He wasn't worried about the car. He caught a bus to the High Speed Line, and then changed trains at 8th and Market. When he met the world from underground Suburban Station, it was daylight. He fell in step with the masses and went straight to his office.

Ashton was the first one in the executive suite. He walked into his office pulling off his gloves. He was surprised. His latex glove, the left one was torn right down the middle of his thumb. He tried to remember if he had touched anything. He plopped in the chair and thought about the vase. But, it was in a million pieces.

Suddenly, Ashton's eyelids were taking a cue from gravity: they were closing and he couldn't fight it any longer. He hadn't slept a full night since he had found out about his father's death. He needed to take a long overdue nap. He picked up yesterday's newspaper and headed for his private bath. He opened the linen closet and shoved the third shelf. The shelves swung open into a safe room, his private secured suite that had only been used for making out with Kali as they secluded themselves from the outside world, and for taking naps. He went straight to the kitchenette and made himself a carafe of coffee. He sat down at the table where he had spread the newspaper and then looked at the cup realizing the coffee would just keep him wide awake. He looked at his watch and thought he could at least afford a couple of hours of snoozing.

Ashton relieved himself of his clothes, neatly hanging his slacks over the chair in the corner. He crashed across the bed and let out a loud sigh. It was good to be still. He needed to be still. He lifted his arm to adjust himself and the watch hit the end of the table next to the bed. He flipped over, removed the watch, and tried to put it on the end table. It fell. He flipped back over on his stomach and let his arm fall to the side of the bed. He scraped the floor trying to scoop the watch into his hand; instead he pushed it farther away. He kept reaching for it and pushing it until finally, he was able to pick it up. He lifted it and it got stuck on something under the bed. He kept feeling under there and thought the protruding object that captured his watch must have been a screw. He gave up, re-shifted his body until he was comfortable and fell fast asleep.

CHAPTER TWENTY-NINE

ASHTON RECOGNIZED THE source of the cold metal pressed against his right temple. His first thought was that the police had tracked him down, but as he eyes began to focus, he was in for the biggest surprise of his life.

"Hey brother," Asa, his dead identical twin, was kneeling down next to the bed. He was staring Ashton in the face. "Long time, no see."

Ashton didn't move. He could smell her. His ex-wife, Redd, was holding a gun. She poked him with it and giggled. He had pissed her off royally; there was no doubt in his mind that she was capable of pulling the trigger. She had just been laying in wait for this moment. He watched Asa stand up and brush off his knees.

"You need to vacuum in here, son," Asa teased. Then he turned completely around.

"How do you like my new look? Been working out," Asa pumped his arms. "Got a new haircut. Like the clothes," Asa waved down the length of his body. He had changed into the clothing Ashton had just taken off.

"He looks exactly like you, doesn't he?" Redd said in her thick South Philly accent. Half Irish, half Italian, she had grown up in South Philly. Her red hair gave away her Irish lineage, but her accent was a dead give-away from whence she came.

"I think that's a trait of most identical twins," Ashton answered.

"Still a smart-ass," Redd sneered as she lifted the gun from his head. He watched her take a couple of steps back.

Ashton shifted around and sat up against the headboard. He saw his ex-wife standing beside the bed still holding the gun with both hands looking like she was ready to pull the trigger at any moment. But, something was holding her back and it wasn't Asa who stood there with the same dufus grin on his face that had irked Ashton from childhood.

"Playing dress-up, little brother," Ashton rubbed his face with both hands. He wanted to uncover his eyes and realize he was dreaming. But, he could still smell her stinky perfume. She was there, and so was his dead brother.

"Aren't you going to ask?" Asa chuckled, then sat down on the bed and leaned over close to Ashton's face.

"Ask what?" Everybody thought Asa was dead. Ashton knew Asa was dying to tell him how he had pulled that one off. Micah had been there, seen the straight line, saw that his body no longer breathed. They had had a funeral that Ashton hadn't bothered to attend. Why should he? His brother's goal had been to murder him and his family. His father crossed his mind briefly and he thought of the tall strangers the neighbor had described to Troy. He shook his head.

"That's not going to make me go away," Asa whispered.

"What do you want?" Ashton asked, still trying to remain calm and assess the gun sitting firmly in Redd's hands. She could pull the trigger before he could get up, and Asa blocked any chance of that now.

"I'm alive, bro" Asa laughed. "I'm alive."

"I get that," Ashton answered.

"Daddy loved me better than you," Asa teased.

"Asa," Redd yelled him, "find the fucking watch."

"Oh, yeah," Asa nodded his hand. "You wear that fucking thing everywhere you go. But, I can't find it. Where is it, bro?"

"So you are still taking orders?" Ashton evaded the question.

"Let's get this over with," Redd demanded. "Jordan's hidden treasure, or not so hidden. You think I had forgotten? It's all I have been thinking about. You and that bitch sitting your asses up on all that money while you shell out a measly $10,000 a month to me."

"Jordan's been dead almost 15 years. What makes you think I haven't cashed it all in?" Ashton wanted to make Asa move out of his way. "Besides, your lover here had millions worth of art. Wasn't that enough to live on for at least a lifetime?"

"Not the way she consumes, you should know that," Asa sighed.

"You didn't tell me how good I looked," Asa stood up holding his hands out to his side. "You think your wife would know the difference?"

"Asa," Redd prodded.

"Alright, alright." Asa bent over to pick something up. "Where's the watch, Ashton?"

"I haven't seen that thing in years. I lost it," Ashton lied.

"You son-of-a-bitch," Redd screamed.

Ashton looked at her seething red lips; he was sure she was about to pull the trigger.

"Hey, brother," he heard Asa and looked toward him just in time to see a rolled telephone book connect with his face. The blow was hard enough to knock him completely out of the bed onto the floor at Redd's feet. He could taste the blood as it swelled into a torrent inside his mouth. He tried to lift his head and couldn't. Then he felt the hard toe of her boot burrow hard into his chest. His body tried to cough, but his blood was stifling the cough. He was conscious. Unlike after the first couple of blows from the inmates during their attack, now he was awake and he was afraid, because he wasn't even unable to roll up in a ball for protection as that blow had caused his body to go completely limp.

They threw him into a chair at the little kitchen table. Immediately, his head slumped forward onto the newspaper he had read earlier. The article was about the investigation into his father's death.

"Look what you did," Redd accused Asa. "How is he going to tell us where the watch is?"

"Oh, I bet that sexy wife of his knows where it is," Asa answered.

"Go, look again. Maybe, you overlooked it," Redd ordered.

"Alright. Alright, Already. I'm going to look again," Asa stormed out of the room and back into the bedroom.

"Look under the bed," Redd yelled behind him. "All I ever wanted, Ashton, is my share," Redd touched his head gingerly with the gun. "I was never in any of those stupid plans to kill you. Though, you deserved it. And, if I don't find the damn watch, I am going to do what Asa and your father couldn't do. I'm going to make you pay. I'm going to make you suffer the way I did when you walked out on me for that bitch."

Ashton tried to speak and couldn't. All he could do was regret leaving home. Regret leaving Kali sitting on those cold steps worrying about him as he drove away doing his best not to look back at her. He was angry, and he wanted her to know he was angry. That had been the first time he had walked away from her, from his family, angry. Now, he was never going to be able to repair that hurt. His head was damaged. He could have fought them if any other part of him had been injured, but he couldn't even lift his head. He couldn't move at all, but he was completely aware of their presence.

CHAPTER THIRTY

HIS EYES WERE so swollen he could barely see, but he knew he was in a moving vehicle. In what direction, he couldn't tell. He tried to turn over, but his head still wouldn't move for him. In front of him, he could see bars. He was in a cage of some kind. He heard their voices coming from behind him. She was driving and Asa was riding shotgun.

"Damn. I think he shit himself," he heard Asa say in disgust. "Don't you smell it?"

"Well, you won't have to worry about cleaning his ass up," she chuckled.

"He's still breathing," Asa's voice was a little closer.

"Why are you fucking worried? This is what you wanted years ago."

"It was never what I wanted," Ashton could hear the regret in Asa's voice.

"Yeah, right. That's why you sabotaged his damn plane and killed the wrong damn people," Redd retorted.

"No, that is not why. Daddy gave me the schematics and told me if I removed that part, the plane wouldn't take off. He didn't say it would take off and crash, for Christ sakes!"

"You are such a dumb-ass," Redd turned the vehicle and came to a short stop.

"If I am such a dumb-ass, why do you love me so much?" Asa reached out and touched her face lightly.

"Jeez, Asa. You are the only person in the world that knows I fucking exist. That doesn't mean I love you," she shoved his hand away.

"I know that's your way of telling me that you love me, Redd."

Ashton awakened trying to scream, but the sound refused to release itself. His flesh was being torn, ripped again and again. He had already passed out several times.

"What the hell are you doing?" Asa shouted as he was coming towards them.

"I was just playing doctor, or should I say surgeon," Redd laughed.

"Oh, my God, he's a bloodied mess. How could you do that?" Ashton could hear Asa's voice just outside his cage.

"I'm bored. And, I'm hungry. And you ruined any chance of him telling us how to get our hands on that money. He's going to die anyway. I'm going to get something to eat. Are you coming?"

"No, I just ate. I brought you something though," Asa was now moving away from the cage.

"No, I don't want that shit," Redd screamed. "Give me the keys to the car. While I'm gone, get his body into the van. I'm ready to go home. We have to dump his ass somewhere."

"Then what?" Asa asked like a little child.

"How many times do we have to cover this? You take his fucking place long enough to get the money he owes me."

"Yeah, right. Right?"

Ashton heard Redd storm out on what sounded like a dirt floor. He heard a metal door shut. He had no idea where he was or how long he had been drifting in and out of consciousness.

"I'm sorry, Ashton. More than you will ever know, brother. I am sorry. I never wanted or planned any of this," Ashton heard Asa begin to cry.

The cage moved as Asa leaned against it. "I wish you were awake so I could tell you everything. I really thought the plane wasn't going to take off. I believed Daddy. He said the plane was to delay you. Hell, I didn't know you and the kids were supposed to die on that plane. You know Daddy. I was as shocked as everybody when it just dropped out of the sky like that.

"When it did, Daddy said I had to get an alibi. A good solid alibi and that's when I sucked Kenny all the way in. I'd been hitting his little ass off and on for years, and I knew he had a crush on both of us, so I used it to my advantage. That is, until he figured things out and tried to rat me out. But, I didn't mean for him to die either. We just started fighting in the car and he drove off at high speed right into the creek. That's how my head got hurt.

"I was lucky. He wasn't. He was stuck in the car, gasping for breath when I got out. I found an old skull cap in the trash and took a cab to Daddy's. The cops had just left the house looking for me. So Daddy made me hide, and then he blackmailed some doctor that was doing illegal abortions for Jordan to get me out of the hospital alive.

"But, Ashton. I didn't have anything to do with that hit on you. That was all Daddy. I didn't even know about it until later. Then, it was really too late to mend fences I guess. I was already dead to you and everybody except Redd and Daddy.

"That bitch is pure hell. You know she started driving and didn't stop until you smelled too bad to stomach. For a minute there, I thought we were going to make it all the way to California. She is freaking nuts, and it's all your fault! And Daddy's. She had Daddy wrapped around her little finger. But, she was pissed when he could no longer supply her cash flow. That's why she poisoned his ass. Hell, I didn't see that one coming. Don't ask me why I am here now, 'cause, I truly don't fucking know. I just hope my life with Kali and the kids is going to be a whole lot better than with her."

CHAPTER THIRTY-ONE

KALI LOOKED AT her watch. She needed to get a move on. She had been sitting with Mrs. Ratcliffe all morning. Though she enjoyed the older woman's company, she had a few errands she had wanted to run before meeting Kacie at the house.

"I know you have to leave soon, but I have so enjoyed your company," the older woman squeezed her hand. Kali smiled down at her. That's what she had liked about living in this small community in South Jersey. She was getting to know people again and they were getting to know her. Mrs. Ratcliffe was the church secretary who had recently fallen and broken her hip. Reverend Mims had asked for volunteers to take care of her since she lived alone. Kali had signed up for Tuesday mornings. But, she was running late. Kacie was coming home early today, because of a school field trip. And one of her classmates' moms was going to drop her off as soon as they returned.

"Kali," the woman still held her hand. "Is everything okay with you? I have been going on and on about my boring life so much that I didn't get a chance to hear what's going on with you?"

"I'm fine, Mrs. Ratcliffe. Everything's fine. Kacie went on a field trip to the Art Museum in Philadelphia today. They are due back soon and I wanted to stop at the grocery store first. There's a little chill in the air and I was thinking of making a big kettle of vegetable soup and some cornbread."

"Oh, sounds good. You must be a good cook."

"I am now. It took a few trials and errors. Ashton will tell you that. But, I cook for the family as often as I can and they seem to enjoy it."

"That's good. How is your family?"

"They are all fine. The boys are getting bigger and I can't seem to fill them up on anything, food, drink, air," Kali giggled.

"Yeah, that's boys for you," the woman still held her hand.

Kali glanced down at the dishes by the bed. "Oh, let me clean these up for you real fast," Kali gently pulled her hand away and started gathering the dishes.

"Kali," the woman smiled. "Is everything alright with you? The reason I ask," the woman paused and reached for her again. Kali came over to her and sat on the bed with the dishes in her lap. "The reason I ask is that, for the past couple of weeks, you haven't really been yourself. Everyone has noticed. You usually run the world with a big, happy smile. When you walk in a room you light it up. These days, we hardly notice you have entered the room and when we do, you seem…startled. Has something happened, sweetheart? Is there something we can help you with?"

Kali stared at her, wondering how to answer the question. She could be honest and blurt out that her husband has changed, that the last time he came home, he came home mean and hurtful, and that everybody in her house was walking on eggshells around him. And, all he wanted to do was find his stupid watch.

"No, I'm just feeling a little under the weather physically and mentally. I think I just need a little vacation," Kali smiled and rose with the dishes. "Otherwise, I am fine."

Kali washed the dishes hurriedly and said her goodbyes. She sped down the little street to the nearest supermarket. While she stood amidst the vegetables, she looked at her watch. She was still behind time and didn't want Kacie coming home to that big, old empty house. She dropped as many tomatoes as she could in as many bags as she could, then went for the corn, which was looking pretty puny. She decided to get the rest of the vegetables in the frozen aisle. As she passed the meat aisle, she changed her mind about the vegetable soup and decided to go for a beef stew. She loaded her cart with large packages of cubed beef, and looked at her watch again. She gasped, and then ran through the store throwing everything she thought she needed into the cart.

Soon, she was racing out of the township onto the back roads leading to her estate. She kept looking in her mirrors for patrol cars, because she knew she was speeding and the last thing she wanted was to be delayed.

She liked living out in the middle of nowhere in Jersey. She had never realized there was so much space in the tiny state until she had decided she wanted no more of Philadelphia. After Adam was born, she had wanted a fresh start.

She and Ashton had had a rocky relationship marred with sordid sex, lies, and murder since the first day they had met. It hadn't seemed like that at first. Not when he had seduced her into a life with him and Jordan. She had become a special lover to both, sometimes in the same bed at the same time with her in the middle. Not something she could ever share with her children. And, she didn't know why he felt the need to now.

He had always been so caring about his children, about her. His protectiveness had suddenly dissolved. She shivered. His loving touch had also fallen by the way side. He was no longer making love to her, he was raping her. She knew that because she had experienced rape before, when Asa had raped her. She hadn't always wanted Jordan, or Jordan and Ashton at once, but they had seduced her. They hadn't frightened her, though she said 'no' many times. They made her change her mind. Ashton and Jordan had conditioned her overtime. She had become addicted to sex with them. It had become her norm, though she knew it was anything but normal.

Yes, she and Ashton had done some things in their lives they both regretted. Neither of them thought the kids should be informed of those details. She wondered why the sudden change. And how could people be so crass in front of their own children? Even Micah was taking him to task on his behavior.

"You little gay-assed bastard, I asked you where was my fucking watch?" Ashton was storming toward Adam as Kali had walked in from choir rehearsal.

"Ashton, watch your mouth. What is wrong with you?" Immediately Kali stepped between her son and her husband.

"Look, bitch. This is not some freaking game. I need my watch," he turned his anger toward her.

"You," Kali poked him in the chest, "calm down. NO one knows what you did with that worthless watch." Ashton grabbed by her wrists and squeezed until she thought her knees would buckle. "Let me go, you bully." She used what was left of her energy and stomped his right foot. He let go, but came back with a slap that sent her to the floor. She reached up to touch her face. She knew, without looking in the mirror, that there was a handprint and a busted lip. There wouldn't be any singing in the choir the next day, not for her. She couldn't let anyone see what he was doing

to her.

AJ and Adam ran to her to help her up, while Katie held onto Kacie, pressing her head into her stomach with one hand over her ear and partially covering her little sister's eyes.

"So, you little faggot, I am asking you again." Ashton reached for Adam and Artie ran between them to Kali.

"You son-of-a-bitch. How dare you talk to your children like that?" Kali was up on her feet. She pushed the boys behind her.

"How dare you talk back to me, you little slut? Yeah, that's all your momma is, boys. A slut. She used to spend more time on her knees with a cock in her mouth than she did anything else. How the hell do you think you got here?" Ashton hit the wall and walked away.

Kali stood stunned trying to figure out what had happened there. Hearing the front door slam behind him, she opened her arms and all of the children ran to her. She hugged and kissed each one of them.

"Listen to me. No one walks alone. You understand. Katie, I want you to help Kacie move into your room, now. The two of you are going to have to share for awhile. Okay?"

"Yes, Mommy," Katie's face was streaked with tears.

"He's not my daddy," Kacie wailed. "I keep telling you, he's not Daddy. I heard him. I heard him talking to somebody on the phone. He is not Daddy."

"Calm down, Kacie." Kali bent down to her daughter. "He certainly isn't acting like Daddy, but it's the illness that's taking over, that post-traumatic syndrome. Aunt Ruby thinks something has triggered it. Maybe, the lost watch. Is everybody sure they haven't seen that dumb watch?" Kali looked around at her children's faces. They were all telling the truth. The last time she had seen the stupid watch was on his wrist the day after Billy's funeral, the day he disappeared for almost two weeks.

"AJ, I need you, Adam and Artie to switch rooms with Uncle Chico. He won't mind. Move his things into your room. Since his is bigger, it will accommodate the three of you. Plus, it's closer to Katie's room. I'm going to need the five of you to stick together. And I mean together, like glue. Your father's more than a little unpredictable, he's hurtful. Now, everybody get moving." The kids began to run toward the stairs. "Not you, Adam. Stay with Mommy a minute."

Kali waited until the other kids were out of earshot and she pulled Adam close to her and whispered in his ear. "Your father is sick. We are going to weather this; but, in the meantime, I need you to be strong and confident. Don't listen to anything he says right now or take it to heart. God knows you are not gay. Just a couple of weeks ago, he was planning to have a talk with you about girls. Trust me, he has seen the way you watch girls," Kali chuckled a little. "I love you. And somewhere in that dark heart that just walked out that door, he loves you, too. You and the others, you close your ears when he calls you out of your name and who you are. I am going to need to you coach the others on this. Can you do that?" Kali stood back and looked in Adam's eyes. She could see them strengthening behind the glaze of tears.

"You are Adam Kenneth Sperling. You are Batman. You are my hero, my rock. Okay? And you are not gay. Just take a look at your Uncle Ricky. Are you anything like him?" she smiled.

"No," he smiled back at her.

"For some insane reason, your father is bent on hurting us. But, we are not going to let him succeed. Now go help your brother and Artie. I'm going to call your Uncle Micah."

Kali made it to her gate passed the other gates of the other large estates on this back road. There were celebrities in some of those homes. Some of them they knew, some they had never seen in the community at all. She pressed the remote and the gate opened slowly. She drove into the circle in front of their large, older home that was now being renovated room by room to reflect their more modern tastes. Kali jumped out and grabbed a few groceries bags and headed to the front door. When she reached for the doorknob, her heart stopped. The door was standing ajar. Kacie had beaten her home.

Kali walked into the door and headed down the hallway toward the kitchen.

"Kacie," she yelled throwing the bags onto the kitchen table. "Kacie, mommy's home." Kali walked back into the hallway and started looking through the house in Kacie's favorite hiding places. "Kacie, I'm not playing with you. Come out, now. We have talked about this, remember?"

Kali sighed and put her hands on her hips. She walked toward the door to get the rest of the bags from the trunk of her car when she heard movement upstairs. "Kacie, come down here right this minute," Kali yelled up the stairs. She looked back at the car through the open door and looked back up the stairs. She wanted to see the little devil in the flesh. The groceries could wait another minute. She ran up the stairs and saw a shadow move in the hallway.

"Kacie Dolores Sperling, stop hiding. Right now. I'm not playing, Kacie. You will lose your television privileges tonight. I promise."

Kali headed toward her bedroom door where she had seen the shadow. The door was ajar about an inch. Kali put her hand on the door to open it gently, just in case Kacie was behind it ready to spring out and say "boo." But, instead of seeing a mischievous child, she wasn't sure what she was seeing. It was like a flash, then she felt her body lift slightly off the ground, and then she heard the sound of her own head hitting something. It sounded like a loud clap of thunder.

The next thing she knew she was laying on the floor looking straight ahead. And lying in front of her, also on the floor was Ashton. He was lying in a pool of blood. As her eyes tried to focus, the heel of a cowboy boot came close her face. She had expected it to step into her face, but instead it stepped across her. She saw another boot with a dark pants leg draped over it and what looked like the hem of a long, dark coat just short of the pants leg's end. Her world went black.

CHAPTER THIRTY-TWO

KALI COULD HEAR AJ's voice. He was calling her. "Mom. Mom. Mom," AJ said, as he held her hand. Her eyes had fluttered and so had his heart.

It was AJ. She didn't have to recognize his voice, only his signature way of getting her attention. He always said Mom three times when he needed her to look at him or to really listen when it was something he felt was important.

She opened her eyes. He was fuzzy at first, but he was close enough to kiss her forehead. She squeezed his hand.

"Mom," AJ's voice cracked as he looked in her eyes.

"What?" she whispered, for a moment wondering why she was in bed.

"Hi Mom," AJ said as his tears washed down on her face.

"Boy, why are you crying?" She reached up to touch his face and realized she had an IV in the back of her hand.

She looked around and saw the hospital equipment next to her bed.

"What am I doing here?"

"Somebody shot you. And Daddy," AJ sniffled. He reached for some tissues and began to clean his face.

"Oh, My God! Kacie," Kali suddenly remembered and tried to sit up. But, the pain on her left side knocked her back down.

"Kacie is fine, Mom. She and the other kids are fine. They are at the penthouse. Uncle Micah let me stay with you."

"Security?" Kali's mind started racing. It had only been a few weeks since Billy had been murdered, and Ashton had suspected it was related to them. Now this.

"Yes, they are under guard."

"Your father?" Kali closed her eyes and almost held her breath. She remembered seeing Ashton lying in a pool of his own blood.

"He's fine. The bullet grazed the back of his head, but it knocked him unconscious. He is awake now, though. He's in ICU, too, under observation."

"Am I?"

"In ICU, yes."

"I have to go see him," she tried to sit up again.

"No, you need to lay back and relax, little girl." Micah entered the room, a slow grin swept across his beautiful brown face. Kali smiled back at him. Her brother-in-law always had a calming effect on her and on the rest of the family as well.

"Ha, ha," she gave up and pushed her head back into the pillow. AJ busied himself trying to make it more comfortable.

A nurse came in behind Micah.

"Gentleman, I need you to leave," she walked over to the side of the bed and smiled down at Kali. "Well, you have had a nice nap."

"How long was I out?"

"Three days, Mom. Three whole days," AJ said before he left the room.

"Who found us?" she yelled at Micah who was just about to close door.

"Kacie," he said as the door closed.

Kali began to pull at the cords attached to her. "What are you doing? You can't do that." The nurse began to restrain her. "Your doctor will be here in a minute. He will explain everything to you, but you have to calm down."

"I have to get to my daughter. She is too young to have seen us like that. Hell, no one should have seen us like that," she screamed, remembering the bloodied scene of her own parents' murder-suicide when she was 17 years old. How her life had changed in that moment, how her future had become unwritten and uncertain. She had to get out of that bed.

CHAPTER THIRTY-THREE

"STOP FIGHTING THE sedation, Kali. Just relax. Kacie is fine," Micah was sitting next to her when she opened her eyes. He didn't dare tell her Kacie was having nightmares, not now.

"You would have been proud. She came home from school and found the two of you. She didn't go into the room. She went to her room and locked the door. She called 911 and then she called me. She did everything she was supposed to do," Micah brushed her rogue curl from between her eyes. She stared up at him, her eyes tearing up.

"Shh, it's okay. Everybody's fine. Even Ashton, although, I must admit I was hoping the bullet would have knocked some sense into his head. Instead, I think some of the sense he had left sapped out with the blood," Micah tried to chuckle, but Kali saw the worry in his eyes.

"What do you mean?"

"I mean, the concussion has caused some sort of memory lapse. And, you think he was in a bad mood these last couple of weeks? He is worse now, that's why I didn't want you struggling out of your bed to his bedside. He can easily get up and come see you. But, he's in there, acting like a big, bullying baby. I have never seen him act this way before. Never," Micah's voice trailed off.

"He's been hurting me, Micah. I didn't want to say anything, but I think…no, I am, I am afraid of him."

"I think your instincts are wise," Micah kissed her on the forehead.

PART FOUR

~ BACK TO THE PRESENT ~

CHAPTER THIRTY-FOUR

THE FAKE ASHTON had called to let her know he would be in New York another day. She was relieved to have Lazarus to herself one more day, but it didn't work out that way. Instead, Lazarus had avoided her. He had taken the kids out early that Saturday morning and informed her they would be all day. At first, she had pouted for being left out. Then she was angry because she wanted his time and then scolded herself for being so selfish. Then she was bored. She jumped in her car and drove to Jersey. She had only been to the house once since she and the fake Ashton had been shot. There was no longer a need to look for the watch, but she was curious to see if the fake Ashton had left behind any clues on how to find Redd.

Kali was happy to find the house still standing, gleaming in the sunlight of the first warm spring day. She unlocked the door and called out. She was no longer in control of the staffing schedules. She didn't know whether she would surprise a housekeeper or a security man giving the place a walk-through.

No one answered. She ran up the stairs to her bedroom and jumped into the middle of the bed. She wished Ashton was there. She wanted a repeat of the safe room sex in the worst way. She wanted her long, thin Ashton. He was just as voracious as her thick, muscled Ashton was. She liked it.

She lingered there for a few minutes, reminding herself that she was on a mission to find out where Redd was hiding. She was no longer in plain sight. Every time she had gone to the swing office, she had searched the Internet and made phony phone calls trying to book Redd for a television appearance. No one knew where she was. The last lead they had was in Rio de Janeiro. And then, nothing. It was as if she had dropped off the face of the earth.

Lazarus had not given her any details of what he remembered, but it was obvious some of it had taken place in the safe room. She had let him chase her out of the safe room without explanation, and she hadn't asked. She knew better. She knew he would let her know what he wanted her to know and when. If she had pressed the issue, he would never open up and let her in. She had to be patient.

Kali started by going through Ashton's old jewelry chest. She had gone through that thing a million times looking for that stupid watch, hoping she would find a hidden drawer or something. But nothing. Then she went through his sock drawer. As she was about to give up, she found a worn-looking business card advertising a pawnshop on Aramingo Avenue.

"Did he pawn the watch?" she asked aloud. "No, dummy, the watch was in the safe room. But, what would Ashton pawn? Did he pawn something or did Asa?"

She stuck the card in her pocket, locked the door, and ran down to her car. She looked back in the rearview mirror, giving the house a silent good-bye when she thought she saw a glimmer in one of the top windows. It frightened her. She wondered if someone else was in the house while she was there. She picked up her bulky mobile phone and tried to call Micah. He didn't answer. She tried Lazarus and had no luck there either. Unbeknownst to her, she took the same route Ashton had taken to Aramingo Avenue 18 months ago. The only difference was she didn't walk straight into the pawn shop; the tiny inkling of what she might find frightened her.

Kali went into a discount store in the same strip mall, and bought the kids shorts and T-shirts to bum around in during the summer. She took the clothes to her car and put them in the trunk. Then, she took a deep breath and walked straight in the pawn shop with the card crumpled in her fist.

"Kalina," a tall man with the neatest dreadlocks she had ever seen looked up from a newspaper. He seemed to not only know her, but to be genuinely pleased to see her. He walked from behind the counter with a large grin on his face.

She stood there for a moment glued, afraid to move. She searched his face for recognition, but found none.

He hugged her. She still didn't move; she just stared.

"It's Jamal. Your cousin, Jamal. I am so happy to see you. How are you?"

"Jamal? Mazetta's Jamal?" Kali pulled the business card out of her pocket and stared at it.

"You work here?"

"I own the place," Jamal said, proudly. "Didn't Ashton tell you?

No, he didn't tell you," Realizing that Jamal backed away from her. "This is a coincidence. But, I am still very happy to see you. I wish Alina was here. She talks about you all the time. I think she has saved every magazine, every newspaper clipping that has you in it. She worships you."

"I, I don't know what to say," Kali looked around the shop. It was neat and clean. Its display cases glistened, but there was no place to sit.

"Come. Come back here into the office," he stepped aside and let her walk toward the back. He noticed her body was stiff and rigid. She was afraid.

"Have a seat," Jamal pointed to the chair. "Can I? Can I, please, let Alina know that you are here? She would love to see you. She could be here in a half hour."

"That's okay," Kali nodded.

"Or, would you prefer we go see her? I was about to close up shop anyway. Business has been slow all day. I can do that," Jamal grinned. "It is so good to see you, little cousin. You have grown into an incredibly beautiful and formidable woman. I know the formidable part because of all the stories Ashton used to tell us about you."

"You know Ashton?"

"Ashton and I had become friends — before his change, I should say. The last time I saw him, he acted as if he didn't know me. So I let it go. It sort of hurt Alina, but we are doing fine."

"Why would it hurt Alina?" Kali asked, not really wanting to know.

"Alina looks at Ashton like a bigger big brother. He has always been kind to us. He is putting her through school, set me up in the shop, and did his best to help Shandie." Kali gripped the arms of the chair, fear and suspicion beginning to grow in her. Jordan had put her through school, too. Ashton had set Kenny up in his own shop. What else didn't she know about her husband, besides being a murderer?

"I tell you what. Come home with me. I live close to your side of town. You will be almost home when you leave my place. Please, you are all Alina talks about. And, you are all the family we have left really."

Kali nodded her head and before long she was in her car following Jamal down a small street just short of center city. It was a clean, quaint street with a bunch of three-story row homes. He pulled in front of a parking space and beeped his horn. She took the spot as he drove away, and then sat there. She watched him walk toward her. He was still thin, and it was obvious that he was still into his clothes. His jeans were pressed hard and he wore one single gold chain around his neck. He opened the car door for her and she followed him through a gate to a very small yard, big enough only for the trimmed shrubbery that occupied it. They walked into a small foyer with three keyed mailboxes. He checked one, and then led her up the stairs.

"I hope you don't mind a few stairs. Alina and I occupy the third floor. We didn't want to hear the tenants over our heads."

"Tenants?"

"Yes, the pawn shop has been a really good investment. I was able to pay Ashton back and buy a few properties. I could have put Alina through school, but Ashton had already put the money out," he stuck the key in the door, but it opened right away.

"Kalina," the young woman squealed. "It's really you," she grabbed Kalina and hugged her. "Oh, my God. I can't believe you are really here. Come in, come in."

Kali walked into the small apartment and noticed it was tastefully furnished. She knew she shouldn't have thought anything less of Jamal. Alina grabbed her hand and led her to the sofa.

"How are you?" Alina's eyes were bright and happy.

"I'm fine," Kali answered, still feeling a bit disoriented. "How are you?"

"I'm real fine, now." Alina was still holding her hand.

Kali remembered the first time Alina had grabbed her hand. She was only six, and her little hands had been sweaty and grimy. Kali had wanted to pull away from them, but couldn't. And now, all these years later, she still couldn't. She wanted to hold onto Alina's hand and she did. She squeezed it lightly.

"You are very beautiful," Kali said. The thought of Ashton sleeping with Alina was creeping down her spine.

"Everybody says I look like you," she giggled. "Well, not everybody. Just Ashton and Jamal." Alina giggled again.

"I didn't know you guys knew Ashton."

"Well, yeah, Ashton told us you didn't like talking about your life with us," Jamal came back into the room and took a seat across from them. "We understood."

"I'm sorry," Kali didn't know what else to say.

"Don't be," Jamal leaned over and placed a bracelet on the table.

"This is the one thing Ashton missed when he came to pick up your things,"

Jamal pointed to it.

Kali picked it up and kissed it. It was the last birthday present her parents had given her. She had worn it every day until Mazetta chased her out of the house with a flurry of fists.

"I kind of held onto it, hoping I could give it back to you one day," Jamal said. "I wasn't there when my mother and stepfather attacked you. I would like to think I would have tried to protect you," he paused. "But, I was in a different place at that time."

"Thank you," Kali looked back at Alina. She was beautiful, and she did look a lot like her.

"Your mother, Mike, where's everybody? You said I was the only one left."

Alina looked at Jamal who nodded his head.

"Mike's dead," Alina held Kali's hand tighter. "Doc killed him a few weeks after you left."

"What?" Kali shook her head. She could still hear the little boy saying, "I wish he was dead" and she had scolded him for saying that.

"Doc had come into a lot of money and was spending it all on liquor," Alina said quietly.

"Doc sold you to Billy," Jamal added. "The money he was spreading was a few thousand dollars finder's fee, hush-money, or whatever you want to call it. I overheard him and Mama talking about finding another girl to sell to Jordan. Doc was real pissed, though, because he didn't get a chance to have you first."

"So, that's how I ended up working for Jordan." Kali remembered being shocked when Billy and Jordan had talked about her aunt and Doc with such familiarity.

"Yeah, my mother used to work for him. So did Doc, until they both became too inebriated to earn any money for him. I got that word directly from my still-whoring mother," Jamal grunted.

"I thought you said there was no one left."

"Mazetta is still breathing, and drinking and trying to sell her old prune of a body to get money for her booze. She is such a mess. She doesn't even acknowledge us when we try to check on her. She is still in the same little, filthy house. It's probably only one of about four houses left on the block that has not been abandoned."

"Wow, so Mike died at Doc's hands? How? Why?" Kali asked. She could still see the two little cousins so clearly she could almost reach out and touch them.

"The reason I was so afraid of Doc," Alina sighed and let go of Kali's hand. Jamal got up and left the room. "He was raping me. Every chance he got, he raped me." Alina looked away as if she were ashamed.

"But, you were six. And you were his daughter," Kali moved closer to Alina and pulled her toward her.

"It didn't matter. He was one sick man. One night, he was falling down drunk and he came up the stairs looking for me. I ran to my room like I always did, and Mike was there like he always was. Sometimes, he would scream and cry as loud as I would and Doc would just pop him in the mouth or threaten him. Well, on that day Mike decided to fight for me. He tried, poor little thing. He went up against Doc, but Doc picked him up like a rag doll and threw him into the door. Mike's head hit the doorknob so hard it left an impression in his skull. Mike slid down to the floor and died. And that sick bastard still had sex with me."

Kali jumped when she heard the clink of the glasses. Jamal set three wine glasses on the coffee table and began to fill them. Kali and Alina both reached for a glass as soon as it was filled.

"I'm so sorry, I didn't know," Kali gulped the wine down. She had been old enough to run. What were Alina and Mike to do? She looked at Jamal.

"Did you know about this?" Kali wanted to be angry with someone. Jamal shook his head. "Shandie and I were so busy trying to get out of the house, we had no clue how badly the kids were being treated. Plus, you have to remember Shandie was 15 and I was 18, trying to find our own way."

"So what happened to Doc? Is he in prison?"

"No, Doc didn't make it to prison. Hell, nothing happened to him really. Mike's death went almost unnoticed, and Mazetta wouldn't allow anyone to come near Alina. Shandie was the one to find them. Mild-mannered, loving little Shandie went ballistic. Doc had rolled off Alina and went to sleep in his drunken stupor while Alina sat in the bed half-clothed, screaming her little head off.

"Shandie tried to get them both to the hospital. Mazetta came home and wouldn't let him take Alina. Anyway, to make a long story short, Shandie committed premeditated murder. Got rid of Doc, got caught and was sent up to the big house. He was in the prison system for three years, long enough to become of age. Every time we got a lawyer that said they could get him off, they would quit. Then one day, Shandie got into a fight and the other inmate ended up dead. He never saw daylight again. He was going to end up spending another 20 years in prison until he was killed a few years back. The whole time he was there, though, Ashton spent all kind of mad money trying to get him out, or at least get his sentence reduced."

"How long have you known Ashton?"

"Since he came looking for you. When you ran off from him," Jamal raised his eyebrows.

Kali lowered her head. She didn't like thinking about those days either. "What kind of relationship do you have with Ashton?" Taking another gulp of her wine, she turned to Alina.

"We are not intimate, if that is what you asking," Alina answered. "He said that would be the first thing that would come to your mind, with your history and all."

"What do you know about my history?" Kali suddenly went on the defensive as she looked from one cousin to the next.

"Everything." Jamal walked over and sandwiched her between him and Alina on the sofa. "Ashton loves you. He explained to us why you had built a wall around yourself and your children. He said that you won't even travel to South Carolina or even talk about your parents or your old friends. He told us that you would refuse to listen if any of us or those people down south were brought up. He worried about you for that. He always wanted to bring you around. He thought you needed us as much as we needed you. He was our link to you. We were his link to the part of you that you wouldn't share.

"Kali. Kalina. Whoever you are. You have only one thing to remember. Anything, anything you need, anyone you need to turn to, Alina and I will always be there. So will, Ashton," he patted her hand. "So will Ashton."

CHAPTER THIRTY-FIVE

KALI WAS PACING the floor. She hadn't been able to reach Micah, and Ruby didn't know where he was. She hadn't been able to reach Lazarus and he had all of her children somewhere. She was headed to the study one more time when the double doors swung open. She turned to see who was there and gasped. All of her children and Lazarus were covered in mud that was sliding down onto the marble floor in the foyer. They all stood there for a few seconds just staring at each other.

"Mom, you are home," Kacie said.

"Where else would I be?" Kali eyes widened as she heard a big glob of mud hit the floor, just short of an expensive Persian rug.

"We were hoping you were working late," Katie giggled.

"Strip," Kali commanded. "Strip! Don't get that mud on my rug. Where the hell have you been?"

The kids began to laugh hysterically. Lazarus tried not to meet Kali's eyes. He looked up at the stairs, at the walls and when he turned to look in the mirror, he broke out into laughter.

Kali ran to the kitchen and grabbed a bunch of trash bags. She tiptoed up to each child who stripped down to their underwear putting their mud-soaked clothing and shoes into the bags.

"What in the world?" she began, and the children laughed uncontrollably again.

"We went to this lake over in Jersey," Adam answered between laughs.

"We jumped in," Artie added.

"It was so cool, Mom," AJ added. "At first we swung across it on tree limbs like the Tarzan cartoon."

"And, then we jumped," Kacie added so demonstratively, the laughter flowed long and hard again. Kali turned away from them as she smiled. Lazarus, the father, had given them the adventure they had been dying for, the type of adventure they had become accustomed to until the impostor had arrived in their lives.

"Girls, report to Jordan's bathroom and wash that gook out of your hair. Boys, to Lazarus' bathroom."

"No," Lazarus protested as the half-dressed kids flew up the stairs still giggling.

"You, the one behind the kitchen." Kali folded her arms.

"Only, if you come with me," Lazarus licked his bottom lip and she wanted to hit him.

"No, I have been trying to get in touch with you and Micah. I think someone is hiding in our house in Jersey."

"How do you know that?"

"I went over there. I was bored."

"Let me guess, I need to fire another bodyguard for losing you."

"Yes, well no, but yes. I guess. That's your thing. I think someone was watching from an upstairs window when I was leaving."

"You sure?"

"No, but I feel like I'm sure," Kali thought about the glint from window. "I was sure creeped out like someone was there."

"Go check on the kids," Lazarus went back out of the door.

"Your clothes, aren't you going to change?" she yelled behind him.

"Yeah, I will. But, not here," he pushed the elevator button.

CHAPTER THIRTY-SIX

"COME ON OUTSIDE. I'm in the car waiting," Micah said as he sat in front of the Sperling rowhouse in Olde City. Lazarus had gone there to spend the night. He couldn't bear to spend another night under the same roof with Kali knowing who she was to him now. When he wasn't sure, it had been one thing. Now that he remembered, it was a totally different ballgame and he couldn't put his children's lives in danger because he urgently wanted to be with his wife.

Lazarus looked out the window and saw Micah sitting impatiently in his little red Porsche. He had the top down. Lazarus grabbed a light jacket and joined him.

"Kali saw somebody in the house in Jersey yesterday."

"I know. I talked to Miss, I Can't Be Still to Save My Own Life this morning," Micah was driving the city streets like no one else was on them.

"You know, driving at the speed of light in a red sports car is going to attract the wrong kind of attention. You need to slow down," Lazarus took in the view as it blurred pass.

"Yeah, I guess you are right," Micah slowed down and obeyed the speed limit.

"I'm just a little pissed. Besides, remember when we could do that shit and not have anybody touch us?"

"When Jordan owned half the Philly PD," Lazarus nodded.

"Yeah," Micah grinned and Lazarus grinned back at him. He reached over and patted his younger brother's bald head.

"Stop it, man," Micah swerved the car a little and they both laughed.

"Whatever you say, Molasses," Lazarus was more relaxed than he could remember or since he awakened in the scuff-walled, makeshift hospital room in Dry Bones.

"Where are we going?" Lazarus asked as they sped across the Benjamin Franklin Bridge.

"To Jersey," Micah was still grinning. Ashton may have been transformed into Lazarus, but his best friend was back where he was supposed to be, right by his side.

The car sped into the circle in front of the house. Lazarus cautiously followed Micah inside. Micah walked in without any concern.

"They could still be in here," Lazarus said quietly, wishing he had known to bring a gun.

"Nobody's here," Micah assured him. "Go put some riding clothes on."

"Yeah, right. I am about three sizes smaller than I used to be."

"Just go put something on. Nightmare has been missing you something fierce," Micah disappeared down the hallway.

Lazarus walked into his old bedroom and immediately the memories gripped him. This used to be his life, the perfect life with the perfect family, and he screwed it up all in one night. He noticed some Gap bags on the bed and dumped the clothes out. There were several pairs of jeans and shirts. He knew Micah had left them there.

Minutes later they were on their horses, running them across the new grass on the rolling hills. He breathed in the fresh air and tried not to think about his current dilemma; and, he knew what he was going to have to do, and do it soon.

They arrived at the waterfall. The one hundred acres of woods hid the waterfall so well that Kali had no idea it was there when she had bought it. Lazarus, then Ashton, and the kids had found it one day as they were exploring the landscape. The waterfall ran into a stream that ran straight into the river. They had been so excited that they had gone home, got camping equipment, and spent the night listening to the rapid water rushing over the little cliff, little by comparison to the one that he had been tossed over by his brother and ex-wife.

Micah was the first off his horse. He grabbed the reins and led the horse carefully down a narrow path. Lazarus followed. They stopped outside of a small cave, its mouth hidden as if behind a curtain of falling water. Micah took the reins from Lazarus, hitched both horses to a nearby sapling, and walked toward the mouth of the cave.

"Whoa," Lazarus cheered. "What? Who is this?"

A man lay hogged tied next to the mouth of the cave. The man's grey eyes widened with fear as the two brothers approached. The man squirmed, but realized if he squirmed too much he would choke himself.

"Is this who I think it is?" Lazarus knelt down in front of the man and ripped the duct tape from the man's mouth. The man screamed as the duct tape took part of his red and grey mustache with it. Then the man stopped squirming.

"You remember, Brady, don't you?" Micah scraped his feet against the small gravel in front of the man.

"Remember him? Hell, yeah, son. I remember this weasel real well. Hello Brady. How are you doing, son?"

"Ashton?" Brady's body stiffened and he realized he had to relax it again or die.

"Ashton, Ashton. Did you just call me, Ashton?" Lazarus folded his arms across his knees. "He called me Ashton," he said looking back at Micah.

"Yeah, he did. Didn't he?"

"Did you tell him?" Lazarus asked.

"Not a word."

"How do you know who I am, son?" Lazarus said as he looked down at Brady who had started twitching again.

"Asa. Asa suspected it was you. But, he said you had no clue," Brady mumbled as if talking to himself.

"Did you know this?" Lazarus turned to see Micah's expression and realized that he did not.

"I can tell you everything, Ashton. Just let me up and out of here. I swear. Whatever you want to know," Brady shouted.

"Is my wife in danger? Right now," Lazarus said, "is she in danger?"

"Yeah, yeah. She is, if that money doesn't get there."

"Money, what money?" Lazarus sat down on the ground and stared at Brady.

"This money," Micah said as he kicked a duffle bag over to Lazarus. Lazarus unzipped the bag and found stacks of money bound together.

"You withdrew the money in New York?" Lazarus asked.

"No, he made the withdrawals. I made the drops," said Brady.

"The drops?"

"To her. I made the drops to her. He couldn't travel out of country, or he is afraid to, I don't know which. I had to go. I would take it to her in Rio."

"Where in Rio?"

"She's at some flea-bitten hotel called The American. She is registered under the name Lena Roberson, using your wife's bogus ID from when she was with that phony husband, Marcus. She found it when they were searching your little house over in Philly."

"Is she still there?" Lazarus was getting up on his knees. He whipped out a knife he had in his pocket.

"Yeah, she's still there. I am supposed to be on my way down there. When he finds out I didn't make it, he is going to get real pissed. She's pulling his strings all the way from down there. You have to let me make the drop," Brady pleaded.

Lazarus leaned over and cut one of the ropes. Brady was able to move a little without the fear of choking himself. He sighed with relief.

"Thank you, man. Thank you. I tried to tell your brother I could be more help. I just have to follow through. You can come with me. I swear I won't double cross you, I swear."

"Of course, not. I know you will do whatever I ask you to do. How much were they paying you for the drop?"

"Ten percent," Brady answered and Lazarus reached over and cut another rope. Brady relaxed a little more.

"How did they get to me, Brady? Who else knew about the safe room? Or, who told them?"

Fearfully, Brady looked over at Micah. "Leave it alone, Ashton. Trust me," Brady looked from Lazarus to Micah. "Trust me."

Micah walked over and leaned down, placing his hand on Lazarus' shoulder, and then he said, "Ruby. How did my wife get involved in this?"

"You don't want to know," Brady said, his eyes becoming fearful again. He began to struggle against the rope.

"You have nothing to be afraid of Brady," Lazarus assured him. "You have told me this much, I just need to know everybody who was involved in this. We know Redd. We know Asa. We know you. And we know you were long gone before I had the safe room installed. And, Elliott, well I know Elliott. She would have told me if someone had approached her. She feared no one, not even me."

"He was blackmailing her," Brady whispered, and then motioned his head for Lazarus to get closer.

"No, no, Brady. I want to hear this, too," Micah said with a hint of danger in his voice.

"Brady, I am not going to let him hurt you again. I swear." Lazarus cut the rope between Brady's legs.

"Asa threatened to tell."

"Threaten to tell what?" Lazarus asked calmly. He reached behind Brady's back and made an indentation on another part of the rope. "Keep talking. This rope is a little thicker. I am listening."

"You promise you won't let him hurt me?" Brady whispered.

"I promise," Lazarus whispered back.

"Artie isn't Micah's. He's Billy's. He is your little brother." Brady's eyes flashed toward Micah whose jaw was clenching and so were his fists.

"What are you talking about?"

"Ruby. She didn't want Micah to find out about her affair with Billy. She said it was rape, but Billy said it was an affair. Anyway, she got pregnant."

"So, how long did Ruby know that Asa wasn't dead?" Lazarus kept working on the rope until one of Brady's hands was loosened.

"I don't know, but she knew he was planning to take your place. She might have even helped him. But, I don't think she had a choice," Brady added and began to thrash about. One rope was still binding one hand to his foot. He flipped over and started pulling at the rope.

"How did you get involved in all of this?" Lazarus flipped him back over. "Be still, man. You don't want me to cut you." Brady tried to still his body, but he was now shivering uncontrollably as he glanced over at Micah. Occasionally, a light wind would blow a cold spray of water from the falls in their direction.

"I have just one more question, Brady. What was the plan when the money ran out?"

"The children first, one by one. Then her. Kali."

Lazarus stood up. "And, where were you going to be while my family was being eliminated?" Brady stopped and looked up at Lazarus.

"You mean to lay there and tell me that you knew they were planning to kill me and my family? And, the only thing that you were going to do was collect a percentage…"

"Ten percent," Micah chimed in.

"Yes, 10 percent delivering the cash liquidated after each of my children's funerals."

Brady began to shake his head. He tried to adjust himself so that he could get to his feet. As his body turned toward Lazarus he was stunned as he saw the pointed-toe cowboy boot headed his way. He didn't have time to brace himself as the kick that Lazarus delivered lifted Brady's body completely off the ground, up in the air, and over the waterfall.

The brothers stood there as they heard the waterfall muffle Brady's scream. They stood there listening for the final splash, but it was a long way down. Finally, they heard it. Micah picked up the ropes methodically and then held his hand out for the knife. Lazarus handed it to him and Micah flung it all over into the waterfall. Micah picked up the duffle bag and both men stuffed their saddlebags until they were full. Then, Micah threw the empty duffle bag over into the water. They led their horses back to level ground.

"That was you in the window," Lazarus said.

"Yeah, your wife's a nosy little bitch," Micah sighed.

"Yeah, she is," Lazarus answered and gave Nightmare the signal to ride fast. Micah did the same as they rode for a solid hour without a word.

CHAPTER THIRTY-SEVEN

ANOTHER DAY HAD passed and the fake Ashton was not home. Not that Kali missed him, but it made her more anxious. Something was happening and she was completely in the dark. She hadn't talked to Micah, and Lazarus was continuing to go out of his way to avoid her. But, not the kids, he was spending all of his time with the kids, especially AJ.

She had walked in on them the night before. They were the only two in the rec room, but they were standing there head to head. Lazarus was talking and AJ was listening intently. She had started to interrupt but decided against it even though the scene unsettled her. She had seen Jordan and Ashton in that same stance on more than one occasion and Ashton had always walked away a different person.

That evening, Lazarus walked into the living room as they were all on their way upstairs. He was carrying a bucket of their favorite ice cream from their favorite ice cream stand. The kids tackled him and all landed hard onto the marble floor of the foyer. Kacie screamed. She was at the bottom of the pileup. Everyone scrambled up and Lazarus swung her up into his arms carrying her to the sofa in the living room. She was crying and all the kids stood by holding their breath. Kali held her daughter while Lazarus carefully examined her arm.

"I don't think it's broken but, AJ, call one of your uncles. Get him up here to check," Lazarus ordered.

"Ricky's home," Kali called out. She had just spoken to him earlier.

"I'm okay, Daddy," Kacie used the arm that wasn't hurting to extend to Lazarus' neck.

"What did you say?" Kali pulled Kacie away from Lazarus and put her on the other side of her.

"Nothing," Kacie corrected herself. "He smells like Daddy," she whispered.

"I'm sorry, Uncle Lazarus," Kacie said, as Kali put her body between them, shoving her back in his face.

"You are going to be alright," Kali said, as she looked back at Lazarus who was frowning.

"You can go now, Lazarus. I can take care of my child," Kali snapped.

She didn't know whether to be angry or suspicious or scared. She wanted to ask him what he had told the kids, especially since she had been walking on eggshells to keep it all a secret. The last thing she needed was for the fake Ashton to get wind. She wanted to yell at him and ask him what the hell were he and Micah waiting on. For the first funeral?

"Mom," Kacie protested. "It just slipped out. I wish Lazarus was my dad."

"Stop it. Be quiet. Shut up," Kali had never spoken to Kacie like that before, but her fear demanded it. Kali noticed the room became quiet. She looked up and met the eyes of each of her children and Artie.

"Artie, I want you and Katie to go downstairs. Adam, I want you to stay with your mother and Kacie. AJ, I want to talk to you," Lazarus barked the orders.

"No," Kali protested. "No, nobody goes anywhere."

Lazarus stood up and motioned his head toward the door. The kids started walking.

"Take the ice cream," he said to Artie. Artie picked up the bucket as he and Katie went to the door.

"Didn't you hear me?" Kali's voice cracked as she realized how she must have sounded to her children.

"Mom, Mom, Mom. It's okay. Kacie is going to be okay," AJ patted Kacie's arm. "Right, Kacie?"

Kacie nodded. Kali pulled her closer folding the child into her arms.

Adam sat next to them and started teasing Kacie.

Kali watched Lazarus lead the way upstairs and an AJ who was walking taller than she had ever seen him walk before was only a few steps behind. What else could she expect? The real Ashton was home and he had a plan and she wondered if the plan involved her oldest son.

Ricky arrived and insisted the arm get X-rayed. She sent Adam upstairs to deliver the news. He came back announcing he was going to the hospital, too.

Kali didn't want to leave the house. She didn't want the real Ashton turning Ashton, Jr. into a mini-him. She had never thought of that before, but she knew her Ashton was a dangerous man and she knew her son was a loving, innocent young man, at least until tonight. Or, maybe it was yesterday. She couldn't put her finger on when, but he had changed.

CHAPTER THIRTY-EIGHT

THE NEXT SCHOOL morning AJ had prepared breakfast and lunches. Katie had laid out book bags and put everything from their schools that had to be signed at Kali's place at the table. Kali walked in a bit disoriented at how organized her kids were acting. AJ was acting as if he was in charge and they were listening to him. Lazarus was nowhere in sight.

"Good morning," she said as a sliver of cold air passed down her back. She pulled her robe tighter and sat down at the head of the breakfast table.

"Good morning," her kids responded in unison.

"How is your arm this morning, Kacie? Are you okay for school?" Kali reached out and rubbed her baby's arm.

"I'm fine, Mom," Kacie smiled up at her. "Everybody's going to want to know why it is in a sling?

"Can they sign the sling?"

"No, Kacie. People usually sign casts, but your arm is sprained, not broken."

"But, they could sign the sling? Couldn't they?"

"No. No removing the sling and signing the sling. No jostling your arm, period," Kali said firmly. She saw the disappointment in her daughter's eyes, and tried not to fall for it.

"Mom," Adam said, just before he took a large gulp of milk, "what are you getting me for graduation?"

"Graduation? Who is graduating?" Kali looked comically around the room. Her children laughed. "I will discuss it with your father when he gets home tonight." Kali used the standard answer. The kids knew all their presents, especially their birthday presents, were a team effort. But, Kali knew the fake Ashton could care less.

Kali was sifting through papers that had to be signed for book returns, school trips, and next year's class rosters. There was also an envelope addressed to her, in her husband's handwriting, which she put in her pocket. She handed AJ the remaining papers.

"Time to go, everybody. Get moving," AJ said, while standing next to his mother. She was surprised how all the children responded; no one complained that AJ was trying to order them around. No one hesitated to take another bite of breakfast, either. They all moved in almost military precision, grabbing their lunches and book bags.

"Where's Lazarus?" Kali asked AJ.

"Downstairs waiting for us. He didn't spend the night here again last night. Mr. Ahmed spent the night here."

"Where is he?" Kali stood up, looking around.

"He's outside the door waiting to escort us to Lazarus."

"Oh, okay," Kali stuffed her hands in her pockets, fingering the envelope in her right pocket.

AJ hugged her. "We are fine, Mom," AJ stood eye to eye with her. She wondered when that had happened. So many things were changing overnight and so many things weren't moving fast enough.

"Mom," AJ turned to her and whispered loudly, but not loud enough for the kids in the next room to hear. "Adam wants a new 10-speed bike. Lazarus and I are going to go pick it up after school."

"Okay," Kali nodded. She followed AJ out to the other kids and hugged each one tightly.

It had been awhile since Kali had been to the little house in the Olde City section, especially with Ashton. After Marcus, her first husband had died, it didn't seem right to neither make it a home nor even a rendezvous spot. It was just plain awkward. They had gone there together to pack Marcus' things to send back to his mother's, but that had been months and months after his death. They had been through too much to do that any sooner.

Kali and Ashton had brought the twins and Adam, who was still an infant, with them. They had left the kids in the living room while they went upstairs to go through things, sadly reflecting on how things had become so tangled up and to remember all those that had gone before them.

Kali walked into the house and remembered how she had fled there after Jordan's sudden and violent death. She had fled from that same house following Ashton's violent eruption after he had kidnapped the twins. She wondered how she could love him so much. And then she saw him, leaning against the mantle. His body was no longer big and muscular, but it was still hard, buffed and strong. She walked straight into his arms and thought it was just her fate to love him, no matter what form, no matter what actions he took, just no matter what. If there were ever two souls that were born to be with each other, it was theirs. Here stood a man that had been without a memory, yet his mind and body brought him right back to her. Okay, she thought, Molasses may have had a hand in manipulating them in each other's direction, but he had nothing to do with this. They stood there silently holding onto each other like no one else existed in the entire world.

He lifted her into his arms and carried her up the stairs. They fell into the rhythm that belonged only to them. They tore at each other's clothes and, then, attempted to enter each other's space, ferociously trying to become one being. They moved in tandem, they loved in tandem, and they held onto each other the way a desperate man would hold onto a ledge for dear life. They made love until they were too exhausted to move.

"Kali," he brushed her curl from between her eyes.

"What?" she whispered, not wanting to talk or to move or to think, she wanted to just lay there and breathe.

"You have to be ready," he gently stroked her cheek. "Ready for what?"

"The kids' bags are already packed and in a van parked downstairs in the parking lot. The minute you get home from the graduation, you tell Ashton…

"You mean, Asa?"

"I mean him. You tell *him* that you want to take the kids up to the Poconos. He won't follow you because he is afraid of heights. He hates driving through the mountains.

"He did alright driving you to a mountain and dropping you over a cliff.

"She was with him. She was pushing him. You won't be able to push him."

"So, why the Poconos?"

"You are not going to the Poconos. You, the kids, and Artie will get in the van without anything except your pocketbook with your gun in it. The rest is taken care of."

"What am I supposed to do between then and now? I mean, I'm scared. I'm really scared of him. He sounds weird when he calls."

"He is scared. And, he is dangerous. He is looking for someone he is not going to find. Someone is behind schedule, and he is in panic mode."

"What's going on?" Kali sat up and faced Lazarus.

"It doesn't matter. Micah and I are sending him on a wild goose chase. We can keep him away from home until Friday. He is feeling obligated to come home for the graduation. It would look bad if he doesn't show. People will ask questions, and he is not ready to be posed any unnecessary questions."

"What if he comes home before then?"

"He won't."

"But, what if he does?"

Lazarus sighed heavily, and removed his arm from behind her. He sat up, leaned on his knees, and looked far away, thinking about how to respond.

"There is a gun in a shoebox in your closet, the shoebox that holds your red patent leather strappy things with the gold bow. There is a gun inside the bar refrigerator in the living room and another one under your mattress on your side of the bed. Then, there is one in your black coach purse, the one you need to take on the trip. It's in a compartment behind the zipper with the pockets. That's the one you take, so you can stick your hand in it and shoot if you have to. You won't have to remove it from the bag."

"My boots. There is a gun in my boots," she added eagerly.

"AJ has a gun strapped to his right leg. Don't get upset. He knows how to use it."

Kali jumped out of the bed and almost tripped over the sheets.

"You are expecting him to come home and kill us?"

"I think he is scared, and very dangerous."

"What if I can't get to a gun? What if AJ pulls the gun and he takes it from him?"

"He won't. AJ with a gun will be enough to deter him."

"And where will you be?"

"When you get to your destination, I have a destination of my own. But, where I am sending you will be safe. And, when I do what I have to do, it will almost be over."

"Almost?"

"Don't ask, Kali. Just be careful. Be a sweet and loving wife when he comes home. Act natural."

"While I am shaking in my boots," Kali yelled.

"While my mother lion protects her baby cubs. You can do it, baby. You may not know it, but you are a dangerous bitch when you have to be."

CHAPTER THIRTY-NINE

KALI AND THE children were headed upstairs to bed when the front door opened.

"Daddy," the kids yelled and ran toward him. He awkwardly allowed them to hug him. Each one hugged him tight and then ran up the stairs, leaving her alone in the living room with him.

"Ashton, where have you been? I was worried you weren't going to make Adam's graduation tomorrow," she walked over and hugged him. He patted her on the back and stepped away.

"You look like shit. Have you had any sleep?" she took him by the hand and led him to the sofa where he sat down hard. "Can I get you something?" she cooed. "Want some chamomile tea? You look like you need to relax." She stood up and looked down at him. He stared ahead.

"Ashton," she sat back down next to him and reached for his tie. He shoved her hands away.

"Okay," she said, then stood up again. She headed for the stairs.

"Get me a drink," he said. "A straight scotch."

"Okay," she walked over to the bar and opened the refrigerator. She saw the blue container with the gun in it. She pulled out the tray of ice and then put it back. He had said straight, but she had wanted an excuse to confirm the gun was there. She picked up a short crystal tumbler and poured the scotch from the carafe.

"Kids going to bed?" he asked.

"Yes, but you know they would love it if you stopped in their rooms to say goodnight."

"Maybe tomorrow," he took a long swig. "I'll see you upstairs."

"Okay," Kali headed toward the stairs. She turned and saw that he had that far away look on his face again. It made her nervous. Whatever cat and mouse game Micah and Lazarus had been up to had changed this man into an animal ready to break out of a cage. She could feel it in the air. It was the feel of desperation, of danger, of an anxiety that could not be tamed because it was driven by fear. This Ashton was afraid, really afraid.

Kali was standing in her dressing room sliding out of her clothes, when her head snapped back from the strong pull of her hair. He had grabbed her long curls and wrapped them in his hand and began dragging her across the room. It was the same tactic he had used when he had first come home from the hospital after the gunshot. He was getting ready to rape her. She clawed at his face, and began to fight. She was beyond being brutalized. She knew who he was now, and she wasn't making any more excuses for his cruel behavior.

"Stop, Ashton. You are hurting me," she tried to kick him where it hurt, but he used his weight and size to pin her onto the bed. "What is this all about?" she yelled. "What happened to you?" She elbowed him in the neck and it stopped him momentarily.

"Where's the fucking watch, bitch?" He pushed her head into the headboard and it made a loud noise.

"That watch again? I told you I looked everywhere for it. But, I can't find it. It's wherever you left it last," she tried to move from beneath him. He raised his hand to hit her, but it froze in mid-air. She was surprised as he was flipped around like a baby being changed for a diaper. He landed on the floor next to the bed. She looked up and saw Lazarus.

"Stay out of this, Lazarus. This is between a man and his wife," the fake Ashton had gotten up and was headed for a confrontation. Kali remembered the two giants fighting the day Asa had raped her, the day Jordan had died trying to protect her. She crawled out of the bed and ran for her clothes.

"When the wife is screaming in pain, I beg to differ," Lazarus stood his ground. Kali stood in the dressing room near the shoebox with the gun.

"Ashton, be a man. Treat the mother of your children with some respect. Your children can hear her screaming, just like I did."

"You want the bitch, don't you?" Ashton stepped eye to eye with Lazarus. "I've seen the way you lust after her. You think I'm blind. Better yet, you think I am dumb and stupid. I know," Ashton pointed his finger in Lazarus' face and then stopped midsentence.

"You know what?" Lazarus leaned next to Ashton's ear asking in a low voice. "What do you know? What do all of you know? Why don't you let me in on it?"

"Get the fuck out of my house," Ashton stepped away. Kali stepped into her shoes and ran out of the room.

"Come back here," Ashton started toward the door and Lazarus blocked him.

"Why don't you get some rest, son? You look like shit. Maybe when you wake up you will realize you have a wife and family that loves you. Not everybody is that lucky." Lazarus backed out of the room. He looked back at his brother standing there like a logger ready to bring down the whole forest. Lazarus stepped out into the hallway and found Kali hovering around the door.

"My God, the kids," she whispered.

"They are at Micah's. AJ took them downstairs as soon as Asa went into your bedroom."

"He called you?"

"Yeah, now go to Jordan's room and lock yourself in," Lazarus walked down the hall and stood in front of AJ's room until Kali disappeared behind Jordan's door.

CHAPTER FORTY

THE NEXT DAY, the whole Sperling clan watched as Adam walked across the stage picking up his middle school certificate. They all jumped from their seats and cheered. Even the fake Ashton had plastered on a smile and was saying all the right things. She had to admit he at least looked rested, but she knew he was lying in wait to get her alone again. But, that was not going to happen. Not ever again.

Kali was happy the kids hadn't heard her futile screams. She folded her arms around herself trying to steady the shivers; she wondered if anyone noticed how badly her hands were shaking. She hadn't talked to Asa alone since last night and she was going to have to have the conversation about the Poconos. She expected him to be opposed to it now. He was back on his watch trip.

"Ashton," Micah patted him hard on the shoulder. "Son, I know you are a proud papa today. Why don't we all go up to the Poconos to celebrate?"

"No, I think we can celebrate just fine here," Ashton said as he flinched from Micah's touch.

"What's wrong with you, son? Lazarus told me he had to pull you off Kali last night, that you were purposely hurting her. Even I won't stand for that," Micah spoke in a voice low to keep the kids from hearing.

"I think you owe them this trip to the Poconos," Micah urged.

"Then, I am not going. You go. Take your fucking lap dog with you," Ashton stormed out of the room.

"Who wants to go on a trip?" Micah clapped his hands to get the kids' attention.

"We do," they yelled in unison.

Kali mouthed the words "thank you" to Micah and grabbed her black Coach bag. She herded the children to the elevator in the rear that took them down to the parking lot.

The van was sitting in front of the elevator as they walked out. Lazarus was at the wheel. They all climbed in. No one mentioned any luggage, they were all too eager to get away from the penthouse.

They were all surprised when they arrived at the airport and the seven of them boarded a private plane to Durango, Colorado.

CHAPTER FORTY-ONE

THE WEEK IN Colorado had disappeared too fast into a distant memory as Lazarus made his way up to a bar in a third-rate hotel in Rio de Janeiro. The place was dark and almost empty with a patron scattered here and there. He spotted her, but not before she had spotted him. He saw the huntress' eyes light up as he, the new prey, took a seat at the bar.

The bartender gave him a half nod and placed a thin glass in front of him.

"What will it be?" the man asked him, but his eyes were on the redhead making her way from the table she had occupied in the rear near the wide-paned windows.

"Surprise me." Lazarus watched as the man poured a cachaça cocktail straight from a mixer.

"There is always some left," he looked over at the woman who was struggling to get up on the bar stool just two stools away. "Her favorite. Right, Bella?"

"Shut up and pour," she cooed seductively.

"You're buying?" the woman asked pointing to Lazarus who was assessing her closely. Lazarus lifted his drink to her, and then nodded to the bartender who began to mix another cocktail for the lady.

"Are you staying here?" she asked bluntly, and then drained the last dregs of the drink she had brought to the bar with her.

"No, I was just here to meet a business associate," Lazarus answered.

"She stood you up?" the redhead smiled.

"No, he and I met and completed our business," Lazarus pulled out a wad of money and dropped a few bills on the counter.

"Keep them coming for the lady." He put the money back in his pocket and stood up.

"Leaving so soon?" She turned around to face him, smiling with a swollen face and sullen eyes.

"Yes, I have to get an early start tomorrow." He took a couple of steps back and she literally jumped off the barstool.

"Are you American? You sound American with a hint of some sort of accent," she asked in her own thick, south Philly dialect.

"Puerto Rican, from New York," Lazarus lied, but thickened a Spanish accent for her ears only.

"New York," she smiled. "How I miss New York."

"This is a big city, what could you possibly miss?" he asked.

"Americans," she sighed. "I miss Americans."

"Why don't you go back?"

"I will. One day," she replied. "Do you really have to go now?" she reached out and touched his arm. He almost recoiled, but took a deep breath and stepped away.

"I really have a long day, starting very early tomorrow," he began to walk away. He could hear her heels clicking on the floor as she followed him.

"Your name?" she asked. "You didn't tell me your name."

"Arturio. Arturio Davis," he answered and she began to laugh.

"Davis. A Puerto Rican Davis?" she laughed harder.

"Davis-Ribiero. Mother's Puerto Rican. Father's black. Raised by mother," he put his hands in his pockets and tried to walk away again.

"I'm sorry." She grabbed him again. "Why don't you stay, Artie? I could really use some company, some American company."

Lazarus turned to her and stared down at her. He smiled and shook his head. "I know I am going to regret this," he said. "But, I have to go out into the jungle tomorrow morning. I'm leaving about 4:30 am. I will just be out there for the day checking on some property for a friend. If you really want a little American companionship, you can tag along. I'll pick you up outside. I have a green Jeep.

"It's just a friendly invitation. If you are not out there when I drive up, I will keep going. It's up to you," Lazarus saluted the bartender and left.

CHAPTER FORTY-TWO

LAZARUS WENT BACK to his room and removed his large, dark shades. Sitting on the edge of the bed, he held his head in his hands. He missed Kali and his children. He wanted this to be over and done, but he had to be patient. Lazarus sat up and looked at the mirror facing the bed. He knew he looked nothing like the man he once was, and he knew that he would never be that man again, and that saddened him. But, what saddened him more was that his children were going to have to believe that their father was dead, and his wife would have to go on with her life without him.

He had enjoyed every minute in the Mesa. He sat there remembering the incessant chatter from the children as they were filing out of the airport. They were expecting to catch a cab or a van, or travel in the mode they were used to traveling in, a limo. But, instead, an RV was parked at the curb. When the door swung open, everyone's mouths dropped when they saw Elliott sitting at the wheel.

"Ms. Elliott," Kali screamed and was the first one on the RV. Lazarus thought she would squeeze the life out of the woman. Then each child, including Artie, gave her equally big hugs. They all missed Elliott as they fondly called her. She was the common sense, the steady hand, the advisor, the event planner, the mother, the grandmother, the aunt that everybody needed, not just the best executive assistant on the planet.

The whole family had suffered a terrible blow when Elliott walked away from PDSI. Elliott knew them all; she knew them better than anyone. She had been there for Ashton and Kali through every child, through their quick, thrown together marriage, and through every achievement. She was the extended family that filled the holes left by the real mothers and grandmothers they needed.

"It's so good to see you," Kali had said while fighting back tears of joy.

Lazarus had been surprised when he thought he had seen a watery glaze in Elliott's eyes. She had never been known to cry. Now, he was thousands of miles away from the softball games in Ray's pasture and the talent shows on Ray's porch under the virgin southwestern skies canopied with bright stars, but none as bright as the Sperling children entertaining their parents.

He had been proud to attend Bobby's middle school graduation and so happy that all the children welcomed Bobby into their clan like another brother. He watched them bond out there in the middle of nowhere, and he found himself bonding with Kali again while mourning what he was about to lose. And, he had no one else to blame.

Lazarus tried to go to sleep, but couldn't. All he could do was to stare at the stream of streetlights on the ceiling of his small hotel room and try to remember every inch of his wife's face, the feel of her soft skin, and the taste of her lips. He ached for her. He ached for the noises his children made as they existed, growing up, and just being. He missed them.

"Are they all in bed?" he had asked Kali as she was coming out of the huge modular home they had bought for Ray and placed in the middle of his pasture. Ray and Bobby would move in as soon as the Sperling clan would vacate it. But, Bobby had already moved in with his new brothers and sisters. Lazarus couldn't remember if he had ever seen Bobby so happy. He hadn't realized how lonely the boy had been out there in the dry weeds and rocky cliffs. His nearest friend probably lived at least five miles away.

"Those restless ones are resting," she sighed and sat down on the step. "This is the best trip they have ever had. The best trip, I have ever had."

"Come here," he reached out to her and grabbed her hand. He pulled her to him. Out there, under the cavernous night sky, they could be Ashton and Kali. During the day when the world surrounded them, they tried not to touch each other, tried not to look at each other too long, tried not to run into each other's arms. He was their bodyguard, their adopted uncle or, at least, that is what they tried to imply. But, everyone knew.

They just knew the roles they were supposed to play, and left it at that. The kids didn't slip up and call him Dad. Kali was no longer defiant in whispering his real name. He was Lazarus. Even to Ms. Elliott who had begun to spend hours sitting on the porch with Ray by her side. She was at least ten years older than the man, but that didn't stop Ray's heart from melting every time the woman waltzed into a room or sprinted across the pasture with all the kids in tow.

Elliott never expressed it verbally that she knew who Lazarus was, but he could tell that she did when he walked past her and when their eyes met. At first, her eyes would glaze over sadly and, occasionally, she would reach over and touch him, his arm, his hand, his face. Then, she would just watch him. Their eyes would meet with a smile. They would nod and keep going or, sometimes, they would have the same crazy conversations he had grown to love when she was with him almost every day of his life.

"This is a good trip," he held Kali in his arms as if she were a normal extension of his own body. "But, it is going to have to end. Soon. At least, for me."

"No," Kali held onto him burrowing her head into his neck, not wanting to share him with the rest of the world and wondering if she could just step inside his body and stay there forever.

"I've got to go, Kali. I stayed longer than I had planned. Ray is going to watch out for you. So, is Elliott. Neither of them will let you or the kids out of their sight. You are safe here."

"No. You can't leave me again. Suppose you forget me again. I can't take it. I can't go back to that evil twin of yours and pretend any more."

"You won't ever have to endure him again. I promise. But, you will have to face him again. Ray will let you know when you have to go back. I don't want you to be afraid, but I want you to follow his directions. You understand?"

"Do what I say, when I say, where I say and how I say. Don't ask why," she whispered, remembering the days of Jordan.

"I'm not that bad, am I?" Lazarus stepped back from her and tugged at her chin. She shook her head. "But, in this case," Lazarus sighed, "it might be best to abide by those rules. You know me and Molasses, how we are when we are planning something."

"Nothing can go wrong," she reached up and wiped her eyes. She hadn't cried since they had arrived in their peaceful little haven. Neither had the kids cried about anything, not even when they crashed into each other playing hard.

"Life itself makes things happen unexpectedly. Micah and I just try to put a little wiggle room in our plans for the unexpected. This time, there is no wiggle room. We have things that have to be done," he kissed her forehead and she leaned into the kiss. She didn't want his lips to move from that spot. She wanted to remember the warmth, the softness, and the moisture in that one little space.

He lifted her into his arms and walked her to the RV parked behind Ray's house. She opened the door for him and he placed her gently inside. She took his hand and led him to the back of the van, where an almost full-sized bed took up the little space. She scooted onto the bed toward the headboard. He crawled onto the bed behind her and then over her. They stared into each other's eyes and smiled. His lips met hers hungrily. Her hands met his head and her fingers twisted through his hair as they took the air completely out of the room. When their bodies demanded they come up for air, Kali giggled.

The first time Ashton had undressed her without her noticing, she was 17 years old. Here it was 17 years later, and he could still do that with ease. She was completely naked. She grabbed his face, and sighed sweetly, "Ashton, what on Earth did you do with my clothes?"

CHAPTER FORTY-THREE

H E WASN'T SURPRISED at all to see her standing in the doorway of the hotel so early in the morning. She was desperate. She had probably snorted away all of her money waiting for Brady to show up with the next influx of cash. He was sure Asa was in a panic, too. Asa was probably lying to her telling her it was on the way while he frantically tried to access other funds that Micah was busily playing hide and seek with, moving the accounts. Lazarus was sure Asa either thought Brady had stiffed him or was dead. Either way, it was probably sinking in that his days as the fake Ashton were numbered. Brady's disappearance could mean two things to him. One, someone else knew that could present a danger and or two, when Redd found out she would either rat him out or kill him herself, the way she had done the real Ashton. That's why Asa had totally lost it and attacked Kali.

"Buenos Dias," Lazarus got out and opened the door for her. She hopped in holding onto her purse protectively.

"Ready for an adventure, Bella?" he asked.

"My name is Lena," she extended her hand. He shook it limply.

"Lena. Somehow, you don't look like a Lena. I was actually thinking last night that you looked extremely familiar, and, this is not just a line, I swear." He joined hundreds of other cars on the highway out of Rio. He was amazed at how busy the city was. It did remind him a great deal of New York, the way it constantly moved.

"I hear that frequently," she looked around into the darkness. Redd wasn't sure why she trusted this man enough to follow him into the jungle. Maybe it was because he was willing to walk away from her; so many men wanted her to cling to them when she met them. It was easy to get what she wanted from them. This one was different. He was still wearing those big, dark sunglasses in the middle of the night. That intrigued her. She thought of all the vampire movies she had seen, and became more than intrigued. For the first time in a long time, a sensual longing began to manifest in her loins. She laid her head back on the seat rest and relaxed. She was ready for the ride.

They drove for hours. The roads became two lanes, and the two lanes, supposedly, became two lanes on a mountain trail. Lazarus expertly drove the road carefully gauging if another car or truck was headed around the narrow highway. At least once, he had to stop and pull as close to the mountain as he could to let an oncoming car go by. He could hear her gasp. More than once, she had pulled a flask out of her purse that sat on the floor next to her feet. Finally she emptied it.

He had watched her in the beginning, before the roads became increasingly dangerous. He wondered how she had reached this low point in life, and when she had become so dangerous. He hadn't known this woman for over a decade now, and he didn't know whether to hate her or pity her.

She touched the back of his hand and stroked it. He held on tightly to the gearshift, trying not to pull his hand away. She looked up at him smiling, thinking her touch was somehow going to turn him on, not realizing her touch was searing and repulsive to him. Did she not know that the last time she had touched him, was to torture him? No, she didn't. He smiled down at her. He thought about Kali.

CHAPTER FORTY-FOUR

"HOW MUCH LONGER?" Redd whined. The narrow road along the mountainside didn't seem to faze her any longer. She had emptied the silver flask and it was before 9:00 am.

"We should be there in a few minutes. I'm trying to recognize the turn-off. There," Lazarus pointed to a dirt road that appeared between two narrow cliffs. He slowed the Jeep and made the sharp right onto the road. The jungle thicket covered both sides. He was thankful it hadn't rained and the little road was dry. He drove about a quarter mile before the thicket became a clearing that surrounded an odd-looking house embedded in the trees.

"It's beautiful," she said as she stumbled out of the passenger side, and then turned to grab her purse. She pulled it close to her body, as if she expected him to snatch it and run. She followed him to the door and watched closely as he looked for the right key.

"Is this your place?" she rubbed his back as he was walking into the door. It was all he could do not to cringe, so he started talking.

"A friend of mine owns it. He asked me to check it out and pick up a few things while I was here."

"You have been here before though?"

"Yes, many times." He walked into the living room with the cathedral ceilings draped by the jungles' natural vines.

"This must be hard to keep up. You would think the jungle would overtake it and you would lose it forever," she said as she began to walk through and touch everything. Her pale hands ran across the light-colored sofa, and then she touched the ceremonial ornaments sitting decoratively around the room. She stopped in front of a small marble mantle, and tried to lift a large porcelain, milk-white vase sitting there. It wouldn't budge. He raised one eyebrow. She was getting jittery and he wondered if she sensed something. First, he thought, she was clutching the purse as if it were a lifeline; now she looked like she was testing the vase for weight. Had he made a mistake?

If she knew, he wondered what triggered the knowledge that it was him. And, then he wondered if she was even aware of it, or maybe she could just feel it in her bones the way he had felt his knowledge of Kali.

"I have to go upstairs and see that everything is okay. I'll be right back," he said, watching her out of the corner of his eye. As he reached the landing of the stairs that overlooked the living area below, he saw her dig in her purse. She looked stunned as she only came out with the flask, the usual junk in a woman's purse, and a wallet. She hurriedly put everything back with the exception of a small gold makeup mirror. She sat down at the table in front of the window and opened it. Then, he watched her hurriedly snort its hidden contents with a little straw she produced from her pocket.

He strode back down the stairs as she paced across the living room. He sat on the sofa with his back to the corner of it; he kicked off his shoes and put his feet up on the coffee table.

"There's food in the fridge, if you are hungry. I'm not much of a cook," he said.

"I'm not hungry, darling," she giggled nervously.

"Is everything okay?" he asked and patted the sofa to see if she would sit down.

"I'm fine," she lied and sat down on the other end of the sofa with her back to the opposite corner.

"I guess you didn't expect the real jungle, did you?" he smiled at her.

"No, down here when people say jungle, they mean jungle," she almost choked on the word.

He wiped his nose with his finger and smiled. She looked at him strangely.

"Residue," he said. "A little residue." He pointed to her nose. She wiped it away without any sign of embarrassment.

"Just needed a little pick me up," she said and looked around the room. He saw her shiver.

"You can't be cold. It's got to be almost a hundred even this far up," he crossed his legs.

"No, I am fine," she scratched her head and pursed her lips. "The place is beautiful," she said again. "This friend of yours must be wealthy."

"Well, I would just say comfortable and appreciates nice things," he said, nodding his head as if to agree with himself.

"So," she put her finger in her mouth. "What are we to do now?"

"Well, we can talk. We really haven't done much of that," Lazarus sighed.

"Yes, I noticed you are a quiet man," she reached back for her purse again and put it in her lap.

"Did you get what you came for?" she asked.

"Is the lady ready to go already?"

"Well, I was just up for a ride. If you are too tired to drive, I can drive back," she offered.

"Me thinks you are not sober enough to drive me down that mountainside. I tell you what, give me an hour or so to recoup and we can head back down. You can relax if you want to. I'm going to go out and check on the car. I left something in it that needs to go into the garage. I'm sure my friend has some more of that white powder you like lying around somewhere," he put his shoes on and headed for the car. She watched him carefully. He saw her get up as he left through the side door. He knew she was searching for the coke. He had left her a nice size bag in the front bedroom.

Redd was thinking about seducing the thin man when she had noticed his hand on the gearshift. It looked familiar. She had reached over and began to stroke it. It had been awhile, and she was going to enjoy a little rendezvous in the jungle. At first, she thought his hand had quivered at her touch. That excited her so she stroked it some more. She lifted his long fingers one at a time and noticed something in the brightening morning sunlight. The finger pad was, smooth; it had no print. That revelation sent a chill down her spine, but she shook it off. Ashton was dead. She was just missing Asa, she convinced herself. That hand of his had reminded her of Asa's. She had reached into her bag and felt the little firearm that fit perfectly in a side pocket. Then felt around and pulled out a flask instead.

The stranger didn't talk much and she was kind of happy about that. Redd laid her head back against the headrest and enjoyed the slightly cooler air. If it hadn't been for the hand, she could have fallen asleep easily. Instead, she started thinking about Ashton. It had not been her intention to kill him but, once she started inflicting pain and seeing his blood run freely, she began to enjoy it in her haze-afflicted mind. She looked at the thin man next to her. Impossible, she thought. Ashton was mere bones spread against the rocks of the lower Mesa. She giggled. The man looked at her strangely, and then he licked his bottom lip. That made her nerve endings feel as if someone was viciously running a jagged ice cube across them.

She reached over and let her hand glide down the side of the man's neck. When he turned toward her, she saw what looked like a small scar. Plastic surgery, she thought and another chill ran down her spine.

Twenty minutes later, he walked back in to find her sitting loosely on the couch. She was feeling good. She looked up at him and smiled.

"Enjoyed my friend's wares?" Lazarus plopped down on the sofa and removed his shoes again. He threw the keys on the coffee table. Her eyes focused first on his long angular feet and then on the keys.

"Your friend is in the business?" she asked as she wiped her nose realizing that first the hands, then the feet were no coincidences.

"He just dibbles and dabbles. Extra money for extravagances like this," Lazarus said, waving his hands. She recognized the gesture, too. There was no doubt.

"I should have known you would know people like this. You and your criminally-oriented family," she snorted and sniffed.

"Did I give you that impression? Is that why you were so agreeable to following me, a stranger in the woods, little girl?"

"You were always so clandestine." She shook her head.

"You are funny," he grinned. "You talk as if you have known me for years."

"I did. Once. Before I turned you into this," she flipped her hair and smirked.

"How would you know me? I have never met you before," Lazarus put his feet on the floor and leaned on his knees.

"I know who you are, you bastard. Asa suspected that you were still alive. He said," she chuckled, then wiped her nose with the back of her hand, "some dumb bastard who had permanently lost his memory had shown up in Philly. He said he thought the freaking bastard was you, but he wasn't sure of it.

"Damn bastard. He could never get anything fucking right. Then, he turned it around. He assured me you were dead when we threw your ass off the fucking cliff." She curled her legs beneath her body and held her purse tight.

"I removed the gun when you were taking one of your drunken stupor naps on the road," Lazarus licked his bottom lip. He saw her shiver.

"It's in the car. It's still loaded. You are welcome to go get it," he threw the keys at her.

"I'm not afraid of you. You are just as weak and just as stupid as your twin brother."

"Lady, I don't know who you think I am, but I wasn't born a twin. So I know for a fact you have the wrong man. We can go back now, if you want?" He stood up.

"No, no. Hell no. I am not going anywhere with you," she said, curling up tighter like a defiant toddler.

"Okay," he sat back down. "We'll sit here until you sober up a bit, but I am not leaving you out here alone. This is no place for a woman out here alone."

"Oh, now you are my big, bad protector. Where were you when I needed you? Oh, that's right! You were taking care of your bastard kids trying to win that bitch back. Billy told me. He told me everything.

"Just like he told me that he kept asking you to help me and Asa out of Germany and you took your own good time picking up the phone. You let us sit over there and suffer for months. For months, so you could have it all set up nicely to serve me with divorce papers when I got off the plane," she yelled.

"Go ahead, Lena. Whatever you need to get off your chest, do it before we get back into the car. So, please, let it out. But, also please know I am not who you think I am."

"Really? Really. You think I am as clueless as that bitch you married. I may not have recognized you last night, but I did this morning. I know those hands. I know the way you walk, the way you lick your bottom lip, and the way you smell," she shifted around the sofa as if she were trying to decide what to do with her own body.

Lazarus laughed and shook his head.

"I should have known you were crazy, either crazy or a prostitute. I was hoping for prostitute," he said just before he ducked. Her purse flew at his head and landed near his feet. He picked it up and looked inside.

"Wow, you lifted the whole bag. You are a crazy thief. Maybe when you finish your meltdown you will reward me with some…"

"Fuck you, fuck you, fuck you," the words seethed through her teeth.

"Wow, did your parents teach you that word? If I had children, I would teach them how stupid it sounds to say that, especially from a woman, and super especially from a beautiful woman, Lena."

"Don't. Don't call me that bitch's name," she screamed. "It wasn't even her name. She lied. Just like you lied. Your lies got her husband killed. I bet she didn't even miss him. Just like you never even missed me.".

"Okay, your name isn't Lena. What is it?"

"Oh, Ashton. You think you are so damned smooth, don't you? You think you are the master manipulator. You think, and think and think while other people just do it. Like I just did it. I was sick of your ass succeeding and forgetting that I existed. You do remember that I exist," spit flew from her mouth as she spoke. Lazarus wiped his face with his shirt sleeve to remove one of her projectiles. He got up and moved to a chair facing her.

"Okay, I'll bite. You are obviously in a talking mood, lady, whoever you are," he held up his hands and shrugged.

She stared at him, and then placed her hands in her face. A loud moaning sound emerged, but when she removed her hands from her face, he realized she was laughing. She was laughing hysterically.

"Okay, maybe I won't bite. Let's go," he picked up the keys and went to the door.

"I'm sorry," she said. "I'm so sorry. I don't know what came over me. But, then you sat there looking scared to death. Oh, God. I'm so sorry. I guess. I guess he's been on my mind so much lately." She tried to stand up but her knees weakened. She lowered herself back to the sofa gingerly. "I didn't mean it. I'm not crazy. I swear. I just probably need something to eat."

"There's canned chili and baked beans. I think some cans of soup, stuff like that. There may be some crackers in there not opened. What would you like?"

"Let's start with the crackers," she took a deep breath. "Oh, and bring the can of baked beans."

"Don't you want them warmed?" he asked.

"No, I will eat them cold," her voice trailed off. He left the room and returned with an art deco tin plate of beans and a row of crackers. He put them on the table in front of her and went back to his chair. She picked up the plate eagerly and began to eat.

CHAPTER FORTY-FIVE

"**G**OD, THIS IS so good," she ate hungrily. "I'm so sorry. You remind me of him."

"I think I got that. Who are you anyway?"

"My name is Redd."

"The model Redd? Wow, I knew you looked familiar. What happened? Why are down here living under an assumed name?"

"It's a long story," she began to scrape the last of the beans off the plate.

"You want more?" he asked.

"No, I am fine now. What was in that coke?" she asked as if she was suddenly genuinely embarrassed by her behavior.

"Coke," he shrugged. "I don't touch the stuff myself. You probably shouldn't touch that bag again. But, maybe it wasn't just the coke. You were drinking pretty heavily on the way up here. Your brain is probably going a little bit haywire."

They sat there for a minute staring at each other. He was a bit disappointed. After kicking Brady over the waterfall, he had conjured up this monstrous beast of a woman in his head. Oh, he knew how dangerous she was and how she had tortured him to near death. But, sitting across the table from her, having a quasi-normal conversation gave him a glimpse of how they used to be. But, he wasn't going to blame himself for her madness.

"Let me make you some tea. Then you can pretend I am your bartender."

"My bartender?" she shook her head and her eyes lightened up for the first time.

"Yeah, I used to tend bar in a past life. And, I realized what they say is true."

"What's that?"

"That you are everyone's psychologist. People used to come in and describe their whole worlds to me and didn't think anything of it. Who was I to tell? I would never see the majority of them again. And the ones that came back would give me updates on their lives. Go figure," Lazarus walked away and left her smiling down at the table.

"You are so easy to talk to. I can see why your bar clients would come back," she said. Lazarus noticed some color was returning to her face as he put the mug in front of her. She sipped the tea right away.

"Perfect. How did you guess I like one part tea, three parts sugar," she giggled.

"Wild guess. Figured you needed a rush from the other white stuff," he sipped his tea and put the mug down and twirled it.

"So, who did you think I was?" Lazarus was curious about her. He wanted to know what part he had had in her derailment into insanity.

"My ex. Your voice is different. Your face." She touched her own face. "But, your mannerisms are a lot like his."

"As I recall, I smell like him," he teased.

"Yes," she giggled. "You must wear the same musk oil or something. Why did you bring me out here?"

"For sex," he picked up the tea again. "Isn't that why you followed me?"

"Maybe. Or maybe it was that big wad of money you pulled out at the bar. That took a lot of guts you know. In these parts, people have died for less."

"That happens anywhere, but I am not afraid. People tend to fear me," he took another sip of tea.

"You are one of those," she said and didn't appear afraid of being in the presence of danger.

"Yes. I tend to kill people now and then," he said offhandedly.

"Always the quiet ones. I knew you were quiet for a reason. Do you plan to kill me?" she leaned over the table seductively. She was intrigued.

"I'm on hiatus. Already did what I came down here to do. Just thought some companionship would help pass the time."

"I have killed twice out of the four times I attempted the deeds." A slow grin formed across her lips. "Each time, it was sort of anticlimactic."

"Was it your ex or someone related to your ex?" He took another sip of tea.

"You are good," she giggled. "You know, I don't know to this day, why." She marveled at the porcelain mug with the jungle imprints.

"I knew I liked you for a reason. Tell me your sordid story. Then I will tell you mine. How's that? Maybe we could write about it. Call it,

'How I Became a Killer'? Or, something like that," they both laughed.

"I don't know. I was ticked I guess. I don't know whether it was his fault or mine. He loved me once. He loved me so much it drove me absolutely crazy. His love was so overwhelming, I couldn't breathe. I guess because I didn't love him like that, but I loved him. I didn't realize how much though until it was too late. I blew it. I blew it, big time. But, I had a little help.

"You see, I was dating his brother, Asa. The first time I saw him I thought he was the most gorgeous man on earth or should I say, boy. I met him in high school. I was going to the catholic high school for girls, and he was going to the one for boys. Every once in awhile, the boys would come to our school for some event or vice versa. On one particular day, I can't even recall for what event, the boys came to our school. I was sitting in the cafeteria when someone passed me this big note. It was a large piece of paper that had been folded to about yay big," she held up both hands as a way to measure it.

"I opened it and it was a pencil drawing of me. It was perfect. Then, someone pointed him out. Like I said, he was gorgeous. I couldn't tell what he was. He had that exotic look, like you, sort of. Are you ever going to take those dark glasses off?"

"I can't. I have a condition. These aren't cosmetic. He lifted them quickly and exposed his camouflaged eyes beneath the black contact lenses and then put them back in place.

"That's a shame. You have beautiful, beady little eyes," she almost choked on her tea.

"Ha, ha. So you killed him because he was cute?"

"No, silly. I fell in love with him. We dated for three years. My whole senior year and the first two years of college. He was my," she shook her head, "my everything. And, then I met the other one."

"Other one?"

"His twin. I hadn't met him before. Asa lived with his father, and his twin lived with his grandfather. I had met his father and his stepmother, and his brother by his stepmother. But, I had never met the rest of his family and then one day we went to New York to visit his twin. His brother was going to Columbia. Asa and I were at Temple."

"So you killed his brother?" Lazarus waved his hands as to hurry up.

"No, silly. Not then. Let me tell my side of the story."

"Damn girl, I want to talk, too."

"You will get your chance." She was obviously enjoying getting her story out. "Anyway, I'll be short. I fell in love, sort of, with the brother. Asa was goofy and fun and free-spirited. Ashton, oh God, Ashton, was quiet, serious, and so damn sophisticated. I was just wowed, is all I can say. When he entered a room, I mean he entered the room. Women loved him." She put her cup down and smiled. "And he wanted me, the minute he laid eyes on me. He wanted me. And I wanted his world."

"His world was different from yours?"

"Oh, yes. There was a sophistication, an air, about him that made me want more than the fun and games I had with Asa. Plus, he kept telling me how I was meant to be a runway model and he was going to make it happen."

"So you got a late start in modeling."

"If you call 19 years old late. I graduated high school early," she got up from the table and twirled around as if she were wearing a free-flowing frock. "He didn't lie. Before I knew it, I was working and he was managing me every step of the way. For a minute, I had the best of both worlds. I had a double set of men worshipping me, competing for my attention. Then, he asked me to marry him.

At first, I hesitated. Asa was the one that had my heart, but I liked being on Ashton's arm. He knew everybody. He was opening doors I didn't realize existed before, and then there was goofy, my art boy, who was becoming increasingly skilled in photography. He was earning a lot of money on the side just shooting pictures, selling them to magazines and companies. But, none of that seemed important. He was a behind the scenes kind of guy. Ashton knew how to look and act in front of a camera. He wasn't just another gorgeous version of Asa, he was smarter."

"So why did you kill him?"

"It was because I couldn't bear the pain any longer," she sighed, returning to the table and propping her chin on her hands.

"He hurt you?"

"In the worst way. First, he got me to agree to adopt children that turned out to be his biologically. I knew it. I knew the minute he brought them home, he was lying. They looked like her, even when they were only a few days old, I could see her."

"Who? Her?" he teased.

"The bitch his grandfather left his penthouse to. Even left her like half a million dollars. She was supposed to be some high-class hooker that worked for the old man, but I knew the moment I saw her that she had her hooks into Ashton. I could feel the tension in the room when she walked her highfaluting little ass in the room."

"That's why you killed him?"

"You are damn anxious. And, according to Asa, he may not be dead. That is, if he can make up his mind. Hush. Be patient," she reached over and patted his hand. He was surprised that his skin hadn't flinched this time. He was enjoying the story and how animated she had become as opposed to the lethargic woman she had been on the trip up the mountain.

"Oh, there is so much more," she grinned. "He divorced me. This bastard was rolling in dough. I mean rolling in it. His grandfather left him millions in his will, but there were millions unaccounted for and everyone knew who had it. Ashton was his grandfather's right-hand man. He knew everything about his grandfather's affairs. Later, I found out, he was his grandfather's number one henchman. So, please, he wasn't an angel. He had been killing people long before I laid a hand on him.

"Anyway, it wasn't so much that he divorced me. It was the when and the where, and the how he did it."

"What do you mean?"

"He took his hands off my career after he brought those babies home. He said he didn't have the time between running his company and taking care of the children. He wanted me to become a stay-at-home, or at least closer to home, mom. And I couldn't do it. Every time I looked at those creatures, I thought of her. He tried for awhile to work things out, but I wasn't cooperating in the least. I wanted out, but not completely out. I still had Asa. All I needed was Ashton's money."

"You are dragging this out," Lazarus faked a yawn.

"Asa and I were stuck in Europe on my last working trip over there. This rich German with supposed connections to the fashion industry there had suckered us into Germany. Instead, we found ourselves in some sordid sex game.

"At first, it was fun and outlandish. It was like this big, roaming orgy. For the first couple of days, it was wild: sex, drugs, loud music, luxurious surroundings, gorgeous people, freaky people, rich people, and just plain people, but then the excitement wore off when we realized our passports had disappeared. It took us three months of abuse to get out of Germany. I won't go into the sordid details, but I could never get Ashton on the phone.

"And, his father. That bastard was feeding us the line that Ashton said he couldn't do anything to help us and then, months later, picked up the phone and opened our way out of Europe. Though I had been wrong to believe that Ashton was refusing to help, I still think he should have been concerned enough to find me after not hearing from me for so long." She hesitated as she tried to think of a reason why Ashton should have looked for her and then she laughed. After all, she had gotten him used to not hearing from her when she was with Asa.

"Now, Billy was the cunning one. He pitted the twins against each other constantly. He even suckered Asa into trying to kill off Ashton's whole family."

"Is that why you finished it off?"

"No, darling. But, by then I was buying into it. I was so hurt because he had methodically moved all of his money into his children's accounts right after they were born. When he divorced me, he had so little money, the judge only gave me a mere pittance in alimony. Trust me, it wasn't enough for a maggot to live on. Asa tried but he couldn't give me what Ashton had given me."

"What about your career? The money you made?"

"I goofed the money because I lived with a wealthy man. I had fun with it. And my career was dead. Very dead. Back then, a woman in her thirties was washed out and worthless. It's different now."

"Why don't you go back?"

"Like this?" For a minute, it looked as if she would cry and, then, she went straight for her purse. He watched her remove her paraphernalia and line the powder up perfectly before she inhaled it.

"Besides," she started up again as if she had never stopped talking, "he owed me."

"Do you regret it?"

"I did at first. I guess I still do, because I did it partially for the wrong reasons. He owed me the money, but he had nothing to do with leaving me stranded in Germany. And, even though I knew the truth...," her voice trailed off a bit. "It was their father, Billy, who had

had the audacity to laugh at us when we went to see him. He laughed at us. He said that we were pathetic, and he compared me to her, compared Asa to Ashton and told Asa how proud he was of Ashton and how disappointed he was in him.

"Can you imagine, your own father turning you so against your own brother that you end up trying to kill him and, after you fail, you end up on the run for years under an assumed identity? Looking back, it was all that jealous old bastard's fault for everything that went south. So, I killed his ass. Went into the kitchen to get some tea and found a very interesting package under the kitchen sink. Didn't know it could make someone foam at the mouth like that. He even shit on himself.

"Anyway, Asa and I were at our wits end when Asa started taking a stroll down memory lane, when he used to pretend to be Ashton and get him in trouble. So I got to thinking, why not take his place long enough to get our hands on his money."

"So you killed him? I mean, tried to kill him?" Lazarus folded his arms on the table and laid his forehead on top.

"I know I tried. If he survived, it was because the bastard was too resilient. That could be him walking around now with part of his memory missing. Thank God, if that bastard is really him, it's the part that keeps him from remembering anything about what happened to him and, maybe, he will never come looking for me.

"I almost killed his idiot brother, too," she giggled. "He was supposed to step into Ashton's shoes long enough to grab the cash and run. But, then he liked the new life. Wanted to hang around. I got so pissed I shot him in the head. Only grazed him and I didn't get to finish the job because she walked in and surprised me. Just knew it was the end of her, but both of them survived. So, I blackmailed him. He has been good at making sure the money was flowing, but he has missed a drop." She folded up her mirror and put it back into her purse.

"No, he didn't miss," Lazarus sat up. "That was the other thing I had to do while I was down here. He asked me to deliver something for you." Redd's face paled and she swallowed hard as she wiped her nose. She reached inside her purse. She knew Asa wouldn't entrust anyone other than Brady to make that drop, or he would have made sure she knew whom to expect.

"It's not there, remember?" Lazarus took a deep breath. "It's no longer in the car either. I thought it best I move it. It's up there." He looked at the planters hanging across the cathedral glass ceiling.

"What?" Her voice quivered and she heard the distinctive cadence in his voice. She sighed. She should have listened to her own instinct.

"Your gun," Lazarus removed his glasses and wiped his face with the back of his sleeve. "Thank you. Thank you for the explanation. I was wondering why you hated me so much."

"I don't hate you, darling. I am so sorry I hurt you. I told you I regretted it. I told you how I was manipulated." She leaned toward him trying to reveal her cleavage, which used to get his attention every time.

"Yes, you did. But, my memory is back, Redd. And I remember vividly, every last puncture wound, every last slice, every last stab." He pounded the table with one hand, lowering it as if he were stabbing it. "You enjoyed it. Admit it," Lazarus demanded. Redd stood up and began to approach him. She was bold, he thought, not just crazy.

"It was not that anticlimactic for you when you kicked me over the cliff. Asa wasn't moving fast enough for you. I should probably thank you though because, if he had tossed me, I wouldn't have gotten caught on that branch. That old, dead branch was strong enough to hold me. And the temperature outside was cold enough to keep me from bleeding to death.

"You know, even though I went to Catholic school, I used to doubt in the existence of a God. But, Kali, who has endured more than any woman should, would always tell me that God was watching over me, no matter what I did. As I sit here listening to your twisted logic, I realized that God was truly watching over me. Wow, how amazing. There is an existence out there taking care of me. Not for me, no I am beyond His kind of help, but for Kali. She's the one He is really watching over. And my children," he popped the contact lenses out of his eyes and grimaced as he squeezed his eyes shut.

"When I first woke up after you almost killed me, I was so scared. I was petrified. Somebody wanted me dead in the worst way. But, they didn't succeed. That's how I gained my strength and courage back. I kept thinking they didn't succeed.

"If you had told me you were suffering I would have given you some cash. But, that wasn't what you wanted. You wanted to lie around with Asa and blame me for your pathetic lives. Is that what Daddy told you? I bet that's what he said, wasn't it?

"There is one thing I can say about my father, he worked hard. He earned his own way. It might never have been enough for him, but he got the point. He went out and got as much as he could for himself. Even if he was sitting around stewing about what he didn't have, he didn't sit around waiting for someone to fulfill his basic needs.

"You are one spoiled, useless bitch. But, I do want to apologize. I should never have tried to take your heart from my brother. For that part of your story, I regret it. I regret that I just didn't leave you and marry Kali when she was pregnant with our children. There are so many things that we both should and can regret."

"Will you regret killing me?" she asked. Her eyes were half searching for the planter he had referred to because her brain was still sharp and focused. Her body would never be found, if there were a body at all left. There had been a time when she could convince him to do anything. She took a deep breath and let her eyes meet his. All she had to do was to make him feel sorry for her.

"I am not going to kill you. I didn't come here to kill you. Outside in the car is a bag filled with cash. About one million, give or take a few dollars I used for expenses down here. It's yours for you to disappear and never look back. If you look back, you will be like Lot's wife. I will turn you, literally, into a pillar of salt. Do you understand?

"As for my brother, forget him. He thinks he is in love with my wife. You know how I am about sharing my women. I don't go for that," Lazarus walked over to the coffee table and picked up the keys. He walked over to her and dropped them in her hands. "Go check."

"What's the catch?" she asked and knew this was ending too easy.

"You stay here. I will send someone back to pick you up. I don't want to be seen with you."

"You will send someone to pick me up?" She shook the keys and hurried to the door. He stood in the doorway as she searched the car, and then watched as she checked the duffle bag she found in the rear. She looked back at him and grinned mischievously.

"What if I send someone to pick you up?" she jumped into the drivers' seat. "I will tell my son to send you a thank you note."

She sat behind the steering wheel and put on the seatbelt.

"Your son?" She heard him ask as she walked toward the car.

"You didn't let me finish the story," she yelled back dangling the keys in the air. "Before Asa came out of hiding and found me, I had built a new life with another man who really loved me," her eyes teared up. "We had a son. But, I lost him because of Asa. I lost him. His father took him from me, and I didn't have a pot to piss in, so I couldn't fight for my son. With the money Asa has been sending me and this, I can fight for him, now," she turned the ignition.

"You don't know how to drive that car," Lazarus walked up to the door and tried to reach for the key. She swatted his arm.

"I can drive it better than you can," she pushed the gas pedal to the floor. Lazarus escaped within a second of getting his foot run over. She hurried down the driveway, not noticing the bag jerk out of the rear of the jeep. The bag had been tied to a fishing line from the side.

Lazarus picked up the bag, went back inside, wiped the place down, and bagged everything that she touched. He locked up and went down the back stairs. He jumped into the original Jeep he had driven up into the mountains, and headed back to Rio to return the bag of cash he had borrowed from an old friend. She had been right about one thing. Drug dealers, thieves, and murderers were his friends. He could have lured anything up to that cabin. Turns out, all it took was a wad of cash, a jeep, and a bag of uncut coke.

CHAPTER FORTY-SIX

KALI PACED THE large suite in Las Vegas overlooking its glitzy skyline. She had registered in the exact suite, under an alias, as instructed. She had bought something silky and clingy and wore nothing beneath, also as instructed. She picked her watch up from the dresser. He was late. This made her anxious. Vegas weather was sunny and hot as usual. She wondered if his flight from wherever he was traveling had been delayed. It was unusual for him to be late for anything.

He used to tease her that she was going to be late to his funeral. She would correct him saying, 'you are supposed to say you will be late to your own funeral.' "No," he would say. "You will be on time for yours; it's mine you will be late for."

She stopped in front of the mirror and, for a second, thought she could see Kenny standing behind her, waiting to dress her to Jordan's delight. She would never forget the first day Kenny had come to prepare her for Jordan. She had thought it was a tortuous and ugly joke. She had willingly shed her clothes to be with Ashton. She was barely getting used to shedding her clothes for Jordan and, now, here was this skinny little guy who thought he had the right to touch every inch of her nude body and who thought he had the right to dress her from head to toe.

Their relationship began as a bumpy ride. If Jordan were not in the room, she would push Kenny's hands away, especially when he wanted to wax her private parts. That was too much. But, she had grown accustomed to him, and to his hands. They could soothe away the stress of her situation with such ease. Some days, he would bathe and oil and massage her. And, his hair and makeup skills were to die for. He would do her makeup and hair, and then start packing up his kit.

"Where's my clothes?" she would ask, knowing sometimes it would be only a g-string and other days it could be an evening gown with a split all the way up to her armpit. But then, there was an occasion when the makeup was the only thing she wore, maybe with a pair of six-inch stilettos.

"Stilettos," she chastised herself. She had brought a pair with her. Kali was supposed to have them on. She had just finished the last strap when there was a light tap on the door. She peeked out of the narrow scope of a peephole and frowned. She didn't recognize the man. She ran back and put a robe on, then opened the door just wide enough to get a full look at a man who looked like Steve Erkel wearing high waisted, high water pants, a huge pair of square glasses and a short afro. The man who resembled the *Family Matters* television character was standing there with a large bouquet of flowers.

"Flowers for Patti Jones," the man said in a long, southern drawl.

"You can leave them right there," Kali said, noticing the man wasn't wearing a hotel uniform.

"No tip?" the man said as he put them down.

"Just a minute," Kali went to shut the door and the man's hand grabbed it. He stunned her. She jumped back frightened as the man picked up the flowers and stepped inside.

"Now, is that any way to treat your long-lost husband," Lazarus began to laugh. Kali snatched the flowers from his hand and feigned throwing them his way. He took the flowers back and threw them on the floor; he grabbed her and pulled her into his arms.

She pushed the afro wig from his head and flung it down where the flowers lay. Then, she took his large, square glasses and threw them into the air.

"Oh, I have to get you out of this polyester shirt," she began to rip at the shirt.

"Careful, I have to wear something out of the room," he teased.

"You can just wear me." Her mouth began to devour his.

"Oh, is Niecy horny?" he grabbed her butt and lifted her as she helped him roughly out of the shirt. She didn't care if she ripped it. She wanted him to rip her. He laid her on the bed and let his hand slide up the blue silk gown. He raised himself over her as she tugged at his belt.

"Down girl," he laughed.

"Up boy," she giggled as he began to help her remove his pants. He didn't have on any underwear or socks. She squealed loudly.

"Boy is up, ain't you Taylor?" he leaned in for the kiss. The kiss was deep and succulent. He had been dreaming of the taste of her since he had left her bed in the Mesa. He had been dreaming of that taste all of his life he thought as he dove into her mouth, his heart traveling up and through to hers. This was love he thought, not sex, not lovemaking, just love at its purest. His hands held her head, holding it firmly as their tongues lashed, and licked, and teased each other.

Their bodies were meshed as they rolled back and forth finding their own unique synergy that no one else understood. They were impervious to the world; no one could penetrate the bond between them. Their love was too strong, too wrong, and too powerful to contend. They both had survived Redd, Billy, prison, past marriages, death, and even Jordan. When their brains met, when their auras intertwined, and when they were occupying each other's space, they created a brand new universe.

Lazarus' hands began to tug at the silk that didn't budge as it was wedged underneath her body which was wedged underneath his, so he ripped it off her and she screamed with pleasure. His head moved away from her hungry lips and his tongue began to tease her behind her right ear. Her body arched as deeply as it had arched the first night he had seduced her. His tongue began to follow a path beneath her chin. He stopped, and sucked the tip of her chin. She tried to bring her mouth to his, but he pulled her head back with a gentle yank of her hair. His head ventured down to the indentation of her throat. He nibbled, she squirmed. He ventured down between her breasts as her nipples stood at attention. He took one into his mouth, her fingers grappled, finding a hold on his hair. Gently, she yanked his head back and he found the other breast.

She tried to lift her head, but he held her in place as he worked his way down to her belly button. She knew where he was headed. She knew what he loved more than anything and she knew how he could make her scream. She began to tense up with expectation, and then he lifted her hips. He rose up with her hanging halfway in the air. At first, he teased her with light wisps of his tongue, and then the long, soft rubbery moist tongue penetrated her. She thought she would break her own neck from the intense orgasm she experienced just from that one un-intrusive intrusion. She went limp as he buried his head further and further into the center of her universe. Then she tensed again, again, and again.

Kali thought he would never let her go. She tried to walk using her hands to get a balance, to twist away, to be free of the explosions reverberating through her body like fierce waves in a violent ocean sweeping her out to sea. She screamed for mercy, and he went deeper. Then he began to pull and tug with his lips, her lips, her source of pleasure. Then he let her hips slide down his chest. She was getting ready to lift her legs, free them so she could run, though she didn't know why, when she began to rock beneath him. He was slowly making his way home, announcing his intention. Then he knocked on the door loudly, not giving her a chance to say don't come in. He was in and he was riding her hard. They both screamed when he came an hour later, without going limp once.

She tried to crawl out of the bed to go to the bathroom. He grabbed her foot and put it in his mouth. She smiled at him. "Gotta go, son." She tugged her foot.

"Not yet," he said trying to pull her back. She resisted and kicked him with the other foot. "Oh, no you didn't," he grinned down her.

"Don't make me wet myself," she started giggling as he now had hold of both of her feet, and he was taking turns licking each one from the heel to the toes.

"Ashton," she screamed delightfully, but urgently, too. "Stop."

"In a minute," he said as he grabbed her up in his arms and lowered her to the floor and entered her. At first she fought, hoping she wouldn't pee on the floor, but as he kept sliding in and out with such easy, titillating friction she lost the desire to pee and had only the desire to squeeze Taylor as tightly as Neicy could squeeze. She lost track of time as he lifted her and twisted her and sucked her into an absolutely frenzy, then suddenly they both dropped. They lay in each other's arms as the room was darkened by the darkening skyline.

"Ashton Taylor Sperling," she whispered.

"Kalina Denise Harris Roberson Sperling," he laughed.

"Roberson. Why would you add that?" she sat on up on her elbows. His head was laying on her tummy.

"I don't know. I guess with all my memories flooding back, I got to thinking about the kid. How he died too soon. How he died because someone wanted me dead."

"It wasn't your fault, Ashton. None of this is your fault. You don't control other people's crazy notions. Your father and your brother were…are crazy. Come on," she pushed his head away. She used the bed to help lift herself up and she reached back for him. He took her hand.

"Let's shower. Then, its Taylor's turn," she got up and led him into the bathroom.

"Taylor was having a pretty good time," he squeezed her hand.

"Niecy was beginning to think Taylor hadn't had any in a long time. But, Niecy knows better, because Taylor took Niecy out to play before he left."

"But, that was a whole week ago and you know how Taylor gets," he teased as Kali pulled him into the shower turning the cold water on. They both screamed.

CHAPTER FORTY-SEVEN

LAZARUS WALKED INTO the study to find the fake Ashton sitting in Jordan's old chair. His head was being held up by one hand whose fingers were twisted into his graying hair.

"Where, the hell, have you been?" the fake Ashton stood up. His eyes were red and glazed over.

"I was out west with some friends, but you knew that." Lazarus walked in and sat down on the leather sofa, the same one he used to sit on to talk things over with Jordan. It was funny how easy it was to remember now, but he was getting scared. He was forgetting things. He had forgotten the name of the hotel he had told Kali to wait for him in, and he had wandered around Las Vegas for two hours until he finally remembered. That was not normal.

As long as he could remember Kali and his children, he reasoned, he didn't have to remember anything else. Not even the sight of Redd's car flying off the cliff ahead of him. She had taken the road too fast and met up with an oncoming truck. She tried to swerve and couldn't compensate, because she couldn't brake. He had made sure of that. He kept wondering why she was so far behind when he had finally gotten on the road. She should have been at least 40 minutes ahead. But, there she was.

He saw the Jeep go up in the air and then pause for a few deadly seconds before it pointed downward, her red hair flapping. He was too far away to see her face, but he knew that it was filled with fear. The scene frightened even him.

A trucker got out and stood on the side of the road for a few minutes but, being in a precarious spot, he got in his truck and began to take the incline. He pulled up beside Lazarus and rolled down the window. They looked at each and just shook their heads. The trucker picked up his CB radio and reported the accident. Lazarus sat there and then looked at his watch. He waved a business card at the truck driver, who took it and nodded gratefully, but the information on the card was bogus.

"Where's my wife?" The fake Ashton plopped back down in his chair looking defeated.

"She's not back, yet. They went to the Poconos, right?" Lazarus crossed his legs and folded his arms. He knew the mood Asa was in, because he had watched him go through it a million times. He was feeling abandoned, or afraid, or just sorry for himself.

"What's wrong, son?" Lazarus licked his bottom lip.

"Like you would give a shit," he threw a folded newspaper in Lazarus' direction. "The city is in mourning, you idiot."

Lazarus unfolded the paper and a smiling young Redd stared back at him.

"She died in Brazil, it says," the fake Ashton sobbed openly.

"That's right; she was your ex-wife. I didn't know you still loved her," Lazarus folded the paper and walked it over to the desk. "I'll leave you to grieve. Maybe, you should talk to Ruby," Lazarus said as he left the study. He had one more person to deal with before he handled his brother.

CHAPTER FORTY-EIGHT

"RUBY, RUBY, RUBY," Lazarus smiled at his brother's moody, insolent wife as she opened the door to their apartment.

"Micah isn't home," she stood in the door.

"I know," Lazarus put his hand on the door and pressed it open while Ruby tried her best not to let it swing open any further. "What have I ever done to you, Ruby?" he asked.

"Dr. Sperling to you," she said, still trying to block his entrance.

"In my eyes, you will always be Papa's little brown babe." He walked past her with ease into the living room and pulled off his jacket. He let it drop into one of the chairs, eased himself onto the sofa and kicked off his shoes. He put his feet on the coffee table.

"Is this some sort of sick joke?"

"I don't know, I was thinking of asking you the same thing, Ruby Booby," Lazarus reached over for his jacket and pulled out a cigar.

"No smoking in this household. And I would appreciate it if you put your clothes back on and left."

"Is that how you talk to all of your patients?"

"All of my patients don't force their way into my home, strip, and try to smoke."

"I take it Micah is not allowed to take his shoes off in here anymore either. What happened to you, Ruby? Did the MD come with a brain drain?"

"Ha ha. I laughed at your joke, now leave."

"Why, Ruby? I just want to know why," Lazarus put the cigar in his mouth and felt his pockets for a lighter. "Where does Molasses keep the lighters?" He got up and started looking around.

"Get out," she yelled. "Or, I will call Micah."

"Micah knows where I am. I know where Micah is. Do you?" Lazarus found a lighter and flicked it, putting the flame to the cigar. He blew the smoke from his nose. Ruby crossed the room and reached for the phone. Lazarus sat back down. "No ashtrays," he sighed. "Let's see what my brother has hidden in this household that he uses as an ashtray."

"He doesn't smoke," Ruby had picked up the phone and held the receiver to her ear listening to the other line ringing. Micah wasn't picking up.

"There is a reason for that, you know." Lazarus came back with a juice glass filled with water.

"Don't you dare," she yelled when she saw him with the glass. "That's just plain nasty." She hung up the phone.

"He's not going to answer you until I tell him we are finished talking," said Lazarus as he dropped an ash in the water. Ruby headed for the door. "It's inevitable, Ruby. Our talk. It can be just a talk, you know." Lazarus propped his feet back onto the coffee table making himself comfortable on the sofa.

"Is that a threat? Are you threatening me? Does my husband know that you are in his home threatening his wife? The mother of his child?"

"Hold up," Lazarus held up a finger. "I was with you all the way up until the last part," he chuckled. "Although, you could be right. The DNA test should be back soon or is it back already?"

Ruby's eyes widened. "How dare you?"

"Is that all they taught you to say in psycho school? Maybe I should become a psychiatrist."

"Don't start. Don't start. I saw her picture in the paper today, and I know you had something to do with it. Just like Brady. Brady has suddenly just disappeared," her voice trailed off.

"Not really," Lazarus shook his head. "His body is somewhere the eye could see him, if they found him. He's definitely not invisible. Or, maybe, hmm, I never thought about it, but, bodies do decompose if they aren't embalmed right away? I guess he will disappear eventually. Kind of sad, you know. We had some great times in college. We tore New York up. Nobody partied harder than me, Brady, and Troy."

"You can't be serious." Ruby began to pace the floor looking back at Lazarus. She needed a clue, she needed bait. She needed to change his mind. She turned to him, crossing her arms and looking him in the eyes, she spoke slowly and firmly as if to a child considering sticking its hand in the fire and she was too far away to snatch it to safety. "Okay, you had me for a minute there. My husband and his little brothers have you thinking you are Ashton and you almost had me believing you. I told Micah to leave this alone. Now I am telling you. You are not who they say you are. I'm sorry they have convinced you that you are Ashton, but trust me, it's a sick joke. You have to let it go. Leave it alone. Just leave it alone. Leave it alone!"

"Ruby, calm down, sweetie." Lazarus patted the sofa next to him. "Come on. Sit down. Let's talk this out. Tell me how you got involved in my murder."

"Lazarus, Ashton lives. I don't know who you are, but you are not Ashton."

"Do you think for one minute, Ruby," Lazarus shook his head with a smile on his face, "do you think that a few stern and authoritative words from a psychiatrist will change my mind?"

"I had nothing to do with what they did." Ruby sat down hard in the chair behind her desk and wrapped herself in her arms. She began to rock. "Don't hurt Artie, you vicious psychopath. Artie needs me. He does. I know you are already thinking about letting her raise him. I can see it. But, he needs his mother. I know she loves him. I know you love him, but you can't come close to loving him like me." She began to weep.

"How did they find out about the safe room? How did they find out where all my bank accounts were? And, don't say Elliott. I know that before she quit, Elliott threatened to cut fake me's balls off. Besides, Elliott had nothing to lose or to gain. Elliott was happy being Elliott. She was and is no threat to me. But, you, you don't like my wife, first of all. And secondly, you were sleeping with Billy behind Micah's back. Sounds like a little blackmail, a little hate. Put them together and they spell ambush Ashton, coach up Asa, and everybody lives happily or not so happily ever after. What was the deal, Ruby? Rough her up in exchange for more information? I don't know, though, could another woman stoop so low as to do that?"

"You have it all wrong, Lazarus." Ruby looked around the room through heavy tears. Lazarus left the room and came back with a box of tissues.

"Then set me right."

"They didn't just blackmail me, they threatened me. They promised me that when your children… Artie would be with them if I didn't keep my mouth shut."

Lazarus blew a slow, deliberate ring of smoke and sighed. "Ruby, you are still lying to me. Because, you and I both know all you had to do was tell Micah and it would have been over."

"But, Artie," Ruby sniffled.

"But, you are a doctor with access to DNA testing that could have proved them wrong."

"I was scared."

"Micah wasn't. Artie belongs to him, regardless of DNA. So, your story is still a little weak, if you know what I mean." Lazarus let the ashes drop into the glass. "And, I have got all day and all night. Knowing Micah, he will just go to the penthouse for the evening, or stay in the office and work."

"I hate you, you smug son-of-a-bitch. Everything is your way or no way! Jordan died and you stepped into his shoes automatically. You orchestrate everything, my life, Micah's life, Artie's life. I sit back and watch how you have literally repeated Jordan's family hierarchy. The only difference is that you have little girls you are messing up. I was tired of your reach around my throat."

Ruby ran out of the room. Lazarus sat there and waited. He knew she was looking for a gun, any gun that Micah had hidden throughout the apartment, but they were all gone. There weren't even any knives or spray cans in the place.

Slowly, Ruby walked back into the room, her face still stained with tears. "What now?" she asked as she crumbled onto the sofa.

"You use the same tactics you used to bring me down, but this time, we bring Asa down."

"And, if I say no," she choked back more tears.

"Kali WILL RAISE your son."

CHAPTER FORTY-NINE

KALI TOOK A deep breath before opening the door to the penthouse. Both Lazarus and Micah had coached her over and over as to how to behave and what to say. That was all she had thought about on the long trip home. By the intense look on her children's faces and their closed mouths, she suspected Lazarus had been talking to them as well. She closed her eyes and remembered his touch.

It was funny how Ashton had transitioned into a totally different man but with the same drive and personality, though most people would scarcely notice. She was still in love with him. She still wanted him, but the more she watched him and listened to him, she didn't know whether she should be more afraid of his impersonator or more afraid of his alter ego.

Ashton's new alter ego was calculating and devious. When she had read the newspaper about Redd, she knew without a doubt, he had paid Redd a visit.

"Daddy," Kacie was the first to yell as they burst through the door. The young child leaped into the fake Ashton's arms. He caught her and smiled. "We had such a great time, Daddy. Why didn't you come up to see us?" Kacie asked angelically as Kali held her breath. Kacie hadn't run to this man so eagerly in a long, long time.

"I wanted to," he actually kissed her cheek before putting her down. Then all the children hugged him and kissed him. Kali watched the scene with amazement. She had been worried that the kids would avoid him to keep from slipping up and telling him where they really had been. Instead, they began to chat about horseback riding and swimming and fishing, things they had actually done, but not for a minute in the Poconos.

Kali interrupted them. "Real baths, please! Everybody scoot. Give your dad some air. Go, go. Take your things with you," she scolded playfully. They grinned at her, but obeyed her as they ran with their rustling baggage and wares up the stairs. "Now it's my turn." She sauntered up to fake Ashton. "You didn't come looking for us."

"I knew where you were," he lied. He had tried to find

them. Micah had told him they were staying at a friend's cabin, but refused to divulge the address until he got his act together.

"Did you enjoy being alone?" Kali asked as she stepped out of her shoes.

"No, I actually missed you," he reached for the curl between her eyes. She backed away from his touch.

"I wasn't sure if I should have returned." She picked up her shoes and headed toward the stairs.

"I'm sorry, Kali," he said softly, but loud enough for her hear.

"Excuse me?" Kali said defiantly.

"I said," he walked up to her and took her hand, "I'm sorry. I realized while you were gone how much I have hurt you. I'm sorry." His words sounded sincere, but his touch made Kali want to hurl. She pulled her hand away from his.

"I haven't been myself for a while. I don't know how to explain it," he moved closer to her, but she stood her ground and kept her face sober when she wanted to laugh in his face. She wanted to laugh real hard and tell him that he was not Ashton and never would be Ashton, but she kept quiet. Micah and the real Ashton had assured her it was only a matter of time before the impersonator would be permanently gone from her life.

"I'm going to take a shower. The cabin was one of those bare bones, bare necessity kind. I'm ready for some real amenities."

"Yeah, go relax. I'll be up later," he held his hands up and backed away. He watched her slowly take the stairs up as if she were really tired. He knew that she was wary of him and he couldn't blame her. He was going to make it up to her. He didn't know how, but he was going to find a way. With Redd gone, there would be no more guilt when he wanted to love her. With Redd gone, he had no one left to love him, no one left that even knew he existed. His father had helped him avoid prison, helped him set up a new identity in another country, but then had banished him.

Billy would have nothing to do with him until he had shown up on Billy's doorstep. Asa thought his father was welcoming him with open arms until he saw Redd and realized it was him, Asa. Billy had been growing old wishing and hoping to make amends with Ashton. He had discarded any love or concern for the son he had raised to be the man Asa had turned out to be. It was Billy that had put the divisive spirit in

Asa's heart. It was Billy with all the bright ideas on bringing Ashton down after Jordan had died. And it was Asa who tried to please his father and hurt his own brother, his own mirror image. All Asa had ever wanted was to be a part of Ashton's life. All he had ever wanted to do was be just like Ashton. Everybody liked Ashton. And everybody had treated him like Ashton's leftover brain, even Billy.

Asa stood in the middle of the foyer and thought about the penthouse and how badly he had wanted to live there with Jordan and Ashton. He remembered crying a flood of tears when Billy would drag him back to Germantown. It wasn't because of where he lived; it was because of whom he had to live without, his twin brother.

Ashton used to treat him so special when he would come over. Ashton's face would light up and he would grab Asa by the hand and drag him to his room. Ashton would share his clothes with Asa, his toys, his music — anything he had. They would even share the same bed though Jordan had given him his own suite. When they were little, they would fall asleep in each other's arms. When they got older, they would stay awake all night talking. When they both became sexually active, they became more competitive. Ashton started becoming the ladies' choice and Asa started becoming the twin they ran from. Billy made him feel worse by comparing his grades to Ashton's and then he was furious when Ashton decided to become a lawyer and all Asa wanted to do was paint and take pictures.

But, the more he thought about it, none of it was Ashton's fault. Not once did Ashton pretend to be Asa and get him in trouble. At about 13 years of age, Asa started feeling inferior to his brother who had more sophistication even at that age. Jordan had introduced Ashton to dignitaries; Billy had kept them from him. They were so alike and so different. Jordan had treated him with love every time he was in his presence, but Billy convinced him that Jordan didn't want him to live with him, and he believed him.

It wasn't until he had taken Ashton's place in this home again that he realized Jordan had wanted him, too. He had sat in Jordan's room one day going through some of Jordan's personal papers still left in a small file cabinet in the back of his dressing room. Asa was looking for a clue to more money that may have been stashed away. Instead, he found a heated letter from Billy to Jordan, vowing to keep Asa as far away from him as possible. Billy was going to let Jordan keep Ashton, but he wasn't going to allow him to corrupt all of his sons the way he had corrupted him. The letter never said why Jordan was allowed to keep Ashton, but it alluded to an agreement that could not be broken.

Asa had sat in that dressing room and cried, and then his anger had overtaken him. He had walked in his bedroom and saw Jordan's pride and joy, Kali. For some reason, he directed his own anger toward Kali. It didn't make any sense to him then and it didn't make any sense to him now. But, Kali reminded him of the pain he had suffered by not growing up with Jordan, not knowing him the way he wanted to know him. But, she had, and so had Ashton.

The more he thought about it, Asa realized he wasn't angry anymore. There was no one else to push his buttons. Billy was gone. Redd was gone. And as far as he knew, the only man that he had known to share his dislike for his brother was gone. Brady had disappeared with over $800,000. He wasn't surprised. He hadn't really trusted him, but Redd did. Redd had used Brady to contact her son. He had used Brady to blackmail Ruby for her part in Jordan's death. If Jordan had been taking the right medication, his heart wouldn't have given out on him so quickly. It might have been stronger, strong enough for him to survive the shock or to fight back. No one but the four of them knew that that whole rape scene was meant to upset Jordan to death. Billy was tired of waiting for his cut, so was he, and so were Redd and Ruby.

It was funny that Ashton had never considered that Ruby and Redd had become and remained good friends over the years. They had always been a foursome. Micah and Ruby would meet Ashton and Redd. Asa was never invited on couple's nights. He was always expected to find something to do with himself. And he did. He took pictures. One night, he had snuck into the penthouse and set Kali up with a mickey. She had come into the kitchen, warmed some milk, and he had laced it. When she awakened the next morning, she had no clue of the pictures he had taken of her.

He had saved those pictures and cherished them. He didn't know why, but he knew that he was falling for her. He had been surprised by his attraction to her, another reason he had battered her. He was supposed to hate her. She was the reason Ashton had abandoned them. She was the reason Jordan had withdrawn from Ruby. Brady had lost his job because of her. She was always in the center of their conversation. If they talked about Ashton, somebody brought her up, the only woman that Jordan had ever truly cared for. Everybody wanted to know what made her so special that Ashton would be willing to die for her. He wanted to raise his hand. He had the answer.

CHAPTER FIFTY

"**W**HERE DID YOU get that?" Asa strode swiftly across the room where Kali sat combing her hair.

"What?" Kali looked at him with surprise. He almost lost his words as she went back to combing her hair with the bejeweled wide-toothed comb.

"The comb," he tried to calm his voice. He didn't want to alarm her. He had made up his mind that he was going to win her heart for him, not for the Ashton who used to be, but the Ashton now.

"Oh, this is cute isn't it? One of the kids, well, Adam found it at the local general store. They have all kinds of neat things in there. You will see. They bought you something every time they went into the store. Don't tell them I told, but they are planning a big surprise for you tomorrow."

"Can I see it?" he held his hand open. Kali stopped and pulled a few strands out of the comb and handed it to him.

"Do you want one?" she grinned.

"It just looked familiar. Redd used to have one a lot like this," his voice choking against his will.

"My God, Ashton. What's wrong?" Kali jumped up and put her hand to his face. "You look like you are about to cry."

"I can't believe her death has affected me, either." He walked over to the bed, embarrassed by his own reaction.

"Death? What are you saying?" Kali sat next to him. "Is Redd dead?"

"Don't tell me you hadn't heard?" he said sarcastically.

"No," she lied, shaking her head. "I have been roughing it, remember. And we didn't listen to the radio on the way home. We sang, not too well, I might add," she rubbed his back. "She was awfully young. What happened? Where was she?" Kali asked.

"Oh, honey, I'm sorry. Here I am getting choked up over a woman that hated me," he wiped his eyes and squeezed his nose between his eyes.

"No, no. It's okay," she whispered. "You did love her once. You had a life together." Kali kissed him on the cheek.

"Let me run you a hot bath," she stood up. He grabbed her hand.

"They found her body in a river down in Brazil. She had been in a car that was reported to have gone off the side of a mountain."

"Oh, my. Oh, what a horrible death. I'm so sorry for her," Kali knelt in front of him and smoothed his hair away from his face. "Have you contacted her family? I mean is there something they will need help with? Or, is it over already? The funeral?"

"I, I didn't think of that. I wish I had. They had the funeral two days ago. It was a closed casket."

"Did you go?"

"I drove down to funeral home in South Philly, but I couldn't get out of the car," he admitted. He had wanted to see her in that casket, but when the funeral home told him it was going to remain closed, he didn't know what else to do. He went back to his office and tried to destroy all of his phone bills, knowing that if the police wanted to trace them, it wouldn't do any good.

He called Ruby. She said they had nothing to worry about. She said there was no one left to tell anything, that all they had to do was to continue to go on about their lives. When he asked about Lazarus, Ruby had said that there was nothing to worry about there, either. The medical records indicated permanent memory loss. They had laughed at the irony. Ashton would live the rest of his life as someone else in his own company, and in his own home, with his own wife and children without a clue to his real identity. Ruby thought it was karma; Asa thought it was sad and a little part of him regretted it. The only saving grace was that the real Ashton was not dead. After all had been done over the years to make that happen, Asa wasn't sure that he could actually continue to live if the other part of him was really dead.

CHAPTER FIFTY-ONE

"WHAT IS IT that you really, really want out of life, Ashton? You seem to have lost your enthusiasm for the company. You have handed everything, literally, over to Lazarus to run. The way you acted when I first hired him, I am shocked that you trust him so much." Micah sat in the office facing his brother who was leaning back in the chair. The family had been home for a week now, and he was acting happy. Micah couldn't remember Asa ever being that happy before. He was finally living Ashton's life. He had wanted to be Ashton his entire life. Micah watched him sadly. At one time, Asa had been talented and very loving. Their father had changed all of that. He had drummed hatred and jealousy into the malleable heart of a child, and that lust to be someone else had developed into this.

"Don't tell me you no longer trust him, little brother? I gave him the reins because he is good at it. Doesn't mean I like him any better, though," the other Ashton said.

"Is that why you keep Troy nosing around?"

"I don't fully trust him. We still don't know a lot about him."

"Do you feel threatened? If so, why is he still here?" Micah asked, leaning forward as his brother toyed with the ashtray Kacie had made for her father.

"Okay, I don't trust him." He folded his hands. "I just want to make sure somebody is watching him, just in case."

"In case, what? He runs off with the company money?" Micah half chuckled.

"No, my wife," Ashton answered sternly.

"Your wife? Kali doesn't give him the time of day. Where did that come from?"

"Kali doesn't give him the time of day. That's where that comes from," he answered. He wanted to say he wasn't stupid. Everybody thought that of him when he was Asa. But, he could feel the tension and he could see the diverted eyes. And, he had to be ready, just in case the medical records and Ruby were wrong. If his brother's memory ever came back, there would be hell to pay.

"Well, all I am saying is, you need to ask Troy to back off. He will run him off and the company might start sinking again. So, what is it that you want to do? What is it that you have wanted to do all your life?"

"Run this whole town," a big grin widened on the fake Ashton's face. "I want to run for mayor."

"Mayor. Ashton, your company almost tanked. How can you run the city?"

"Like I am running the company now, surround myself with the best."

"So, you think Lazarus is the best?" Micah stood up to leave.

"You are still getting paid, aren't you?" Ashton laughed.

"Well, I will see about throwing your hat in the ring, and go from there," Micah began walking out of the room.

"Are you serious? Just like that. You're going to help me run for mayor?"

"Is that what you want? If it is, we are running out of time to get your paperwork in," Micah smiled at the idea. It made great sense. It would slow down his plan a little, but it would be worth it.

"Let's do it," Ashton jumped from his chair and hugged Micah.

"I love you, man," he said as grateful as a child on Christmas morning. "Micah, I just love you, man."

"I love you, too, big brother. Whatever you want, I will always help you get it."

CHAPTER FIFTY-TWO

"YOU ARE SCARING me," said Ruby, as she paced the floor of her home office. Artie was upstairs in the penthouse as usual. This was the first time she and Micah had spoken in weeks. She had become accustomed to him coming in late at night after she had gone to bed. Sometimes, he would crawl into bed quietly and other nights he would sleep in the guest bedroom.

"It is not my intention to frighten you. All I want is for us to get back what we had. Or, at least what I thought we had."

"But, you are so distant. You won't even look in my direction anymore. And I know you know. You have never even let me explain."

"Ruby, I am here right now. I wanted to just talk. I want to know why. And, I have to know where we stand."

"So you will know whether you will let me raise my own son?" Ruby brushed a tear that had escaped down her brown cheek.

"I would never take Artie away from you. Where would you get that idea?"

"You know where. I know you know. You tell each other everything. Always have."

"I used to think you told me everything," Micah sighed and put his face in his hands. "How did we get here? When did you start feeling so insecure? I loved you," he began to rub his bald head.

"Loved me," Ruby almost choked on the words. "Loved me? Has your love gone somewhere?"

"I don't know. All I know is that my wife has been caught up in a plot to kill my brother, his wife, and his children? How am I supposed to feel?"

"Is that what you think? Is that what Lazarus told you? He is just as warped as he was when he was Ashton!"

"When he was Ashton. You make it sound like people change identities on a regular basis, especially those who were brutally beaten, stabbed, and left for dead. Waking up not knowing who they are, and why they'd been brutalized. How could you stand by and let it happen? I can't fathom it. When I look at you, I don't know you anymore."

"It wasn't like that. I had no part in their plans for murder. The only thing I agreed to was getting our share of the money. They didn't tell me about their plans to take anybody's life. Do you think I would stand by and let them hurt your nieces and nephews? Even her?"

"Her," Micah laughed. "Her? You call Kali, *her*, the woman who proudly says you are her best friend? I have heard her on many occasions talk about you with awe, with love, and respect. And all she is to you is *her*."

"Her, who sleeps with my husband like it's a run to the corner store?" Ruby shouted. "Oh, you didn't think I knew?"

"We had sex," Micah got up and started walking toward Ruby. He reached for her, and she turned away.

"Yeah, sex. I know. Jordan's view, your view, Ashton's view. It's just sex. A release. A biological function, right?"

"You didn't used to have a problem with that." Micah stood in the middle of the floor, watching Ruby pace farther away from him.

"I wasn't married to you, then. I was working for Jordan, remember? Working. I didn't willingly go into the business to have sex with all of you. I didn't have a choice."

"Oh, and Kali did?"

"She had a choice when she slept with you. She was married to Ashton. She wasn't working for Jordan. Jordan has been dead a long time."

"And, apparently, so has our marriage. She and I didn't start having sex until you helped Asa take Ashton's place and you started pulling away from me. Was that why? Yeah, that's why you became so aloof. The guilt was eating away at you, wasn't it?"

"I made him go back." Ruby stopped in front of her desk and leaned on it. "I couldn't believe it when he told me Ashton was dead. They were supposed to kidnap him and get access to the money, and then they would disappear into South America.

"But, that's not how it happened. He said Redd had been injecting Special K, the street version of ketamine, to stay high. Someone in Germany had turned her on to it, and she was shooting it up regularly. He left her alone with Ashton to get some supplies and food; while he was gone she went berserk. And when he told me about it, I was devastated. I made him go back to find Ashton, because he thought he was still breathing when they threw him off the cliff. Asa found him in a little hospital clinic, and he threatened the doctor. He told the doctor that he would either make sure he no longer remembered who he was or the doctor would end up just like Ashton." She could no longer brush away the tears as they poured down her face, streaking her makeup. "So the doctor made sure there was enough damage to cause permanent memory loss, pure retrograde amnesia." Ruby reached for the tissues.

"No, the doctor didn't. He couldn't bring himself to do him any more harm."

"But, his medical records?"

"Were false," Micah answered.

"But, but," Ruby began to stutter.

"Ricky doctored the records to make the report worse. We thought you may have had something to do with it. We couldn't give you the whole record, just in case."

"Just in case?" Ruby wiped her eyes and stared at the mascara and makeup on her fingers, then noticed her own hands were shaking. "Now what?" her voice quivered. She knew Brady was dead. She knew Redd was dead. She couldn't be sure she was under the protection of being Artie's mother. She hated the Sperlings. She had grown up being used by them. Jordan had lured her into his world when she was only 15. She was only trying to get back what they had taken from her.

"Who shot Asa and Kali and why?"

"Asa was having a hard time pulling off being Ashton, no matter how much I coached him. So, we decided to make it look like a head injury. Kali wasn't supposed to be home."

"No, but she and Kacie were supposed to find him." Micah shook his head thinking about the effect it had had on Kacie to find both her parents in a pool of blood, appearing lifeless.

"No, Kacie was supposed to be out with her school and her friends. At least, that's what I thought. No one was supposed," she began to choke, "I was supposed to find him. But, I got stuck in traffic."

"And, Kali almost lost her life. And my niece almost lost her sanity."

"I know it's twisted. But, I couldn't control them."

"All you had to do was tell me what was happening. A lot of people would still be alive."

"Like Scully, the prison guard. Like those men who beat Ashton in prison. Like Kali's cousin who tried to help Ashton with his dirty work in prison. What was his name, Shandie? He died helping Ashton, didn't he? Like Kenny? Like Marcus, her husband? Like Rita, Troy's sister? Like, like," her voice trailed off.

"Ashton didn't kill Marcus and Rita. Nor did he have anything to do with Kenny's death, or Jordan's death or Billy's death. All Ashton did was fall in love with a woman, a woman that made you jealous. Why were you jealous? I loved you. I married you. And, you slept with my father? So don't act as if sleeping with Kali was some deadly betrayal. You pushed me into her arms. You pushed her into mine. All we were seeking was a little comfort from our insane worlds. Nothing, nothing was making any sense.

"I just need to know, Ruby. And, I will leave you alone. I won't take Artie from you. I won't let Lazarus use you to get back at Asa. I will move upstairs. You and Artie can live down here. But, I don't want his relationship with his cousins, or Kali, or Lazarus for that matter to change one bit. I just need to know," Micah pleaded.

"What? What is it that you need to know?" She began to walk toward him.

"Was there ever an inkling of love for me? Or, did you marry me so you could stay connected to the lifestyle you had become accustomed to? Tell me, Ruby, was I the lesser evil?"

"I loved you, Micah. I love you now. It just hurt. After all I had given Jordan, he just walked away. When he died, he left me out of the will. Oh, I know he gave me an old, useless Bentley that you could drive. That was a sordid joke between us that he couldn't let go.

"Yes, I was jealous. And, I let Billy and Asa get to me. And, I am sorry. I am so sorry. I never knew that that alliance would end up with so many lives crushed, our marriage crushed, my life in danger." She gulped as Micah walked toward her with his arms open. She ran into them.

Micah's body was warm and welcoming as they stood in the middle of the floor embracing. She felt his tears against her neck. He ran his hands through her hair. He lifted her face and kissed her. Ruby began to relax in his arms as his hand caressed the back of her neck. As he stepped away from her, she experienced a prick, not unlike a bug bite. She wiped the back of her neck and thought his hand must have been roughened. She didn't know whether he was still getting manicures or not. She no longer knew her husband. He stumbled backwards and plopped into the chair.

"Are you alright?" she asked as she went to the chair behind her desk. She sat down and folded her hands.

"No, Ruby. No, I am not all right. I don't think I will ever be all right again. I gave you my whole heart. I would have gone to hell and back just for you. And, now, I want to wipe all this pain away. I want to forget, the way Lazarus forgot. I don't want to even comprehend how you could have been a part of all this. Ashton, Lazarus, my brother, my best friend, the only constant in my life, loved you, too. What am I supposed to do?"

"I don't know, Micah. I don't know, either. All I know is that I will never, ever betray you again. I swear," Ruby said, and then her eyes widened in surprise. She took one last look into Micah's reddened, tear-laden eyes and her head fell forward. Micah sat there and watched his wife. He knew she would never lift her head again.

CHAPTER FIFTY-THREE

"A BRAIN ANEURYSM? How classic." Troy was blocking Lazarus' way into the office.

"Excuse me," Lazarus waited for Troy to move.

"Who is next?" Troy asked.

"I don't understand what you are getting at, detective. Maybe if you let me into the office, we can discuss it like grown-ups." Lazarus looked at his watch. Troy stepped aside, and Lazarus walked into the suite. He stopped at his assistant's desk and picked up a few folders. Troy followed him. "You were saying?" Lazarus looked at his watch again.

"Ashton doesn't trust you. He thinks you had something to do with Ruby's death."

"I believe there was an autopsy. I also believe it was her husband who was present and not me. I still don't get it."

"I don't get it either, but it's making the hairs on the back of my neck stand at attention." Troy entered Lazarus' office and sat down.

"You have this puppy dog loyalty to Ashton, don't you?" said Lazarus. "Has it always been that way? Oh, no, wait. You were responsible for sending him to prison for something he didn't do. You thought he killed your sister. And, it destroyed him, didn't it? That's why the puppy dog loyalty, huh? I guess that means you don't believe he will ever forgive you?"

"My and Ashton's relationship has nothing to do with the fact that I recognize a killer when I see one."

Lazarus laughed and opened his briefcase. "Cigar?" Lazarus pulled out a couple and tossed one at Troy.

"No, thank you," Troy brushed it away.

"Tell me your story, son. There's a lot going on under that brooding, singular brow of yours."

"What did you say?" Troy sat up and leaned forward. *He knew this man from somewhere, but where,* he thought.

"Nothing. I was just wondering what makes a man like you tick. I wouldn't be surprised if it wasn't a man like you that made me who I am today," Lazarus lit his cigar.

"Meaning?"

"Meaning, it was probably some hot shot detective that threw my chopped up body over a cliff and left me for dead. You think?"

"Not a man like me. I run myself and my shop by the book."

"Yeah," Lazarus put his feet up on the desk. "You belong in one of those black and white cars, don't you? Your whole life is defined by black and white. You are a very predictable man, Troy. I feel sorry for you."

"Well, I am just here to put you on notice. If anything happens to Ashton, I mean, if he breaks a fingernail, I am coming for you," Troy pointed his finger close to Lazarus's face. Lazarus didn't blink or move. Troy stood up and straightened his tie, then stormed out of the door.

CHAPTER FIFTY-FOUR

KALI ROLLED OUT of the bed at the row house. She looked back to see Micah still lying there staring into space. The best she could do for him was to hold his head to her breasts and let him cry. She never asked if he had anything to do with Ruby's death. She didn't want to know. In the mornings, she would hold Artie before he went to camp; in the afternoons, she would hold Micah in a totally different way. In the evenings, she would pass Lazarus in the hallway on the way to their separate rooms. And, she ached every minute of the day for this life to be over.

Kali walked into the office one day and found the three men in her life in a huddle around the conference table. "What's going on?" She noticed fake Ashton's satisfying grin.

"I just threw my hat in the ring. I'm running for mayor," he said proudly.

"You can't be serious?" Kali joined them at the table. She looked directly at Micah. She was afraid to look in Lazarus' direction. Troy had already accused her of having an affair with him. Troy was everywhere these days, annoying the heck out of all of them.

"It's what I have wanted to do since I was a kid," he grinned wider. Kali watched thinking she had never seen him so happy. And, lately, he had been in the best mood about everything. He was even playing with the kids, buying her little presents, and acting as if he were enjoying life. She would smile at him sweetly and thank him for his gift while holding in a silent scream. She hated him; he was enjoying the life he had stolen from his brother.

"You never mentioned that before," Kali said. Micah knocked her knee under the table.

"I was afraid you wouldn't take me seriously. Like you are doing now." He gave her a pouting smile. "But, these guys think I can do it. And, I think I can do it. Especially with you and the kids behind me. Think about it. We'll be back on all the magazine covers and the newspapers, too. Heck, I see *60 Minutes* or *Barbara Walters* in our future."

"I see it, too," said Micah. "We have got a lot of planning to do. Kali, I want you to find out what big venues are available next month. We want to kick this off right with a big fundraiser. I mean, a big venue to hold one of the biggest, if not *the* biggest campaign kick-off this town has ever seen. Money and votes. Money and votes." Micah's lips were smiling, but his eyes were still dark and blank, almost lifeless.

Kali sighed as she acquiesced to the mood in the room, and sighed because she knew Micah had a plan and Lazarus knew exactly what it was. And after everything that had happened, she didn't want any part of it. Ruby was dead. She would never understand why, and she knew they would never tell her why Ruby had to die.

Micah was the first one to leave the office. He had returned to work but moving around in the world, in a ghostly manner. There had never been any doubt that he loved Ruby with all his heart, and he was truly mourning her. Kali watched him leave; his shoulders were not as square and tall as they once had been.

"He is still hurting, Ashton," she said, looking at both of them as they sat across from her. They looked at each other.

"Your brother needs you," Lazarus told his impersonator. "He just needs you to hang out with him. Take him out for a beer or something. Go for a walk."

Ashton rose up from the table and pushed his papers together. "Yeah, you are right. Maybe the game tonight. We haven't been to a football game in a long time." He seemed to pick up momentum, the more he thought about it. He walked past Lazarus on the way out.

"Thanks," he patted Lazarus on the back and then winked at Kali. "I'll be home late tonight. You can get home, okay?" He blew her a kiss.

"Yes, I drove down here anyway." She blew the kiss back.

When the door closed, the tension in the office elevated quickly. Kali sat there staring at her hands she had folded on the table. She could feel the heat of Lazarus' body all the way across the shiny, wide wooden table. "I guess I better get home to the kids," she whispered.

"I guess so," Lazarus whispered back. But, neither of them

moved. "Have you been in the safe room lately," he asked as he pushed away from the table.

"No, it's been awhile," Kali pushed back from the table, too.

"Would you like to visit the safe room?" He held his hand out toward her. She shook her head. Kali stood from the chair and began to walk toward the sofa. The way she moved frightened Lazarus. She moved her legs with great effort. She lifted her feet as if they were weighed down with bricks. Her shoulders were rounded, and she held her stomach.

"What's wrong?" He started toward her, and she jumped away from him nervously. She held up her hands for him to stay away and eased herself onto the sofa.

Lazarus sat on the coffee table in front of her. She pulled her feet up on the sofa, turning away from him. He remembered her lying on another sofa in this same office 13 years ago. She had just been lured back to Philadelphia and had no idea whose Christmas party she had been brought to attend with her new husband. When she had seen him, she had fainted out of fear. This time she wasn't fainting, but she was afraid again.

"Kali," he called her name gently. He reached for her again, and again she recoiled. "What's the matter, Kali?" he touched her anyway. She shivered. "Kali," he called her again and reached for one of her feet. He removed the shoe and began to massage the foot. She tried to kick him with it. But, he held it firmly and then kissed the top of the foot lightly.

"Stop it, Ashton," she said as she began to cry.

"Are you afraid of me, Kali?" he asked and grabbed her other foot. She tried to scoot further in the sofa.

"Should I be? Ruby was. I could see the fear in her eyes when you walked into a room."

"Troy's been talking to you."

"You know he has."

"And, he's making you doubt me," he removed her other shoe.

"You are doing all of this to me." She wiped her tears with the back of her hands and lay flat on the couch.

"I love you, Kali," he kissed the bottom of her foot. It brought her a fleeting moment of pleasure.

"I am not having sex with you," she sniffled. "I am already having sex with your darn brothers." There was no doubt in her mind that he already knew about her and Micah, especially since Ruby's death.

"Kali," his hand began to massage and stroke the calf of one her legs.

"Don't be calling my name," she said as she tried to shift her body out of his reach. "Just leave me alone."

"Kali," he lifted her legs and sat on the sofa, laying them in his lap. "It's really almost over. I promise."

"Will it be over for me the way it was over for Ruby?" she asked.

"You know, little girl, I have never wanted to hurt you. I do everything I can to protect you. But, sometimes, you are still so naïve." He pushed her legs from his lap and stood up. He walked over to the desk, sat down behind it, opened the drawer, and pulled out a cigar.

"Naïve, naïve. I think that's an inaccurate description of me these days," Kali protested.

"No, Kali, you are nothing but naïve. But, it was bad enough that you put that damn Kenny's name in my son's name after he betrayed both of us."

"What are you talking about?"

"I woke up with you introducing to me Adam Kenneth Sperling. Kenneth, after Kenny Blackmon."

"Kenny died because of you," Kali sat up. She couldn't believe her ears.

"Kenny didn't have to. He certainly didn't have to keep lying, keeping me in prison, either. Now did he? But, you couldn't look at it that way. All you saw was poor Kenny."

"Poor manipulated Kenny. You, your father, Asa and, oh my God, Jordan manipulated that man to no end. He did what he did to protect himself."

"He did what he did for money. Kenny was not some innocent bystander and neither was Ruby."

"What do you mean?"

"I mean, it could have just as easily been Ruby raising our children instead of you raising Artie. That's why Ruby's dead. You are alive because the bitch is dead. Is that reason enough?"

"But, Ruby loved me. I loved Ruby."

Lazarus flicked his cigar roughly and then stood up. He stamped it out and walked toward her. "Naïve, I can take. Stupid, I can't. Not from you. Not from the woman Jordan loved. Not from the woman I love. And not from the woman that's going to have to keep this family together when the shit hits the fan. You understand?"

Kali nodded her head, the tears poured faster. She knew she had given Kenny more than one free pass, but it was the only way she could live with herself. She had been living her entire life without a friend, a real friend in the world. Sure, she had Ashton, the kids, Micah, Ricky, and Chico. And, she thought she had had Ruby. But, there were days when Ruby would walk into a room and not even make eye contact with her. She had convinced herself that that was just Ruby, not always the friendliest. But, they had been friends and had enjoyed each other's company. At least, that was what she had wanted to believe. If that's what she could believe, that meant she didn't have to admit how alone she really was.

"Don't fall apart on me now, Kali. You are the strongest woman I know. You have to hang in there just a little bit longer," he stroked her hair and pushed the curl from her face.

"Why me?" she asked as her body hiccupped under the sobs rising in her chest.

"Because. I don't know why you are the one who has landed in the midst of all this. I don't know why I am who I am. Does anybody really know, Kali? All I know is I love you more than I love my own life, more than I love my own children and I love them with every fiber of my body, my mind, my soul. But, I love you. And, for that reason I am going to ask something of you that I could never ask anyone else to do."

"What's that, Ashton?" She choked on his name. She knew he only wanted to be called Lazarus, but she loved calling him by his own name. She loved everything about him, pre-Lazarus and now.

"I want you to mourn me," he whispered. "When I am gone, I want to you to truly mourn me."

"I don't want to hear it," Kali screamed at him. Her whole world was one big tumultuous rage because of him and now he was asking her to mourn him.

"You can't leave me again," she began to weep, burying her face in the corner of the sofa. She heard him moving toward her. She curled up into a ball. Lazarus took one of her feet in his hands and began to massage it again. "Where are you going?" she asked as she wiped her face with her hands.

"I am going to have to leave for awhile. Just for a while."

"What are you planning to do now?"

"Don't ask. Just listen." She felt his tongue on the top of her foot and she tried to pull it away. He put his hands under her waist and flipped her over. He leaned over and kissed her lightly on each eye.

"I never ever wanted to see you hurt again. I pledged my life to keep sorrow out of those beauties that used to shine so brightly every morning that they made the sun jealous. I am so sorry, Kali. I am so sorry. But, I promise you. You will never be hurt by me or my family ever again. I swear," he said as he lifted her head to meet his. He kissed her so deeply she thought the two of them would join forever. She kissed him back, grabbing the big head she had loved to hold onto tightly.

He lifted her up and walked toward the private bath. She buried her head into his neck and closed her eyes. She wanted to remember this. She wanted to remember his smell, his touch, the texture of his hair and his skin. She would never ask where he was going, not now and not before. It was their unwritten rule, and she hated it.

They entered the safe room and he laid her on the bed. She let him wipe her tears with tissues and then undress her one item at a time. She reached for his clothes, but he held her hands and laid them beside her. "Let me," he whispered as he unbuttoned her blouse.

Kali watched him closely as he went about disrobing her with focus and with a gentleness that made her entire body sigh. When she lay before him completely nude, he climbed over her and began to disrobe himself. She saw the thin body of the man who was once buff and bulk, and was enthralled that his muscles were still defined and strong. No matter what he called himself, he was still taking great care of himself. She reached up and let a finger caress the big scar that went down his sternum. She knew the history, but it never ceased to amaze her that he was still walking among them. *A lesser-driven man would have died from these injuries,* she thought. But, Ashton Taylor Sperling was never a lesser man.

His face came to hers again and he began to kiss her lightly all over.

"No more tears, my little wonder woman. You won't ever cry again. If anything, you will make them cry. Understand?"

Kali nodded. She wondered if the talk he was giving her was the same talk he was giving their children. They were changing. They had all changed. And she had seen her husband, her lover take each one and spend time with that child. Then she would see them, his head to their foreheads whispering only audible enough for that child to hear. And, she had seen them mature right before her eyes. He was teaching them to be strong, and he was passing on his gift of strength to her and to them.

That afternoon, Ashton touched every inch of her body with his hands and with his tongue, tasting her and savoring her taste so that he would never forget. She in turn devoured him.

CHAPTER FIFTY-FIVE

THE HUSTLE AND bustle of preparing for the campaign launch was exhaustive. The more Kali tried to stay out of it, the more she was dragged into it. Her fake hubby was becoming more and more dependent on her. She hated him for it, but she smiled sweetly through it all. She watched the kids as he did everything he could to win their hearts, and they too responded the way a loving son or daughter should respond. She hated that, too. They were training their children to be liars.

It was only three days before the launch and she had driven the children out to Jersey. The only good thing that had transpired of late was that Asa wasn't lurking over her and trying to keep up with her every move. She had taken the children horseback riding and now they were all tired and moody. She left them to their own devices and to allow them to entertain themselves.

Kali went for a walk. Fall had taken most of the greenery away, leaving mostly naked trees across the 100-acre spread, but it was still beautiful. She had a couple of hours of daylight left and decided to take advantage. She headed for the corner of the property that touched the river. She had thought about climbing up to the waterfall and thought better of it. She didn't want to do that alone.

Kali reached the river in a little over 15 minutes. Over the years, her stride had quickened as she learned to keep pace with her long-legged husband. He used to tease her about having to slow down for her, and she had teased him back saying she could outrun him anyway. He never asked her what she meant; he would only laugh at her. But, she was teasing him about his age the best way she could without making him self-conscious. There was a 13-year span between them. Kali was in great shape herself, so sometimes she would try to outrun him. No matter how hard she tried though, it still wasn't possible. His age never slowed him down. And, it wasn't until he had gone through that excruciating experience with Asa and Redd that he began to show any age at all. Now, he was graying a bit, and the soft skin around his eyes had developed a couple of lines. It was a wonder he hadn't aged more. But, recently, she had watched him play basketball with the kids, and he was still running circles around them. The only one that was giving him a run for his money was A.J.

She thought about A.J. Her 15-year-old baby was now standing as tall as his father. And, the once light, buoyant child with nothing to think about but crushes on little girls was now serious all the time. He was stepping in and taking charge of his brothers and sisters, and, she noticed, he was keeping Artie close. She was proud of him for that, but it scared her, too. He was the child that spent the most time with his father, the most time in the head-to-head conferences, and the most time in secret rendezvous. Many times when Lazarus was nowhere to be found, A.J. had someplace to be. She wasn't sure if Asa had noticed, but she had.

She wondered if Lazarus had noticed the changes in their children. For instance, Adam was still adventurous, running through the house on occasion and creating havoc among his brothers and sisters; but, he was also taking the pen to paper more. Kali had found some really sinister stories he had written. She sighed as she thought it wasn't like he had no real-life examples to give him those types of thoughts. Artie, who was obviously missing his mother, was still quiet like his father. She wondered if he would ever suspect his father of murdering her. And would he grow up to seek some sort of revenge? The thought frightened her. Her daughters concerned her most, because Katie and Kacie were exhibiting cunning traits of deceit behind endearing eyes and innocent smiles. Something they had learned up close and personal from their own mother.

Kali was excited to hear the water running. She wished that old river could wash all of her worries about her children and husband away. She walked up high over the embankment. She had no intention of going down those slippery rocks to the river until something caught her eye. It looked like a book bag.

"Oh, my God! Which one of my children has been playing down here by the river?" she shouted toward the bag. "Well, Kali, you are not going to know until you look in the bag, now are you?"

She eased her way down the rocks and saw the black bag with a muddied white stripe half buried under more mud. She kneeled down and yanked it free. Instead of a book bag, it was a duffle bag. She shook the mud free and turned it over.

Now don't you feel silly, she thought. It doesn't belong to any of us.

She was about to let it drop when she realized there was still something inside. She unzipped it and reached into the bag. She found a wallet and a black plastic bag. She walked back up to a large rock and sat down. She opened the bag first and pulled out four stacks of money banded and each band had a red bank stamp on it. She counted the first stack and realized there was $5,000 in $100 bills in the stack.

"Whoa," she said loudly and then looked around to see if anyone was nearby. "This is, oh, my God, this is $20,000 by the looks of these other stacks." She stuffed the cash back in the bag. "I wonder if this was a bank job," she began to feel afraid out there alone on the side of the rushing water.

When she opened the wallet, the first thing she saw was a picture of a little white boy with blonde hair and two missing front teeth. She smiled at the picture and pulled it out of the protective plastic. On the back of it read "I Love U, Robby" and then beneath it "7 years old." Kali flipped through the rest and found credit cards and discount cards. She didn't pay attention to the name until she reached the drivers license. The name startled her, she dropped the wallet.

"Brady," she whispered as she stared at the ugly man with the nappy red hair and thick mustache and remembered a conversation with Troy.

"You need to be careful, Kali," Troy had cornered her in the office one day after he had left Ashton's office ."Ashton's worried about how close you and the kids are to this Lazarus character. He doesn't think it's healthy. Neither do I."

"Troy, you can't be serious. Ashton is the reason he's here. Didn't he tell you that?"

"To run the business, Kali. He's ready for him to leave the house. He's even asked him to leave on more than one occasion," Troy had insisted.

"Troy, Micah and I keep telling you that Ashton isn't all there these days," Kali made a twirling motion with her hands over her head. "One day, he loves Lazarus and the next day he dislikes him for some reason or another. Lazarus is not a threat to us. A few months ago, I couldn't say that about Ashton. Why don't you give it a rest?"

"I would. But, I have to agree with Ashton. There's something strange about this Lazarus character. I am not buying the amnesia story. I believe he knows who he is, and whoever he is, I believe he has a grudge against this family," Troy had

leaned close to her face. She turned away from him.

"Kali, too many things have happened that's connected to this family since that man has come around. You need to be careful."

"You are the cop, Troy. I bet you can't find out anything about him. Is that what's making you so paranoid?" Kali tried to walk away. Troy grabbed her arm.

"Redd's dead. Ruby. Brady's missing. Billy was the first to drop."

"Redd has been out of this family for a long time. Ashton divorced her over a decade ago. They hadn't been living together…why are we talking about Redd? And Brady, heck, the last time I heard that name he was testifying against Ashton in a murder trial for murders he didn't commit. And, as I recall, you were the one responsible for him going to prison for those murders," Kali pulled away from Troy and stormed out of the door.

"Kali," Troy called after her.

"Shit, Troy. From where I stand, if Lazarus had something to do with those two, that means he was protecting this family. Your logic is all screwed up," she yelled before slamming the door behind her.

"You and your big mouth, Kali," Kali began to empty the wallet. It had about $100 in cash in it. She stuffed that in the black bag, too, and then pushed the plastic bag into her coat pocket. She looked around for a flat rock, and then made her way back down to the muddy shore. She picked up the duffle bag and threw it into the river. She did everything she could to dismantle the wallet and then sent it flying into the water as far as she could throw. She picked up the flat rock and began to dig. She didn't stop until she had made a slushy hole about a foot deep. She threw the little boy's picture in first. Then she took the rock and beat the credit cards and driver's license to unrecognizable shreds of plastic and dumped them into the hole. She didn't know why she was burying them, but she did.

It was dark when she made it back to the patio outside of the kitchen. "Mom," the children ran to the patio door. "Where have you been?" the chorus of voices demanded.

"I had an incident with the river," she stood outside the door. "Katie, go get mommy a robe." She began to peel out of her muddy clothing and shoes. She knew from the looks on her children's faces that she had frightened them. Kali put on the robe and left her clothes in a pile on the patio. She stuck the bag of money in her robe pocket.

"We can go after I take a shower and get dressed." Kali walked in past the children, but A.J. followed her to the stairs.

"What were you doing by the river?" A.J. asked in a tone that startled her. She turned to look straight into his eyes and, for a moment, stepped back in time. He looked the spitting image of his father the first time she laid eyes on him.

"I went for a walk. I slipped down some rocks. But, I am fine. You didn't alarm anyone, did you?"

"No, mom. No, I didn't. I knew you would be back."

"Good. Let's keep this adventure to ourselves. Okay?"

"Okay. Nobody will say anything. We are good at saying nothing," A.J. answered as he walked away.

They drove back to the penthouse in complete silence. Kali was now drawing the kids into more deception, more complicated webs. She was relieved that none of the men were home when they arrived. She took the bag of money into the study and found a large envelope. She was stuffing the money into the envelope when Asa surprised her.

"Hey, honey, where have you been?" He walked over and hugged her. She let the bag slide to the floor under the desk.

"We went out to Jersey and rode the horses. I guess I let the time slip by us. You need to go out there soon. Nightmare misses you," she patted Ashton on the butt.

"I missed you," he said lifting her up onto the desk.

"Wanna hear my speech? Lazarus has been coaching me all afternoon. It's a hell of a speech."

"Sure, I would love to hear it. Go for it," Kali sat and listened intently. He was right. It was a hell of a speech and he delivered it with such passion she was almost proud of him.

"That was awesome," she said as he finished. "I can't wait to hear the public take that in."

"I can't either," he said, looking at his watch. "I will see you upstairs," he said, leaving the room as zestfully as he came in.

Kali reached under the desk and grabbed the envelope. She sealed it and started sliding into her coat as she ran for the elevator. Kali walked the dark streets of Philadelphia a couple of blocks until she came upon a small church she passed often and had always thought about visiting, but never did. She stuffed the envelope into the mail slot and ran back home.

CHAPTER FIFTY-SIX

"WHAT DO YOU mean you are going away? You have school." Kali was sitting on the edge of A.J.'s bed.

"I won't be gone long, mom. It's a just a few days. I can take my schoolwork with me. I have already asked my teachers."

"You didn't ask me," Kali watched her son continue to pack his clothing. "You are 15 years old. You don't just tell your mother that you have to go away for awhile without any explanation. You can't go anywhere without my permission."

"Mom," A.J. shook his head as he zipped the bag. "I'm not running away from home. I will be back."

"Be back from where?" Kali ran her fingers through her hair.

"Mom," A.J. sat next to her on the bed. "Think of it as camp. I have already told what's-his-face and he's okay with it."

"What's his face?"

"That man in your bed at night," A.J. said sarcastically. Kali slapped him.

"I will not be disrespected by my own son." Kali stood and faced him.

"I meant no disrespect. I know you are only doing what you believe you have to do. And, I am only doing what I believe I have to do, Mom. You have to let me go."

"Is your father going?" she whispered.

"Yes, but he will be a day or two behind me. So, let me go," A.J. countered without the pleading teenage voice that he used to have when he wanted something. He was taking charge and it made her bones creak with worry.

"I don't like this."

"I have to go, Mom."

"Why you?"

"Because, it has to be me."

CHAPTER FIFTY-SEVEN

EVERYONE IN THE house had left except her. She was alone. She was rarely completely alone, but here she was in this 26-room apartment and she was the only living, breathing thing in it. She needed a drink. She made her way down to the study and poured herself a scotch. She had no plans to be anywhere, so it didn't matter if she got tipsy or not. She took a sip from the scotch and tried to get comfortable on the sofa. It wasn't working. She moved to the desk chair, and that wasn't comfortable. She took her drink and headed back up the stairs and then Jordan caught her eye.

"You smug, bastard. You see what legacy you have left behind. Liars, thieves, sex-addicts, power mongers, rapists, murderers. You, sick, bastard," she said as she sat down on the stairs in front of the life-sized portrait of her benefactor.

"You created this mess," she yelled and then drained the glass and frowned as the liquor burned her throat. "And, now. Now we are creating the next generation of little Sperling crazies. I hope you are happy. My baby boy is out there somewhere doing God knows what in the name of protecting his family. Just like you. Just like my Ashton.

"You knew something like this was going to happen. You used to say you didn't like the dynamics between the twins. You should have done something about it.

"Instead, you were busy seducing little girls for your pleasure. Setting us up for destruction by your righteous little boys. I hate you," Kali spewed. She tried to stand up, but the scotch had already taken hold.

"Whoa. I should have poured a smaller glass," she giggled. "Oh, Christ. I am sitting here talking to a painting that that stupid ass Asa painted. That stupid-ass that thinks, now I believe this," she pointed to Jordan, "that thinks he is Ashton. And we call him Ashton, even though we know he's Asa. We are just as screwed up as he is. And, it's all your fucking fault.

"If I had only run when you came into the room that day," she began to cry. "But, where was I to run? I didn't have anybody. I certainly couldn't have run back to that hell house in the Badlands. It was either be raped by you or by that drunken, stinking Doc.

"But, then maybe little Mike would have lived. And, maybe Shandie wouldn't have died in prison. And, maybe my children wouldn't have been born," her voice trailed off as memories began to flood her mind. She shook her head trying to chase them away, but they wouldn't let go of the hold they had just taken.

"Well, well, well. Look what we have here," Jordan was standing in the doorway of her bedroom with a large bouquet of roses. She had just rolled out of bed naked with Ashton. He had introduced her young body to sex and she loved every minute of it. They would climb into bed early and make love to the wee hours of the morning. She was 17 years old, only a month or so from her 18th birthday when Ashton had seduced her and introduced her to Taylor, his nickname for his penis. He was teaching Niecy, her vagina's nickname, how to be horny. And she was horny all day long. All day long, she craved his touch and his dynamic entry into her universe. And then it ended, their depraved little sexually intense universe opened her up for fair game when Jordan walked into that door with that lewd old man's grin on his face.

She had held her urine to the last minute, enjoying being spooned by her knight in shiny armor. She jumped out of the bed and was going to run to the bathroom as the door opened. Grabbing a pillow, she tried to hide her naked body. She was already afraid that Jordan was going to kick her out on the street when he found out she was sleeping with his married grandson, so when he walked into that door her heart sank.

"Oh, don't hide," Jordan walked over to her and tugged on the pillow.

She held the pillow tightly. She was dancing around because she didn't want to urinate on the floor, especially in front of the men; she wanted to retain some dignity.

"Come on, Kali. Let Jordan see," said Ashton as Jordan took a firm grip on the pillow. "He just wants to see you, Kali." She turned to see Ashton lying there naked, dreamily stroking Taylor. "Let him see you so you can go to the bathroom."

Jordan snatched the pillow quickly. Kali tried unsuccessfully to hide herself with her hands. "You are more beautiful than I had imagined. God, you are absolutely... I don't know. I'm speechless. That's how beautiful you are, young lady," Jordan sighed with pleasure. "Go ahead," Jordan smiled at her. "Don't want you to have an accident on the rug. Ashton, get her ready for me. I am going to take a shower.

"Go on," Jordan motioned his head toward the bathroom. Kali had run past him.

Kali was still sitting on the toilet stunned as Ashton sauntered into the bathroom and turned on the shower.

"I think you should probably douche. I know he's not going to want to taste me inside Niecy."

"What are you talking about?" Kali shivered.

"You think I have a taste for pussy. Jordan loves it. He is the one that gave me the love for it. He started me on it at a very young age. I am too embarrassed to tell you how young I was when I ate my first pussy."

Kali covered her mouth as a tear escaped from her eye. She saw Ashton's hand extended toward her. "You have to get up, Kali. I need to go pretty bad myself."

Absentmindedly, Kali stood up. Her mind was trying to process what was going on. "Do you think I am going to have sex with Jordan?" she finally blurted out hoping, she was loud enough to be heard over his loud stream of urine into the toilet bowl.

"Well, give me a second. I'm going to explain that to you," Ashton said as he continued to pee. She was amazed how long it lasted and how much pleasure he seemed to take in the release. He shook his penis and went back to the shower testing the water. He reached back and guided her into the shower. He took the soap and began to bathe her, the way he had done many mornings and evenings before. He stepped out the shower and brought her a disposable douche bottle. "Remember how to use it?" he asked as if it were reminder how to use a turn signal in a car.

She stood there helplessly still shivering and watched him kneel with the bottle in his hand. She felt the cold nozzle as he inserted it inside her and squeezed. The cold liquid mixed with the warm spray of the shower ran down her legs.

He took her by the hand, guided her out of the shower, patted her dry with a thick absorbent towel, and then tossed it aside. He led her to the massage table in his dressing room and lifted her onto it. She heard him pour the oil in his hands. He began to massage her entire body until she was completely oiled down. She lay there shivering.

"I'm not having sex with Jordan," she said, finally shaking away the stunned, frightened feeling.

"Yes, you are," Ashton said as he picked up a comb. "Let's detangle those curls a bit. I know he likes to run his fingers through a woman's head of hair. And, I love to play with your hair so I know he will, too."

"I can't," Kali jerked her head out of his reach and started grabbing clothing. She didn't know where she was going, but she was not going anywhere near that old man to have sex. Ashton grabbed her and pulled her to him. He kissed her

gently on the forehead.

"I didn't want to go into this. But, I guess I just have to tell you like it is, little girl." He held her so tight she thought she was going to lose her breath. She struggled as best she could. "You have already agreed to have sex with Jordan when you agreed to work for him."

"I agreed to no such thing."

"Come on, Kali. You had to know."

"I knew no such thing," she tried to squirm free of his grip, but he was too strong for her. He was scaring her.

"Do as I say do, when I say, how I say, where I say it. No questions asked. When I say jump, I mean jump or else," Ashton whispered into her ear.

"That doesn't mean I agreed to have sex with him," Kali protested.

"It means you agreed to whatever he asks you to do," Ashton blew her wet rogue curl from between her eyes.

"You knew this?" Kali tried to fight loose, but his grip kept her in place.

"Kali, Kali, listen to me," Ashton sighed. "My grandfather is a very dangerous and powerful man. He is the last man on Earth to make angry. If you want to wake up tomorrow, you will go into his room and well, the rest will follow."

"Aren't you going to protect me?" Kali's view of her knight in shiny armor was now tarnished.

"No, sweetheart. I want to wake up tomorrow, too," Ashton kissed her on her cheek. "I can help you though," Ashton whispered. "Listen to me. Your mind is a wonderful thing. It can take you places. Let your mind take you someplace else. Think of someplace you always wanted to go or, better yet, close your eyes and pretend it's me. You like having sex with me, right?" Kali nodded her head. "Pretend he's me. Close your eyes and just let go. Besides, where else are you going to find a lover in this city who can keep you in a penthouse with all these beautiful things and put you through one of the most expensive schools in the country? Think about it, Kali. You really don't have to do anything else, except have sex.

"Besides, if by chance he lets you out of the agreement, he won't let you walk out of that door with anything that he bought you. You would end of walking out of here butt naked, getting raped by the first cop to pick you up. Then, he would drop you off at a homeless shelter where you would get raped by some drugged up stranger at night, or he could send you home to Auntie and Uncle down in the Badlands and your uncle could rape you for free. Just think of Jordan as the lesser of all the other evils. And get, this," Ashton grinned at her. "He won't stop us from seeing each other or having sex. He'll actually encourage it.

"Look, Kali. He's in his '70s. He is not going to want to do it every night. He'll probably be satisfied eating your pussy and spooning you on occasion. I don't think he has that much oomph left in his trunk, if you know what I mean."

"I can't," Kali tried to free herself as Ashton lifted her and walked her through the bedroom to the hallway.

"Make it easy, Kali. Give him backlash and you will regret it. I swear to you every time you piss him off, you will pay for it," Ashton opened the door to Jordan's bedroom. Jordan was standing there in nothing but a white terry robe. Ashton carried her to the bed and laid her down. "She's all yours, Papa. Do you want to me stick around?"

"No," Jordan grinned. "Kali and I need some time alone to get reacquainted. I have been away from home about, what, four weeks now?"

"Yeah, about," Ashton agreed as he winked at Kali. She lay on the bed as stiff as a board.

"She hasn't had a chance yet to tell me about school. Have you registered yet?" Jordan walked over to the bedroom door and shooed Ashton out before he closed it. "So," Jordan opened his robe revealing a nude, thin, older body and then sat down on the bed. "How is school? Do you like it?"

CHAPTER FIFTY-EIGHT

IT WAS IN the air. It hung thick with anticipation. Each morning, when she awakened, her heart was pounding louder and her world had taken own a unique, unclear surreal look. She looked down at the huge, lustful body next to hers one morning and then buried her face desperately in her pillow to muffle the scream she couldn't hold back any longer. She stopped as she realized he was taking her into his arms to comfort her, and she held her breath as he stroked her head, holding it against his massive chest.

If only he knew what she knew, he could easily twist her head and break her neck before he ran. He would run, she thought and they would remain in danger, but he couldn't run if she followed her instincts and trusted Lazarus and Micah. She thought of Ruby fleetingly and sighed. There was no doubt that Lazarus and Molasses were going to handle this, but when? Her heart began to race again.

"What's going on? Are you alright?" Mr. Imposter asked.

"I had a bad dream. I dreamed my children…" her voice trailed off. She couldn't tell that lie. She was afraid for her children, but she had never dreamed or imagined the worse for her children.

"The children are fine," he tried to reassure her. He had long ago abandoned those plans, even before Redd's untimely death. He couldn't bring himself to do that to those young ones who reminded him so much of himself and his brother.

"You are right, you are right. It was just a dream," Kali casually released herself from his grip and got out of the bed. "Busy day ahead of us," she pointed to the clock. "I bet Micah is already at the office."

CHAPTER FIFTY-NINE

KALI BURST INTO the study to get her portfolio. She had left it on the desk the evening before trying to outline how to fund the mayoral campaign even though she didn't quite understand why they were going through the motions. She saw the look of disdain on Asa's face as soon as she walked in the door. Troy was standing in the middle of the floor across from him with his back to the door. She took a deep breath and breezed in anyway, she thought of it as her latest fact-finding mission.

"Have you seen my portfolio?" she asked walking past Troy without speaking. She enjoyed ignoring him. She hated him.

"It was on the floor," Asa answered with a fierce frown on his face as he tapped it on the desk.

"Along with this," Troy said, waving a single stack of money.

"Oh, My God, is that where I lost it?" Kali walked over to Troy and snatched the $5,000 wad from his hand.

"This is yours?" Troy asked suspiciously.

"Yes." Kali stuck it in her portfolio and walked toward the door.

"Wait a second," Troy grabbed her arm. She eyed his hand angrily, but he wouldn't let go. He held her firmly.

"Where did you get this from?" Troy asked.

"My bank," Kali answered. "Am I not supposed to have money?"

"There is a seal on this wrapper. It doesn't belong to any Philly banks." Troy had snatched her portfolio from her hand and was holding the money again in an instant. She pulled her arm free, and then snatched the money back. She looked at the seal.

"That's because the money is from my account in New York, silly. Ashton and I both have accounts there. I don't know about Ashton, but I occasionally withdraw money to give away."

"Give away?" both men said surprised and in unison.

"Yeah, it's fun. I just put a few thousand in the church coffers a week or so ago."

"What church?" Troy barked.

"The one on 19th Street. You know if you walk straight out of this building."

"How much did you give them, Kali?" Asa was chiming in.

"I guess I only gave them 15 since this was still here. I thought the bag felt light, but I didn't have a chance to check."

"So you always give to this church?" Troy was still digging.

"No, I give to different places and people. Whatever hits me," she pried her portfolio out of his hand and then went to the cabinet behind Ashton's desk and pulled out a large brown envelope.

"What are you going to do with that?" Asa asked.

"Give it away. I feel like I cheated the church."

"Did you hand cash to someone at the church?" Troy was still pressing.

"No, that wouldn't be any fun. I stick the envelope in the mail slot. It's an anonymous transaction," she said and strode past both men as determinedly as she could. She grabbed her jacket and headed out of the building toward the church, but changed her mind and took the direction south. She kept walking until she saw a man she had passed a million times sitting on a stack of clothing at the mouth of the subway stop.

"Good morning," she said, stopping in front of him. He looked up at her blankly. "Are you high?" she asked the man. He shook his head. "Are you sure?" she asked, not sure what was making her talk to him that way. Normally she would have been afraid to talk to someone in his condition. She used to marvel at how Ashton would give people like him twenty dollar bills, or check on someone staring off into space to see if they needed a doctor. She had loved him for that. He wasn't afraid to take their hands, or pat them on the back, or acknowledge their presence. She, on the other hand, was like everybody else. She could walk past them and not even think of them until she saw them again. They were there, but not there.

"Do you want to keep living out here like this?" she asked and the man shook his head. "Can you talk?" she didn't know why, but he was making her angry.

"Yes, ma'am."

"Why are you on the street?" She really wanted to know.

"I lost everything, everything," his voice choked.

"Never mind," she said because she didn't want to cry. She pulled the envelope out of her pocket. "Do you read the Bible?" she asked. He nodded. "Have you ever heard the story when Jesus tells the man to take up his bed and rise?" she asked. "God knows, I am the last person to preach. But, here's your opportunity to get your life back." She offered the envelope and the man just looked at it.

"Do you want it or not?" she asked. Cautiously, the man took the envelope as tears poured freely down his face. "Oh, and I would suggest you find a private place to open it. Spend it wisely," she leaned toward him whispering.

Kali walked back towards the Banks Building and, as she turned the corner on 19th Street, she noticed Troy going into the little church. She turned around and hailed a cab. She had to let Lazarus and Molasses know what she had done.

CHAPTER SIXTY

FOREWARNED BY KALI about the money and the tête à tête with Troy, Lazarus didn't know what to expect when he walked into his old office with his brother sitting broodingly behind the desk. He and Micah had discussed all the possibilities at length. For once, Kali's nosiness and pigheadedness had paid off. Neither he nor Micah had left anything in Brady's bag before tossing it over the waterfall, no money, and no ID. So Kali had stumbled onto something big.

Somebody else was supposed to have found that bag. Somehow, somebody else knew that was where Brady had met his untimely death, and was trying to set them up. The wallet had to have been put together after the fact, unless Brady carried two wallets. They had long disposed of Brady's wallet, and had confirmed Brady was dead. His body was now deep in the cavernous underworld beneath the waterfall. They had come back and made sure the body would never surface again.

"Lazarus," Asa hung up the phone. He was in the middle of dialing someone when Lazarus walked into the door.

"Ready to rehearse, or do you feel confident now?" Lazarus asked, taking a seat across from him, then leaned onto the desk.

"Oh, I am confident I can do it, with or without you," Asa said.

"Of course, you can," Lazarus answered, knowing his answer to what to expect was this, the sullen, frightened child-like Asa, though he was no longer child-sized, and no longer harmless. He was a time bomb just waiting to go off. Tick, tick, tick — he could literally see the clock running in the brain of the man who looked like he used to look before the madness had finally set in. And, now, Kali was in the middle of that brain. This giant maniac had fallen for her, and was trying to get hold of her heart, but he would never have it. And, when he realized that, he would surely kill her.

"Troy is watching you, you know?" Asa pushed himself out of the chair and walked up behind Lazarus. Lazarus stood up and turned to him. They still stood eye to eye. His height was not taken from him, only his massive muscular body, only his gorgeous face.

"I was glad when you stopped wearing those silly black contact lenses. Trying to hide who you are," Asa laughed heartily.

"Hide who I am? Who am I?" Lazarus asked, not budging. They were standing so close he could feel his brother's breath as he spoke.

"I am not stupid, Ashton. You and Micah think I am. I am not sure, but I think she knows, too, doesn't she? She knows who you are, just like I know," Asa leaned close enough to kiss him as he spoke.

"Clue me in," Lazarus still didn't move, but he reached down and pushed his chair away from him. He was closed in between the desk and the chair.

"You and Daddy and Jordan always took me for a fool," Asa's eyes were fiery.

"Me. Who am I?"

"Ashton, you think you are so smart. The only thing you are, really are, is the biggest fool that ever lived."

"Why are you calling me you? If I am Ashton, who are you?" Lazarus leaned toward him and their foreheads touched. They leaned into each other.

"I am your biggest nightmare." Asa stepped back and, then, shoved Lazarus who almost lost his balance before he regained it and shoved back.

"Are you on something, son?" Lazarus asked as he watched Asa prepare for another attack and they both lunged. They went crashing to the floor with fists pounding. There was no one to stop them as they completely destroyed the office.

CHAPTER SIXTY-ONE

A.J. BOARDED A small plane and sat next to a man in crisply pressed jeans. "You are wearing his boots," A. J. said as he shook the man's hand.

"He gave them to me, but I plan to return them. He thinks he will not need them anymore. I beg to differ," the man chuckled.

"Then, you agree?" A.J. asked, eager to hear the answer.

"I agree. It's not your father's time to die."

"Thank you," A.J. nodded happily and buckled his seat belt.

CHAPTER SIXTY-TWO

THE TWO MEN fought to exhaustion. Lazarus was the first to lie on his back and refuse to get up. Asa lay next to him on the floor amidst the broken furniture and lamps. They both stared at the ceiling, trying to catch their breath.

"Remember the first time we fought, really fought?" Asa laughed insidiously.

"No, can't say that I remember that," Lazarus answered.

"Give it up. Stop pretending. I don't want to pretend with you anymore. You know and I know who you are."

"Who am I? You have never answered that. You call me Ashton, but I can't be Ashton. You are Ashton," Lazarus said breathlessly.

"You think, you dumb-ass, if you continue to placate me, I will just go quietly into the night?" Asa closed his eyes and let out a whistle. "See what I mean. You are a fool."

"Okay, I will bite. I'm Ashton. Which makes you…his twin brother? The brother that is supposed to be dead? But, you are definitely not dead," Lazarus rubbed his chin. He wondered if his face was as bruised as Asa's. "If you wanted to fight me, you should have thought about that before walking up on stage tomorrow with a bruised and battered face," Lazarus continued to stare at the ceiling.

"You might be right about that," Asa sat up and rubbed his face. "You still throw a good punch, I guess."

"I give what I get," Lazarus chuckled and he didn't know why. Maybe it was because he did remember their first fight. Jordan and Billy had walked in and found them lying on the living room floor just like this. They were eight years old and Asa had broken one of Ashton's toys on purpose. It had been a model plane that had taken him months to finish, and Asa had just said, "Look, Ashton," and then crashed it straight into the floor, demolishing it into a million little pieces.

"Stop treating me like I am stupid, Ashton. I know what you are up to. You think I am going to hurt your family. I'm not going to hurt them. I promise."

"Okay, say I am Ashton. And I am fearful for my family. Why

shouldn't I come out and tell everybody who you are, Asa?"

"Because, if you own up to being Ashton, Troy is going to cart your ass off to jail, for good this time."

"Does Troy know who I am?" Lazarus asked.

"Oh, so he can cart my ass off to prison with you for killing his sister, for killing Kenny? I told you, I am not stupid."

"So, we have a stalemate. You continue to be Ashton and I continue to be Lazarus and life just goes on?" Lazarus asked.

"That's the plan, brother. But, you have to be you somewhere else. Your wife can't have two husbands. Your children can't have two fathers. I guess I understand how you used to feel when I was with Redd while the two of you were married. There is not supposed to be a third wheel, is there? Not even with an old man like Jordan. I bet that used to piss you off when he touched her."

"I lived with it. The same as I lived with you and Redd," Lazarus let go of the charade.

"But, it hurt, didn't it?" Asa sighed.

"Yeah, I tried to convince myself it didn't matter with Kali. But, to have to share both women was a challenge. I took it out on other people. I used my work to justify it."

"I get that. I really get that. I guess your life wasn't the bed of roses that I imagined." Asa sat up on his elbows. "But, the sharing is over. You can still run the company, but you have to move out. Start your own life. Leave her alone. Just by the way she avoids you; I know you have made a play for her. I understand her helping Micah. I am okay with that. But, that's going to end, too. She is a one-man woman and I am one-woman man. She's mine now, so are the children. So is the money."

"So, I am supposed to just roll-over and hand over my life to you?"

"It's best for both of us. We both get to live. You get to be a favorite uncle that comes around about once a month. I get to have the family I always wanted. We both get to live outside of prison walls."

"Sounds like a good plan, but it would never work," Lazarus answered.

"Why wouldn't it? There aren't any other players left other than us and Micah. And, if you tell Micah to keep his mouth shut, he will," Asa looked down at him.

"Troy. Troy won't let it work. He is too suspicious of me now, thanks to you. He is going to keep digging until he finds out who I am. You put him on that trail, remember?"

"Then, we get rid of him, the same way you got rid of Brady, Redd, and Ruby. We kill him." Asa was now leaning over Lazarus looking him in the eyes.

"Brady, is Brady dead?" Lazarus thought it was time to get more information.

"Don't play games with me, Ashton," Asa was almost on top of him.

"First of all, I didn't kill Redd nor did I kill Ruby. But, we both know that they are definitely dead. Now, Brady. Tell me what makes you think he's dead."

"Oh, a little birdie told me he went over the waterfalls. Was given a nice kick over the waterfalls in Jersey," Asa grinned.

"A birdie?" Lazarus was disappointed there was another player out there that he didn't know about. *Who the hell was it,* he thought. Ruby was in Philadelphia when that happened. Who was working with Brady? Whoever it was could have been the person trying to set them up with the extra duffle bag. Somebody had followed Micah with Brady in the trunk of his car.

"It couldn't be Troy. He is still got enough cop in him to want to bring everybody to justice," Lazarus thought out loud.

"God, no. That stupid dick don't know anything except his loyalty to you, to me." Asa rolled back over and lay on his back.

"What about it, Laz? You be your present self, I be you?" Asa lay there waiting for an answer.

"If I am who you say I am, I don't have much choice right now. Do I?"

Lazarus sat up and surveyed the office. "Damn, we have got to do an office makeover quick or both of our covers are going to be blown. There is one thing, Asa. One thing," Lazarus leaned forward on his knees.

"What's that?"

"You have to call off Troy. If he keeps digging, we will be fighting like this in some prison courtyard the rest of our lives."

"Deal," Asa held out his hand and they shook, but Asa wouldn't let go of Lazarus' hand.

"You really don't remember, do you?" Asa asked.

"No, but I knew the moment you guys brought me into this family, that you knew who I was."

"Does she?"

"No. I think she hates me." They both laughed. Asa looked pleased enough to help Lazarus up to his feet.

CHAPTER SIXTY-THREE

KALI WAS STROLLING through the hallway. She had left the girls in the music room; Kacie was playing the piano better and better every day. Katie was lying on the sofa reading a book while her sister practiced a classical piece. Artie and Adam were somewhere in the house. She hadn't heard from them in a couple of hours. As she approached A.J.'s room, she saw a light come on. She rushed through the door to find her son staring down at the bag he had just thrown onto his bed.

"Mom," he turned to her and she ran into his arms. He was taller than she was now; his muscles were developing to the point that they would catch young women's attention, even old ones she thought. He was 15 with a voice that now projected consistently in a deep bass. She smiled as she stepped away from him.

"You are home," she reached up and gently touched the face that now mirrored Ashton's almost exactly. He took her hand and kissed it.

"Of course, I am home. Where else would I be?" he teased.

"Stop," she playfully scolded him. She had been worried. He had been gone for two whole weeks.

"You went without him," she said.

"Without who, Mom?"

"Now, don't be disrespectful. You told me Lazarus was going with you."

"He stopped in." A.J. began to unpack his clothing. He pulled out a small bag and handed it to her.

"What's this?" Kali dumped the bag on the bed and several pieces of turquoise jewelry fell onto it.

"You get to choose first, then Katie, then Kacie. I bought the boys and him something, too."

"Where were you?"

"At camp in the southwest," he smiled.

"You went to see Ray and Bobby?" She smiled back. If only he had told her that in the first place, she wouldn't have worried so.

"No, Mom. I didn't see either of them. And, please. Don't ask any more questions. I am home."

"You were in man-of-the-house training?" Kali sat on his bed and started folding the clothes that he had balled and shoved into his bag.

"Mom," he took her hands. "Most of these need to go into the laundry. Let them be."

"You packed dirty with clean? I didn't teach you that," she admonished.

"Okay, they are now all dirty. I will put them all in the hamper. Did you pick out your piece?"

Kali picked up the pieces of jewelry and examined each one. She took a simple necklace and put it around her neck.

"I knew you would pick that one. I thought of you when I chose it."

"Thank you. Have you talked to Lazarus and Micah yet?"

"No, I just got in from the airport. And, I am tired Mom," A.J. pulled her up from the bed and escorted her to his door.

"It's like that, huh?" She didn't like being dismissed by a teenager.

"Yes, Mom, scoot." He eased her out of the door and closed it.

Kali's first instinct was to force her way back into the room and demand some answers. But, he was behaving like his father used to behave when he was out on a job, as he would call it, when he had a special client. Everything was a secret. Even the contracts that spelled out the payment arrangements were vague and useless to her. She never knew what they were talking about; she just knew it was something that neither PDSI nor their clients wanted known.

CHAPTER SIXTY-FOUR

S HE WRAPPED HER arms around herself and headed down the stairs. It was time she had a talk with Adam to see where his head was these days. As she began to pass the study for the rec room, she heard voices. She doubled back and opened the door to find Troy sitting across from Asa.

Troy wasn't looking too happy. "I'm totally confused," he was saying. "What is precipitating this sudden change? Has he threatened you?"

"Has who threatened who?" Kali walked in and joined Asa at his side. "What's going on?"

"Ashton seems to think I am on the wrong trail. And, that he's been wrong about a few things."

"What things?" she asked.

"All I am saying is that I have gotten to know Lazarus over the last few days a lot better. He's helping me in ways I never would have imagined. He is my friend," Asa stated.

"Who gave you the shiner?" Troy pointed to the bruise beneath Asa's right eye.

"We were jumped out back. We gave as good as we got." He touched the tender flesh beneath his eye and winced.

"Who's we?" Troy leaned forward.

"Lazarus and I," Ashton answered hesitantly. "Now, Troy. Don't jump to any crazy conclusions. We are both pretty scarred up, but we weren't fighting each other."

"Did you report it?"

"Why would we report it?"

"Because some assailants are running around beating people up?"

"Trust me, we took care of it. So, we don't need you to fix it. Troy, all I am asking is that you let things go this time. The last time you held onto something of this type, I ended up serving a life sentence for something I didn't do," Asa banged the desk angrily.

"All right. All right, if you feel that strongly about it, I will let it go. I still think you should find out who this character really is. I don't like him. I don't like him at all," Troy looked from Ashton to Kali as if he were looking for her support.

"Don't look at me. This is between you and Ashton." Kali began to walk away, but Asa grabbed her hand. She went back to him and put her arm around his shoulder.

"See, if Kali thought there was a threat, she would be standing here trying to talk me out of it. Wouldn't you?" fake Ashton looked up at her.

"You know I would. Troy, you know I don't know how to keep my mouth shut," Kali smiled.

"Okay, that's up to you. But, when one of my feelers come back, I will let you know if there is anything to be concerned about."

"Let it go, Troy. Tell your people out there to drop it."

"It's too late for all that, but I won't pursue anything further. That's all I can tell you," Troy rose up and gave Kali his once over like he always did.

She turned her head defiantly and then shoved Ashton's chair back a bit and climbed into his lap. That made him grin widely at Troy. They both sat quietly as Troy left the room.

"I don't think I trust that bastard," he whispered.

"I never have," Kali whispered back and kissed him deeply.

CHAPTER SIXTY-FIVE

THE NEXT MORNING, Kali woke up to find him staring at himself in the mirror. The bruise beneath his eye had darkened.

"Makeup," she said. "Makeup does wonders. I can put it on you."

"I know, I was just thinking."

"About what?" She slipped into a robe and walked up behind putting her arms around him.

"About Troy," he turned to her and kissed her. "I'm afraid I may have only alarmed him and put him hotter on the trail. I need to talk to Lazarus."

"Okay," she stepped back and watched him hurry out of the room. As soon as the door closed, it opened again. She thought he had forgotten something. But, it was A.J. who hurried in.

"Mom, I need to talk to you." He grabbed her hand and began to lead her out of the room.

"Where are we going?"

"To my room," he said as he almost dragged her down the hallway and then closed the door as he led her into his room.

"What's so urgent that you almost pulled my arm off?" Kali shook her hand loose.

"I need you to do some things for me, today."

"Some things?"

"Yes, some things. Mom, Mom. Mom, can you sit down and listen, Mom? Really listen. It's really, really important. To all of us."

Kali didn't like the tone of A.J.'s voice. He was giving her an order, and his eyes narrowed to let her know that he was serious.

"What is this all about?" she insisted.

"First thing, Mom. You are not to ask any questions.

"Who the hell do you think you are?" asked Kali as she fought the urge to slap her son.

"Your son, and the only man in this house that has the power to protect you, right now. You have to listen to me. You can't change midstream. You have to do exactly what I tell you to do," A.J. came back at her in a low, hoarse whisper that frightened her. She had never seen that side of him before. She didn't like it.

"You don't tell me to do anything. You can ask, but you don't command."

"Mom, listen to me. Listen. Shut the fuck up for five minutes and listen. We don't have all day." He took his mother by her arms and forced her to sit on the bed. He kneeled down in front of her and brought his head close to hers.

"I love you, Mom. And I would die before I let you die. So, you have to listen to me, now. Cut the mom and son crap, the adult and child crap, and fucking listen," he leaned his forehead against hers. He had her attention. She was shaking and he hated frightening his mother, but she had to listen.

"You need to make yourself scarce today. Don't answer your mobile. Stay out of the office, get out of the penthouse, go shopping or something. Take the kids with you. About four o'clock, drop the kids off at the row house. Ms. Elliott is staying there. Tell them their father decided that he wants them to attend the next campaign fundraiser.

"After that you leave the house, promptly," he added and took a breath, "come home and get dressed and make like you are the happiest woman on planet Earth. Help build the excitement for tonight. Stick close to him; don't let him detour from tonight's agenda. Make him practice his speech or something.

"Mom, this is something I need to you to do. Swear to me, Mom, that you will do it."

"Do what?" Kali gulped.

"Once you get on stage there will be strips of tape on the floor. All but three will be blue strips. You will stand on the strip that is crossed like a T. Like a T, Mom. You take your place on that tape and don't you dare move. Not even if the world collapses around you. You stay on that tape."

"And, where will you be?"

"I will be with the other kids at the row house. I will be joining them just a little late. I have a date," he smiled. "Plus, I have already made it known that I think Dad's running for mayor is a dumb idea. I have protested and made it known I want no part of it."

"I don't believe you."

"That I think it's a dumb idea for a man who runs a clandestine company filled with fucking covert operations should run for mayor?"

"No, that your profanity-laden mouth will be at the row house with the other kids. Who taught you how to curse like that?"

A.J. smiled and kissed his mother's forehead. "My father."

CHAPTER SIXTY-SIX

KALI WALKED INTO the study about five o'clock, loaded with shopping bags. She was surprised to find Micah standing in middle of the floor with a cigar and a big grin. Lazarus was sitting behind the desk and Asa was stretched out on the couch. They all looked like they had just gotten caught with their hands in the cookie jar.

"Where the hell have you been?" Asa got up quickly and started helping her with the bags.

"Looks obvious to me," Micah took a few.

"How did you get all these things in here?" Asa started opening the bags to take a peek.

"Off! I decided I wanted to wear something special and, boy, was it hard to find." Kali stood on her tiptoes and kissed him on his cheek. He looked straight at Lazarus who nodded his head. Asa returned the nod.

"Have you eaten yet?" Asa was being extremely solicitous. Kali was rewarding him with hugs, pecks, and touches. Lazarus and Micah watched closely as Asa almost floated out of the room with her to get ready.

"You need to go freshen up your makeup," Micah smiled at Lazarus, touching his chin. "I still wish I could have been there."

"Ha, Ha. What do you know?" Lazarus tried to blow a smoke ring and choked.

"I know we suddenly have new furniture throughout the entire suite. I am surprised Kali didn't come in today and see it."

"A.J. took care of that," Lazarus laughed to calm his nerves. He was having a hard time staying put anywhere today. He stood up, put out the cigar, stuck his hands in his pockets, and looked at all the books on the wall.

"Micah," Lazarus said softly. "No matter what happens tonight, I want you to know that I love you, little brother. Outside of Jordan, I have never loved anybody more."

"I love you, too, Ashton. It doesn't matter if you call yourself Lazarus or Ashton. I love you, too," Micah looked away and swallowed hard. "I don't think she would like to know that you love me better than her," Micah giggled and wiped away a tear.

"Oh, I love her with my entire being, just not the way I love you, though. It's a whole 'nother type of love," Lazarus walked over to Micah and the two of them hugged each other for a long time.

"I'm going to run down to the house a minute and hug my children," Lazarus walked out of the study leaving Micah standing in the middle of the floor. Tears ran down his face. He wiped them away and took a deep breath. It was time to get dressed.

CHAPTER SIXTY-SEVEN

"THE THEATER IS packed. How did you get so many people to come out?" Kali was standing behind the curtain with fake Ashton's hand on her butt. He had insisted on a quickie in the shower before they dressed. She could still feel him between her legs and wondered if that would be the last time she would feel him like that. She looked back at him and smiled.

"The people are ready for a change, son," he grinned down at her.

"All I can say is, knock 'em dead." She looked out on the stage and saw the three blue markers. Two were in the slanted shape of an X and one was definitely a T. She concentrated on the T. The stage man signaled them to take their places, the loving supportive family. Lazarus stood on a blue marker and Micah stood on one.

Kali took her place on the T as a popular radio announcer began to give the audience a bit of Sperling history in Philadelphia: nothing about the lineage of prostitution and hired murderers, just all about their wealth, their accomplishments, and contributions (minus the ones under the table) to the city and its community. Son of Billy Sperling, a successful Philadelphia attorney, and grandson of Jordan Banks, an acclaimed jazz musician with countless awards, degrees from Columbia and Penn, and the long list of kudos were announced one by one before the Ashton look-alike took the podium and brought the crowd to its feet on at least five occasions. He was in his element.

Kali was overwhelmed by how well he was received. It made her feel sad. This was where he had belonged. If only Billy had just let him grow up without feeding him hate and jealousy to throw him off track. She thought about A.J. and wondered what it was that Lazarus had been feeding him. A.J. had changed so dramatically; it was frightening.

Ashton finished the speech and the crowd went wild. He turned to Kali first. He lifted her off the tape and gave her a big kiss on the lips. He put her back down and got a big hug from Micah. Kali noticed Lazarus smiling with tears in his eyes. He touched his brother's elbow, and the two men fell into each other's arms and hugged tightly. Kali had to swipe a tear from her face. She had remembered the story that

Jordan loved to tell about how the twins had tried to come out of their mother's womb together. He said the doctor thought they were hugging each other. The midwife had to keep massaging their mother's belly to get them to separate.

Lazarus grabbed Asa's head and began to whisper something in his ear, something that made Asa's eyes light up even brighter. And then it happened. Kali wasn't sure she had seen it at first, but when she found herself suddenly sprayed in blood she had no choice. Asa's face had exploded. She started to scream, but stayed frozen to the tape.

"Even if your world collapses around you, stay on the tape," her son had told her, but it hadn't mattered, she couldn't move, the way she couldn't move when she had heard her parents' last argument, when she had heard her father prime the shotgun to seal her mother's fate. She could have easily been toppled over like a defeated chess piece.

As her mind tried to digest this scene full of blood spewing forward, Kali jumped as another shot hit his head. She watched as Asa's body toppled forward still wrapped in Lazarus's arms. Kali watched as the giant was almost lifted off the ground with the second shot, but she couldn't tell if the second had gotten Lazarus because his head was covered in blood. All she knew was that when they went down, they went down hard and Lazarus's head met the concrete stage floor. Her legs finally let go, but as she lunged forward to get to the twins, someone grabbed her around the waist and dragged her backstage.

She was screaming "Ashton" at the top of her lungs, seeing him lying underneath Asa covered in blood. She didn't know the plan, she didn't really care, she didn't like the way it looked. She saw Micah crawl over the bodies covering their heads with his body as bodyguards ran to the stage, along with medics. People were screaming and stampeding out of the theater. No one knew where the bullets came from. Kali got away from the bodyguard who had grabbed her and tried to crawl out on the stage. She was met by Micah who had been shoved aside by the medics. She sat up and grabbed him.

"Tell me they are not dead!"

CHAPTER SIXTY-EIGHT

KALI AWAKENED IN a hospital bed. The room was darkened and someone was standing next to her. She was afraid to open her eyes all the way, she was afraid to completely awaken. She didn't want to know if it was her Ashton that died on the stage that night. And, she wasn't totally happy that Asa was dead. She had wanted that, but she had never imagined it happening that way. She began to moan weakly.

"Mom, Mom," A.J. said as he held her hand and began to stroke her head. "It's okay, Mom. You are safe."

"Did they both die?" she wailed through the question.

A.J. leaned close to her ear and whispered. "Daddy's in a coma. His head again. He went down pretty hard. Asa's gone. He died with the first shot."

Kali tried to sit up. A. J. held her down.

"You are in shock, Mom. You can't get up."

"I have to go see him," she began to struggle with A.J. who was determined not to let her out of bed.

"Let her go," Micah walked into the room. Troy was close behind him. "Kali, you have to be calm. The kids are out in the waiting room. They can't see you lose control." Micah sat on the bed and she crawled into his lap. She felt A.J. trying to cover her up. At that moment she realized she had on a hospital gown.

"Get another one and let's put it on her backwards," Micah said as he bunched up the sheets.

"Kali," Troy approached the bed respectfully.

"I am so sorry about Ashton. So sorry. You know how I felt about him. And, I swear to you that the son-of-a-bitch is going to pay for this," Troy's voice was slow and determined.

"You know who did this?" Kali asked weakly.

"I don't know who pulled the trigger, but I'd bet my life on who arranged it," Troy answered confidently.

"Really, who would that be?" Micah stroked Kali's head waiting for an answer.

"Lazarus. He's been trying to become Ashton from the first day he walked through that door. Micah, you of all people need to be suspicious. I say he even had something to do with Ruby's death. I don't know how, but my gut tells me he is the source of your pain, Kali. And, I'm going to bring him to justice if it's the last thing I do on this earth," Troy tried to take her hand and she pulled away burying her head into Micah's neck.

"Troy, this is not the time. Plus, if you didn't notice, Lazarus was on that stage and is still not out of the woods. Your boys are telling me there were two shots from two different directions. Sounds like more than one person was the target. If anything, you better start looking for those boys that jumped the two of them in the street yesterday. That's where I would fucking start, if I were a fucking cop. A fucking decent cop who followed facts, instead of his gut. Aren't you tired of sending innocent people to jail? Get out." Micah stood up and almost lost Kali out of the bed. He turned to catch her and put her back under the cover.

"Out, Troy. Just get out," Micah climbed up on the bed and lay beside Kali who was crying and wailing loudly.

CHAPTER SIXTY-NINE

KALI FIGURED SHE had been drugged. This time, she awakened to find all of her children surrounding her, each one of them with reddened eyes.

"Kacie," Kali reached out for her. "I'm okay. Mommy's okay."

"We know, Mommy." Kacie climbed up on the bed and kissed her. Each one of the children followed suit. A.J. hung back and let them.

"Can I get a kiss from you, too?" she waved to A.J. He obliged by walking over and kissing her.

"I was giving everybody else a chance. I have been with you since you got here." He smoothed her curl away from her face.

"How is he?"

"He is still in a coma. But, he's stable, they say. He didn't lose any blood. He didn't get shot. Just, you know. Anyway, I brought you some clothes, if you want to take a walk to see him. We have all been down there already."

"Okay," Kali nodded her head as Katie produced a small tote bag. She looked inside to find toiletries as well as clothes. "Thank you, baby."

"We will see you there, mom. Unless, you need help," Katie offered.

"I'm okay. Where is he?"

Déjà vu, Kali thought as she entered the intensive care unit. Each room was partitioned with large glass panes so that the nurses and the doctors could easily see the patients from a large centralized desk. Everyone was quiet, but constantly moving. It gave her the creeps that he was still on this unit. She entered the room where he lay with his eyes closed, an oxygen tube in his nose, and all sorts of sensors stuck to his body with wires flowing somewhere. Then, there was the drip to keep him hydrated and fed.

She eased over to the bed and took his hand in hers. She leaned forward and smoothed back his hair, which was moist with perspiration, and she wondered if he were working out in his dreams. How many times had she seen that sweat on his forehead after an exhilarating workout in the gym? He loved those workouts, whether he was Ashton or Lazarus. He was proud of his body and he took great care of it. She kissed his forehead first and then his hand.

"Ashton," she whispered, "wake up." She waited for him to respond, but he only continued to breathe rhythmically. She heard the almost silent swish of the oxygen and she gasped. *It's just a precaution,* she thought. He didn't need it, right, the oxygen? She looked around to see if there was someone she could ask and saw Troy standing there watching her. Her heart sank. She needed to get her husband to wake up, but not under the watchful eye of Troy. The last thing she wanted to do was to feed his suspicions. She put Ashton's hand down by his side and stood up straight.

"You have got to wake up," she pleaded in a low whisper once again. She heard the door open and knew Troy was coming up behind her.

"Any change?" she heard Troy ask.

"Well, I wouldn't know. This is the first time I have seen him since the shooting and I haven't talked to anyone yet. I was just about to go out to the nurses' station to ask."

"He looks peaceful," Troy touched her shoulder. She withdrew from his touch.

"Kali, I wish there was something I could say, something I could do to keep you from having to go through this. Ashton would want me to help you. Let me help you. What can I do? I know you have been in the hospital the last two days, is there anything I can do to help with arrangements?"

"Ashton had already made his arrangements. Just like I have. Just like Micah. The resting place, the funeral home, the obituary, everything. We knew with our lifestyles and our business that life is fleeting, too fleeting, so we were prepared for everything except the date and time. Micah has taken care of the phone calls already. The funeral is day after tomorrow."

"Would you like me to be a pallbearer?" Troy lowered his head and looked away as he asked.

"No, that won't be necessary. We already have six people."

"Who?" Troy was obviously a little hurt.

"His sons, his nephew and his brothers," Kali answered, wanting him to leave.

"Well, if you need me to do anything, Kali. He was my best friend. I would like to say a few words at his funeral, if you don't mind."

"Three minutes. After his brothers and the children, then we lay him in the grave. Now, can you leave me please? I need to talk to Lazarus a while."

"I don't understand. I am seriously at a loss. You know, I believe this man is in the midst of your troubles, including Ashton's death. You know I don't trust him. And, I have been a friend of this family since long before you. Ashton and I were roommates in college. I was there when he married Redd. He trusted me. Why don't you? Why are you hovering over this stranger, someone who can't even tell you who he is or where he came from? Why is everybody so intent on me not finding out? You would think, at least, he would want to know," Troy's voice began to raise a few octaves and caught a nurse's attention. She came bursting into the room.

"If you plan to visit, you must keep it down, or I will have to ask you to leave, detective or not. You shouldn't be here in the first place," the nurse stormed back out of the room. Kali pushed her way past Troy and followed her. She wanted to find out about her husband's condition. When she returned, Troy was leaning against the door.

"You didn't answer my question, why do you put your trust in him and not in me? Why are you here holding his hand when you should be home comforting your children, your family?"

"I can answer that, Uncle Troy," A.J. emphasized the word "uncle." He wiggled two fingers signaling Troy to follow him out of the room. He could see that his mother was about to crumble. She was torn, she needed to be with her Ashton, the man she loved with all her heart, but she was under this man's microscope.

Troy walked out of the room and A.J. began to walk out of the unit. Troy was impressed at how tall A.J. had gotten and how mature he had been acting since the assassination.

"My mother is under a lot of pressure, Uncle Troy, can't you tell? Or, what is it that you don't understand?" A.J. looked Troy directly in the eyes. They were the same height now.

"Listen, son. I'm only trying to protect you, your mother, and your family. That's exactly what your father would want me to do." Troy was annoyed that this teenager, whom he had known since he was in diapers, had stepped into his face with an attitude.

"Uncle Troy, nobody, including my father, has really trusted you since you railroaded him to prison back in the '80s. Yes, he forgave you, kept you around as a friend, but trusted you? No, we don't trust you. You are a rigid, little-minded policeman who could turn on any of us as quickly as you turned on your best friend back then. That's why my mother doesn't like you. At least, she is honest.

"As for Uncle Lazarus, he has never said, not one time since I have known him, 'trust me.' You know why? Because he just did everything we needed him to do to trust him. He protected us. He played with us. He taught us how to be happy when our father was miserable and taking it out on us. He had my father's respect. He has our respect. And, we are not going to let you take your guilt trip out on him," A.J. stepped inside Troy's space and Troy had to restrain himself from shoving him.

"I think you had better back down, son." Troy had been surprised by A.J.'s intensity.

"Calm down, boys," a hand slapped A.J.'s shoulder. He turned to see Ray standing next to him. Bobby was standing close behind.

"Uncle Ray," A.J.'s voice choked for the first time when he looked into the man's eyes. Ray pulled him into his arms and stroked his head.

"Do I know you?" Troy asked, stunned by the stranger's presence and A.J.'s reaction.

"No, but we may have spoken. I am Sheriff Ray Rivera from Colorado. If I heard right, you are Troy." the Sheriff let go of A.J. and held him by the shoulders.

"Everything is going to be all right, A.J. You are going to make your father proud. I know being the head of the family now is a big responsibility. But, I think you are going to have to ease into it a little. Calm this down," Ray touched his mouth, "a little bit. It's okay to be angry. You have lost so much in your young life, but anger will eat you alive. Calm down. Don't look at Troy as your enemy. He has valid questions. He cares about you."

"That's what I keep trying to tell him, and Mrs. Sperling," Troy looked relieved that someone understood.

"Look, the boy is under pressure. More than likely so is Mrs.

Sperling. She had come to depend a great deal on Lazarus. I believe he was responsible for bringing order and peace to their household. As he did with mine," Ray reached back and pulled Bobby forward.

"This is my grandson. He was a terror before Lazarus moved in. I share the Sperlings' admiration and respect for that man. And like A.J., I want to protect him as well. So ask away, Detective. I'm sure the only thing you are going to dig up is a man that really, really cares about people. And, a man who can be trusted." Ray walked away with Bobby and A.J. on his heels.

CHAPTER SEVENTY

KALI WALKED OUT of the room and hugged Ray tightly. "Only two at a time. A.J. and I will go the waiting room. You and Bobby go ahead," she looked back and watched Bobby almost run into the room. Bobby kissed Lazarus and, then, sat on the bed. He pulled out a worn copy of a *Star Trek* novel.

Ray stood beside the bed and placed his hand on Lazarus's heart. He said a prayer while Bobby read an excerpt from a scene with Mr. Spock and Captain Kirk. The scene was almost comical so both he and Ray laughed as he tried to read through it.

Kali turned and grabbed A.J.'s hand as they went into the waiting room. There she was greeted by the rest of her children, all with worried looks on their faces. They huddled into one big, group hug. She looked over Adam's shoulder and saw Troy still lurking around nearby. Kali closed her eyes and pretended he was no longer there. She was going to get her husband back and she would fight Troy to the death to do it.

The day passed quickly as each one of the children visited Lazarus with Bobby sitting on the bed still reading. Kali went back in and whispered, "I love you, Ashton."

"No, Mrs. Sperling," Bobby chided. "Don't call him that."

"I know, Bobby," she smiled at the eager teenager who had taken control of the room.

"No, you don't know. He's not Ashton anymore. He's Lazarus. You have to call him Lazarus," Bobby opened his book again and started reading some more.

"His heart," he stopped reading. "Touch his heart. Like this," Bobby placed his hand on Lazarus' heart.

Kali followed his direction and placed her hand gently on his heart. She leaned forward and whispered, "I love you, Lazarus."

"Yeah, Lazarus. You have to remember, he is Lazarus now."

"Okay," Kali could feel the steady beat of Lazarus' heart beneath her hand. She started singing to the beat of a song she hadn't sung since she was in the church choir as a child. *"Amazing Grace how sweet the sound that saved a wretch like me,"* her voice was sweet and sultry.

"He likes that," Bobby pointed to the face of his sleeping friend. "He smiled."

"Did he?" Kali touched his face gently.

"Yeah, didn't you see it?" Bobby shifted off the bed. "Keep singing."

"I once was lost, but now I am found. Was blind, but now I see," she quickly covered her mouth and a tear rolled freely down her cheek. She saw the smile.

"Thank you, Bobby," she grinned, hoping Lazarus would open his eyes next. There was a knock on the door. They both turned to see Micah standing in the doorway.

"I'm sorry. Only two I am told. Can I visit?" Micah looked drained. Kali went to him and hugged him.

"Is everything okay?" she asked.

"Yeah, so far no clues to the murderers, but life otherwise is going on. Did I hear you singing?"

"Yes, I will sing some more when I come back. Bobby's riding shotgun," she smiled. "I will let you visit with him, too."

Kali let herself out of the room and saw Micah kiss Lazarus on the forehead.

"Hand on the heart," Bobby took Micah's hand and placed it on Lazarus's heart.

Micah leaned over with his hand in place, "Good morning, Lazarus. Everything has been done. It's all up to you now. We can't take the rest of the steps without you. So get up and get moving," Micah said.

"You think he will listen to me, his little brother?" he asked, looking at Bobby whose eyes suddenly widened.

"I think he did," Bobby answered.

Micah looked down to see the weary hazel eyes looking up at him. Lazarus smiled.

"Hey, you. It's about time you woke up from your nap. I knew you were tired, but damn," Micah teased.

"What?" Lazarus looked at Micah and then at Bobby.

"Hi, Uncle Lazarus," Bobby greeted him with a hug and a kiss. "Second time."

"Bobby," Lazarus' voice was hoarse. He reached up and pushed the boy's hair away from his face. "Where am I?"

"You are in Philadelphia, in a hospital. Listening to the latest edition of a *Star Trek* novel."

"Were you singing?" Lazarus was still focusing on Bobby.

"No, you have heard me sing. I don't sing that pretty," Bobby took his hand and squeezed it.

"Aren't you going to introduce me?" Lazarus's eyes darted toward Micah.

"Sure, sure, Uncle Lazarus, this is Micah Sperling. He's a very close friend of yours."

"You know who I am?" Lazarus asked Micah earnestly.

"Yes," Micah answered with a smile and took Lazarus' other hand. "You are Lazarus Smith, a very dear, dear friend. You have a really, big group of friends out there in the waiting area. They can't wait to see you."

Lazarus looked from Bobby to Micah and back to Bobby. "I guess I am having another brain fart, 'cause I don't remember this guy," Lazarus looked at his hand as Micah was now squeezing it.

"One of these days, I will have to tell you about this head of yours. It's harder than any granite found on planet Earth. It has survived blows that would have surely killed an elephant. It's quite all right if you don't remember me, I remember you," Micah couldn't resist hugging him again.

"I will take your word for it," Lazarus grinned as a nurse came in and chased both Bobby and Micah out of the room.

Micah and Bobby entered the waiting room to find Kali in the middle of a family huddle. They were sitting on the floor. Each child and Ray was touching her somehow. Bobby crawled to them immediately and reached into the circle to touch her, too. Micah walked over and palmed her head. She looked up at him and saw the biggest grin she had ever seen on Micah.

"Lazarus has risen," he began to laugh hard at his own joke and was almost knocked from his feet by the children.

CHAPTER SEVENTY-ONE

THREE MONTHS LATER

"I HATE THIS," Kali walked into their old bedroom in the row house and saw the luggage already packed and ready to go. She saw the small carry-on bag zippered open on the bed and his toiletry bag sitting next to it.

"It will be okay," Lazarus walked out of the bathroom pulling on a shirt.

"No, it won't be, Lazarus. I am going to miss you. The children are going to miss you. Even Molasses is going to miss you."

"I'm not leaving forever. Just for a spell. We need to put some distance between us, you and me. While we stay in the same town, it gives Troy all kinds of freaky ideas." He pulled her into his arms.

"He's a freak," Kali complained.

"Well, with Ray and Micah working together, he can't find shit." The two of them laughed.

"What about A.J.? Is he safe?" Kali could not help worrying about her son. He was not only looking like Ashton, he was acting like Ashton.

"You mean, Ash?" Lazarus blew the curl from between her eyes.

"Oh, yes, Ash. No more A.J. He's Ash now. Kind of scary, if you ask me. But, Jordan would be proud," Kali pushed her head into his chest. "Don't go," she pleaded. "I can keep my distance, I swear."

"Yeah, right. I told you not to come down here and where are you standing?"

"But, I left something here. I had to pick it up," Kali whined.

"Yeah, what? What on Earth did you leave here the last time you were here?" Lazarus teased.

"My red lace panties." She began to peel off his shirt.

"No, Kali, I will miss my plane."

"That's the general idea," she got him out of his shirt.

"I love you, little girl," he kissed her deeply.

"I love you, old man," she kissed him back as he lifted her on to the bed.

"This is not the last time." He eased his hand up her dress to find her bottom bare.

"It had better not be, and any floozie that you try to replace me with is dead."

"You know how me and celibacy get along. Besides, if I don't shoulder a babe now and then, Troy will continue trying to connect the dots between the two of us." He let out a sigh as he slid into Niecy. "Motive for murder: another man's wife, another man's family. Except it was for my own family."

"That you can't claim."

"Not at the moment. But, I will be back."

"You better!" Kali screamed with pleasure.

EPILOGUE

ROY'S APARTMENT WAS strewn with newspapers, yellow memo pads, and police reports. He had even secured a copy of Lazarus' medical records in Dry Bones. Who was this man? Why were the Sperlings so attached to him? It bothered him that Ashton was almost not mourned at all, how their lives seem to pick up and keep moving. And Troy thought, how he, Ashton's best friend, could not be included in anything, like he was a piece of paper to be tossed in the trash. He loved Ashton and he had promised him no harm would come to him, but it had. And, he was supposed to be paying attention. There was something blatantly missing.

Usually, he was right about these things. He knew a murderer, a thief, a drug dealer when he stepped into the room with one. He was good at what he did. He could use the slightest clue to bring a criminal to justice, but now he was empty-handed. All this paper, and all this info, yet he had nothing to pin Ashton's murder on Lazarus.

No one had seen anything or heard any rumors, and Lazarus was on stage with his arms wrapped around Ashton, both of whom looked happy when the first shot was fired. Troy had stared at the pictures a million times. Kali was frozen with fear, Micah's eyes were widened in surprise, and Lazarus was stunned. Everything was as it should be when you were innocent. But, as he sat looking at those pictures, he was beginning to think no one on that stage, with the exception of him, was innocent.

In another room, in another apartment, in another country, piles of papers and pictures documented every move of every member of the Sperling family. A pair of hands in a pair of latex gloves began to cut and paste a collage of Kali and her daughters. It was the women in the Sperling family he wanted. There was no doubt in his mind that that would be the greatest source of hurt he could ever execute on Ashton. Who would he kill first, he thought, the mother or one of the daughters? He held up Katie's picture to the light. She looked so angelic, so fragile, and so innocent. He kissed the picture.

Lazarus paced the floor of his hotel room in Germany. He hadn't wanted to alarm Kali, but Ray, Micah, and Ash were fully aware that there was still one player left, one that knew who he was and what he had done. He could only hope that whoever it was would come at him directly, if he were alone far away from home. Lazarus looked out into the gray skies over Berlin. His gut had brought him here. He didn't or couldn't understand why, but his instincts had only failed him once before, when he had let down his guard in that prison. That had changed his life forever. He had no plans to repeat that action.

He worried a bit about Ash, though. As a man himself that had killed or been responsible for many deaths, he couldn't help it. It had been his black-clad son and his new best friend Ray who had lain insidiously in the rafters the night Asa was killed. Ash was supposed to take out Asa, and Ray was supposed to take Lazarus out. Instead, he thought as he looked down at his cowboy boots, Ray decided otherwise and put the other bullet in Asa's head. As far as the world knew, both Sperling twins had been laid to rest. And, as far as anybody in the world that cared about Lazarus thought he was completely oblivious to the whole experience.

Once again, the amnesiac had experienced more memory loss, but because he was a friend of the family he was no longer homeless or jobless as a result. Lazarus went to his bag and pulled out a picture of Kali. He kissed it. Whoever was out there had better lay low. The last word in Lazarus' vocabulary was fear, and the first one was vengeance.

Dilsa Saunders Bailey
Books

Fiction

Non-Fiction

Visit with the Author
on
Facebook Page (The Sperling Chronicles)
Twitter (simplydilsa)
www.simplydilsa.com